Stories From Around The Block

A Short Story Collection

Charlie McFadden

Previous books from the Author

The Picture Game
The Fiddlers Elbow

For Emily, as always, my inspiration.

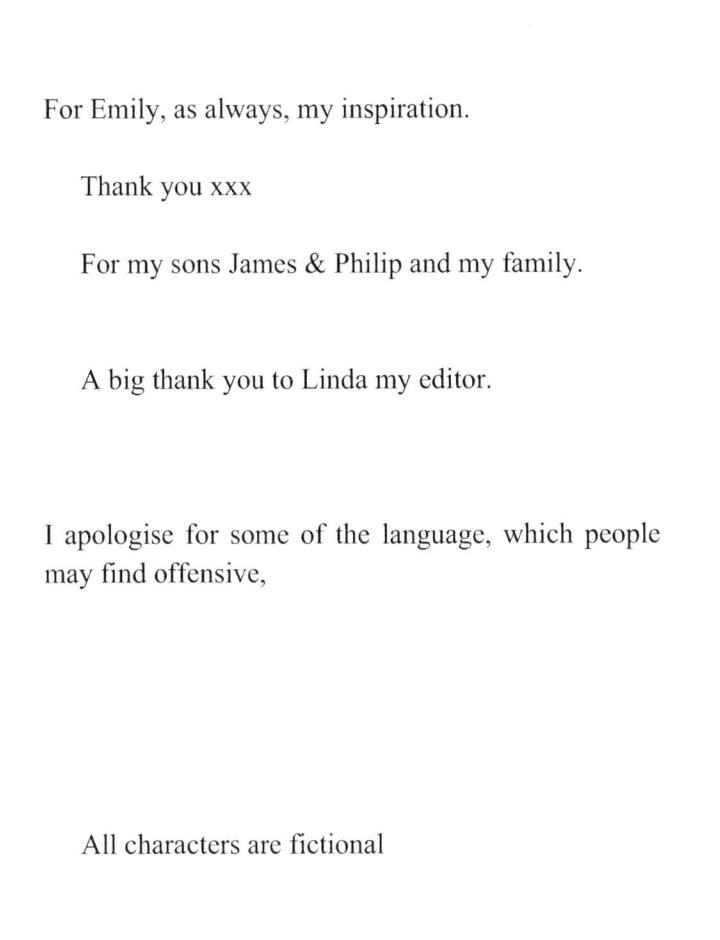

Thank you xxx

For my sons James & Philip and my family.

A big thank you to Linda my editor.

I apologise for some of the language, which people may find offensive,

All characters are fictional

Copyright © 2022 Charlie McFadden
All rights reserved.
ISBN: 9798751819095

Contents

The Race

The Tale that Never Was

The Auction

A Frame in Time

Change is Gonna Come

Art lovers

God and the Devil

Bradley

Jimmy the Dash

A Wedding Suit

The Champ

An Unlikely Liaison

Paedo

Look What You Made Me Do

Red Roses

Perfect Storm

La Bête

The Dinner Party

One for the Road

The Funeral

The Brute

Galina the Mayfly

An Evening in Paradise

The Gift

A Dish Served Warm

Life will change

Just once in a while

And change will change

Just once in a while

The Race

It was August, the last or first or second week, I can't quite remember. Then again, it might not have been August at all.

P.J. had hay to collect and wanted to get a good start on the road. Not wanting to wake Mary his wife, he quietly slipped out of bed. In the kitchen, he cut a thick slice of bread, slathered it with butter and sat for a while with a huge cup of tea. He was fifty-five and one of the many O'Donnell's of Glenbofey. He pulled on a thick woollen jumper and an old grey suit and a work jacket over that. P.J. stood well over six foot and was, to put it kindly, heavyset, or not so generously, a fat lump of a man. It was time to go, he stooped under the door frame and stepped outside. The sky was clear, but the chill was biting. As he buttoned his jacket he gazed up at the stars. The longer he looked the brighter the sky became. He was remembering the constellations he learned at school; the Bear, Orion's Belt and the Plough and his favourite, the Big Dipper. The sun rise in about an hour would be up to greet him by the time he got to Owl's.

First things first he thought, and made his way up to the well to pull off a couple of pales of fresh water for the day. Then to the cowshed, opening the solid rusty gate he made his way in. Six heifers were crowding him, expecting to be let out to pasture, but this morning he was leaving that to Mary. Sandy, his donkey, was standing in the far corner nuzzling uninterestedly at the remains of a turnip. As P.J. approached an ear went up followed by a lazy stare. Both knew the steps to this dance. Taking the lead, Sandy casually moved across the shed and as he did, P.J. followed. Sandy would move again and again and each time P.J. would follow. It was like a waltz, the steps preordained and the heifers the audience. The dance continued until finally, Sandy agreed to take his halter. Sometimes Sandy would perform an encore by refusing to budge but today he could smell the carrots in P. J's pocket and knew he was to be rewarded for his compliance.

Sandy was predominantly grey, larger than your average donkey, a white belly and muzzle. As with all donkeys he had that all-knowing look, a look of calm serenity that belies many a wilful tyrant. P.J. hitched him up to the cart and handed over the carrots as he double-checked the belts and buckles of the harness.

A low throaty, "On, on," and Sandy moved forward out on to the lane, automatically turning right, it was very rare they went left.

About a mile down the road, P.J. called a low "Whoa." Sandy looked over his shoulder as P.J.

shuffled down and picked up a milk churn from the side of the road. It was full and had undoubtedly fallen from the back of one of Mick McCarthy's milk wagons, whilst the sleepy driver snored on his way to the milk depot. "The rascal," P.J. muttered with a grin to no one in particular, pleased with his luck, "Mick won't miss it."

On they went passing whitewashed cottages. In less than an hour they arrived at Owl Rooney's place. As they pulled in, Owl came out from his kitchen. A small man, bright eyes, grey hair and whiskers, he was carrying a cup of tea.

Whoa' whoa', P.J. called out as Sandy slowed and then stopped.

P.J. stepped down, his huge bulk shuddering the timber-framed cart. The sun was now blinking through the clouds as the two men greeted one another. Sandy watched as they spoke but had no real interest in what men had to say, most of it blather. Over the fence stood a black and white milking cow, Bella, who nodded an acknowledgement.

"Good morning," she said.

"Not so bad," said Sandy with a nod, adding "An early one." The pair chatted on a while as the two men conversed in the only language they knew.

From the cottage appeared a young barefoot girl dressed in a jumble of rags. Her hair was red to ginger.

Of course, we have all heard of 'Beauty is in the eye of the beholder, but with an unstitched cleft palette, a chin that was close to touching her nose she was a sorrowful sight. Owl and his wife had adopted her as a baby, her mother only too willing to give her away.

Gloria carried a crust of bread, a piece leftover from breakfast. "Sandy, what have you been up to?"

Her hair-lip distorted the sound but Sandy heard well enough. He flicked an ear in Gloria's direction and turned his head.

"I have missed you so much," she cooed, as she fed Sandy the bread. She embraced his head, stretching her arms around his woolly neck, hugging and scratching.

Sandy answered with a bray that the girl understood. She went back to the cottage and returned moments later with another piece of bread along with a scrubbing brush.

"Now don't be spoiling him Gloria," called P.J. as himself and Owl walked back towards the cottage. "Look what the brushing did to me", he laughed running his hand over his bald pate.

Gloria giggled, but didn't respond other than to keep brushing the donkey's dusty coat.

"How long have you had that donkey now?" asked Owl, lips pursed.

P.J. stood rubbing the bristle on his chin as he thought a while. "It's got to be eight years since the mother has been gone," he rubbed his chin again. "Eight years," then corrected himself, firmly adding "Nine-year in the spring.

"In his prime," said Owl as he too gave Sandy's head a rub.

"Aye, in his prime," repeated P.J.

"He is at that," confirmed Owl, slowly walking around the donkey, he examined Sandy's legs. Owl stood, hands-on-hips, with that authoritative look of a 'donkey expert.' "Have you not thought of entering him into the race?" And before he got a response added, "There's twenty 'dollar' for the winner, ten and five for second and third."

"Ah, I would love to give the fella a run-out, come the day," said P.J., giving Sandy's back a heavy pat with his shovel-like paw. "But…" he trailed off.

They stood together balefully watching Gloria at her work.

Owl glanced back and forth at his huge companion. He was figuring how to put it; it would need tact. A purse of the lips, which was a habit of his, once, twice as he mulled it over. Owl cautiously spoke, "Our Gloria's a jockey, a damn fine one too."

Gloria looked up and with the confidence of a cavalier, she spluttered, "I can ride him, I'll do it."

Owl's face lit up with questioning expectation as he glanced across at P.J.

P.J. waited a moment. He was never one to jump to conclusions, more the type to allow the conclusion to hit him full on the kisser, but this didn't seem such a bad idea. Gloria was lean and sharp of eye, probably only half of the weight of the rags she wore. Yes, he thought she could be a jockey. Before going out on a limb however, he asked, "How much to enter?" adding "Jaysus, you think Gloria has it in her to jockey?"

"I'm a good jockey," said Gloria, affronted at the question.

In truth her jockeying days were very much in their infancy, well not quite in their infancy, she had never jockeyed before in her life, but was willing and able.

Owl was quick to take up the baton on his daughter's behalf, giving out that she had already won races in the fair in Coolclin and had come in second over at Loughfadin on that ol' nag of Meggy Burke's. All tall tales but how was P.J. to know?

"Not a penny to enter and a cup if you win," Owl clapped his hands with impish delight, "Mick the bookie puts up the prize money." Repeating, "Not a penny. Sandy will make ten times his value after he's won. Many a man who will pay top dollar for a winning donkey." Again, all tales but how was P.J. to know?

"This is the girl who will bring home the bacon al'right," said Owl putting an arm around his daughter's shoulder. "Fifty, fifty on the twenty-dollar? He said sticking out a scrawny mitt.

Again P.J. took his time, rubbing his head as he eased his bulk around the cart.

Owl left his hand hanging.

"Yer on!" said P.J. spitting a gob into his palm. Owl followed the ritual as they clasped in a handshake.

Sandy who was taking in what was going on, quite liked the idea. He had been to many a fair and quite fancied his chances. Gloria was ecstatic and with an effortless leap was on Sandy's back but as quickly as she landed, she had slid down the other side and was back on her even before Sandy realised she was on.

"There's no time for that now," said Owl. He didn't want P.J. to get cold feet. "The fair's weeks away, that'll be plenty of time for training."

They all hopped up onto P.J's cart and headed into the opened field. The sun was now up and dawn chorus in full flow, it was going to be a beautiful day. In the field stood ten haystacks and around were scattered smaller piles of haycocks and trancocks. P.J. jumped down, almost turning the cart as he did so. Owl waited a moment, then lit his pipe. Owl was probably close to sixty, and although still vigorous, was never one to get in the way of another man's work. So, taking his time he descended slowly, pensively.

"You're looking a bit stiff this morning," remarked P.J. whose own hip had been giving him trouble for the last few years. "Is it the hip?"

Owl gingerly moved around the back of the cart with an exaggerated hobble and with a look that the Bard himself would have been proud of. He winced "It's these blasted knees." He raised a hand, "No matter, I'll be fine," and picked up a pitchfork by the side of the stack.

Gloria hopped sprightly down and again tried to mount the unsuspecting Sandy, only for the same result as last time. As neither man had noticed and Sandy was only half sure, she pretended it hadn't happened. P.J. was now on top of the stack, Owl passed him up the pitchfork. It was for the men to load the hay, P.J. from the top, Owl from ground level, and Gloria to take charge in organising the distribution in the cart.

"You'll be as well to sling her straight in, Gloria will line her up in no time," said Owl, meaning for P.J. to cut out the middle man, himself.

Well, you couldn't argue with the man's logic.

Owl made himself a soft bed of hay and sat down. He lit up his pipe and as he puffed away, he eyed up the donkey.

Sandy was quietly nibbling an ear of hay just to pass the time, whilst thinking about the race. His mother had often talked of the fairs and the races. There was even mention of thoroughbred blood in her family, but from where and whom, she was a bit vague. But there was no doubt about it, they were from a line of donkey kings. His memory drifted to Toc, a big black and grey donkey, who the hens said was his father. Toc was the strong silent type, a donkey of few words, but Sandy was very fond of him and would follow him about. When Toc was sold, his mother pined for months and months, she never got over it. It wasn't long after, she just fell down and never got up. From then on, Sandy took on the work of the farm.

"G'up," called P.J. waking Sandy from his daydream, "Move on."

P.J. dropped off Owl and Gloria and now himself and Sandy were heading home. P.J's mind was in a spin of excitement, he couldn't wait to tell Mary about the race. "On, on," he slapped the reins down on Sandy's back and before long they were trotting. Sandy too was excited. As they got closer to the farm, he brayed out the news to the cows, who were making their way across the lane into the field, they didn't take much notice but a red coloured hen, named Doris, accompanied Sandy for the final hundred yards.

Despite Sandy explaining, Doris didn't take on board the enormity of the forthcoming event, all she did was complain that the warm weather was not suiting her, not suiting her one bit.

Mary loved the idea of the race but thought that Owl had taken advantage of P.J. After all, it would be Sandy carrying Gloria, not the other way around. P.J. agreed but had shaken on it and in those days, a deal was a deal.

"Well, if we are going, we might as well make a day of it," said Mary. She was a practical woman and at once began thinking of ideas to extending their commitment.

The following morning, P.J. got Sandy harnessed early and their work was finished by the middle of the afternoon. When they got back to the farm they were met by Mary, who fed Sandy a well-deserved juicy carrot. After all, he'd been working and was ready for a rest. Unharnessed Sandy followed Mary down to the field at the back of the cottage, she opened the gate and he skipped in. Hoping for another carrot, he nuzzled the basket she had placed by the side. But all he got for his investigations was a sharp crack on the back, as she hit him with a stick. Unsure of what to do, he raced around the perimeter a couple of times, then wandered back over to her, hopeful. Again, the stick was raised, and the sharp pain jolted his hide, around the field once more he ran. Mary held out the tasty vegetable, hesitantly Sandy wandered closer, and closer, this time he felt sure the carrot was his and was about to take a bite when, crack! "Ouch!" On and on it went until he was completely out of breath and didn't want anything to do with carrots. When completely exhausted Mary threw a halter over him and led him up to the barn. Sandy was confused, he liked his life with Mary and P.J., they were generally kind. P.J. could be stubborn but Sandy knew just how far to push that stubbornness. And besides P.J. and Mary, he had good friends on the farm, all the cows loved him. In fact, it was Tulip who had suckled him after his mother passed away, but all of them were nice, always time for a chat. He did have one enemy however, Sparky the black cockerel. Sparky was mean, lashing out at friend or foe who got too close. He could box you with a wing or stab with his beak. Sandy had many a time tried to defend himself with a kick, but Sparky was as fast as lightning. That wasn't all about him either, besides his viciousness, his language was atrocious too, never a kind word for his hens, just curses and threats. Not a nice character at all, the less said about him the better.

The following few days were hard for all as it was the cutting of the peat for the winter. P.J. and Sandy were out all day. Some days Mary would come along to help with the loading.

Mary was a robust woman, ruddy-faced with thick grey hair. If she put her mind to it, she could match any man in the field but preferred the surrounds of her cottage, planting and tending their small patch of vegetables.

As an orphan, Mary arrived in Loughbally. It was just after the potato famine; times were hard for all. Sweeney and his wife Peggy took her in. Sweeney was a gentle soul with childlike innocence, whilst his wife was stern. Her temper was legendary in the village. The term, "Don't throw a Peggy," was regular parlance. Mary met P.J. at school, and whilst he was not the most handsome, he was by far the tallest. They married at eighteen and twenty-two respectively. It would never be described as a passionate affair but they had rubbed along for thirty-two years and were still very fond of each another. They had had no children, a thing which surprised their neighbours. But life is made up of surprises, even an each-way bet on the favourite is no guarantee.

From inside the shed Sandy could hear voices and a commotion outside. It was early on a Sunday morning. P.J. and Owl decided that as the training was going well, it would be a good idea for Gloria to really put Sandy through his paces. A few moments later P.J. appeared and after their usual dance, he led Sandy out into the big field. Gloria greeted him with her usual enthusiasm and went to work straight away grooming and feeding him carrots galore. P.J. and Owl were in a huddle, discussing the tactics of the race. Go to the front early and keep out of bother was Owl's thoughts while P.J. favoured sitting back until the final furlong. Mary stood waiting as she watched the proceedings. She wanted Sandy to look his best on the day of the race and had made a red and blue sash for Sandy. After Gloria had finished, it was put around his furry neck.

Gloria led him back and forth as all admired Mary's handiwork. Gloria and Mary then joined the men to give their thoughts on how best to conduct the race. As everyone was distracted, Sandy began to eat the sash and would have swallowed it but for some reason, unbeknownst to himself, could only get half of it down his throat. Mary glanced over in horror. A few firm yanks it reappeared from Sandy's throat. Although a bit on the mushy side, she folded and slipped it into her apron as the bemused donkey looked on.

Sandy was saddled up. As soon as Gloria mounted it was apparent that her jockeying skills had been vastly overestimated. It was all she could do to stay seated as the donkey stood still. Whilst her hands gripped firmly to his mane and with her legs around his belly, her backside insisted on dismounting. No sooner she was on, she was off. Her confidence and determination were still strong but there was no hiding it, the technical side was lacking.

P.J. complained to Owl, who shook his head, saying, it had to be the fault of the saddle, so he tightened it an extra hole. Then Owl thought there was too much shine on the saddle and rubbed it over with a bit of dust, then maybe there was too much dust. After an hour of trying every combination, saddle, dust, string, bareback, and Owl himself as jockey, the men were now arguing, close to coming to blows. P.J. blamed Gloria, and Owl the donkey. Sandy himself sided with P.J. If it was not for Mary saying she'd help Gloria in the evenings, their investment was in ruins.

In the evenings of the next two weeks, Gloria turned up for training. On day two the backside and the hands were co-ordinated but now her legs were flapping like a pair of indicators. On day three the hands, backside and legs were all in agreement but as soon as Sandy got up to a gallop, she was off. Mary herself didn't have a problem jockeying when she took Sandy for a little spin, no problem at all. But like P.J., Mary carried a fair amount of timber and with a fuller figure on board Sandy was struggling to get out of second gear.

Now and again P.J. and Owl turned up to watch. It would start with encouragement and quiet advice. But soon the advice got louder, and then louder. With tempers frayed and half an hour of shouting they'd slope off with some excuse or other. Thankfully Mary, Gloria and Sandy were made of sterner stuff. And it was all smiles after a week as Gloria had mastered her unique jockeying style, which was more circus monkey than classic equestrian. Of course, Owl knew from the start it was just a case of the donkey getting used to a rider of Gloria's calibre.

The next thing to do was put them on the clock, check their times. Mary announced that Gloria and Sandy should finish the course in four minutes thirty-two seconds to be in with a shout, and with the mantle clock at the ready, they were set. Around they went, four laps of the field, a more positive crowd they couldn't have hoped for. The improvement was there for all to see.

Mary was logging the time for each lap, and as they passed the winning post on the final lap, she called out, "Four minutes and twenty seconds."

Owl tutted, he disagreed, suggesting it was just under four minutes by his count. "And that's a winning race," he cheered with a bold slap on his 'arthritic' knee.

All agreed, they were in with a good shout and if they played it cute, they'd get decent odds from the bookie. Once again P.J. and Owl put their heads together to work on the tactics, not knowing that Mary, Gloria and Sandy had a master plan in place. Their plan was to go flat out from the start, Mary had mentioned the whip in the final straight, but only if absolutely necessary. It has to be said, Sandy was overruled on that one.

The third Sunday in September was the Ballyfad fair. The one day in the calendar when folks from miles around met up. All manner of things could be bought and sold at the fair, crockery, vegetables, livestock, clothing, just to name a few. Besides the race P.J. was keen to get himself a pair of pigs to fatten up over winter. Mary had been baking all week and expected a good return. She had also potted up a few of her best roses to enter in the Rose competition, a white and pink she thought to be the pick but the reds were not far behind.

The morning of the fair arrived. All preparations were in hand. Owls was taking P.J. and Mary along with him, whilst Gloria was to walk Sandy the four miles to the showground under strict instructions not to ride him. They arrived just after eight, already there was a good crowd. Mary set up her stall alongside Nora Leeson her neighbour. Nora was very interested to hear that Sandy was competing and mentioned that Freddie McFarland was entering too. Freddie along with the lad who stayed with him, not his son, simply known as The Kid, were old hands at donkey racing, with rosettes and silver galore. Nora said Freddie had a new donkey from O'Reilly's racing stable and had won at a fair only a couple of weeks ago. Freddie was in his mid-forties, larger than life, tall with a mop of curly blond hair, a flamboyant arrogant braggart of a man. He'd never done an honest day's work but always had money.

Wanting to view the competition, Mary asked Nora to look after her stall as she wandered off into the coral. A chorus of brays met her as she entered, there was definitely something in the air. All the donkeys were being worked on, as besides the race there was a prize to be had for the best turned out animal. Some had braided manes, others with belts, brasses, ribbons. Gloria was down at the far end with Sandy, who was looking as good as Mary had seen him. Gloria must have borrowed some shoe shine black as his hooves shone like soldier's boots. She was trying to plait a ribbon through his tail but after avoiding a couple of kicks, she gave up.

As Mary approached, Gloria looked up. "Have you seen The Kid?" Mary asked.

Gloria looked to the other side of the coral, gazing a while before pointing to a very slim, straight-backed youth.

"A change of plan," said Mary. "Stick to The Kid... Gloria, are you listening?" She was not, Mary gave Gloria a nudge, "Will yer listen to me." She lowered her voice, "Now in the final chase," Mary looked around furtively, reached into her apron and pulled out a darning needle hidden in her fist. Her eyes fixing Gloria with serious intention, she whispered, "If he's getting away, pull to the inside and make sure no one can see......" Mary winked and flashed the needle.

Gloria looked confused for a moment, then her lip curled into a smile. She took the needle and pushed it into her rags. Another wink from Mary and she was gone.

A few minutes later it was Owl and P.J. who were working their way through the coral, spying on the competition. On the top of their list was The Kid.

They were met by Freddie McFarland who greeted them with a mouthful of gold teeth, a prospector's grin. "Good morning gentleman. What's took you hardworking men out away from your work today?" said Freddie, turning he whistled over to The Kid who was grooming their donkey, "Make sure to keep an eye on him!"

Even in those days, it was not unknown for a donkey to be slipped a little something which would prevent him from producing his best, if you know what I mean.

"We're just out for the day," said Owl, guardedly. "Catching up on a few folks." And with a wave to a rosy faced man close by, "How are you doing Peter?"

Peter the postman waved back, "I'm good Owl, off to get a bit of breakfast now. Good luck to Gloria." Peter had Foncy, an old grey jenny in the race. Foncy had a lovely temperament and was willing enough but years of carrying Peter had almost crippled her. With a bowed back she looked closer to a camel than a donkey. Thankfully Peters' youngest and smallest son Liam was her jockey for the race. She'd competed in every race over the last ten years, but never gotten anyway near the front. However, she enjoyed the race and particularly the gossip as she was going around. If Mick the bookie was right, she would struggle to come last and was listed at two hundred to one.

Freddie proudly took them over to view his donkey and introduced him as Diablo. His coat was shiny black, sharp eyes and alert, it was a beautiful animal, none of the coarse dullness of the rest of the field. They couldn't fail to be impressed.

Owl had his thoughts that perhaps it wasn't a donkey at all, and Freddie had crossed a regular donkey with a thoroughbred horse. He whispered in P.J's ear, "That's a ringer. My arse if that's a donkey.

P.J. was no expert but blurted out, "Is it a mule you's have there?"

The Kid looked up from his duties, and with a sarcastic laugh, "No an Arabian thoroughbred."

Freddie amused, laughed, slapping The Kid on his back, "Yes he's an Arab stallion alright."

The time of the race had arrived, donkeys and riders of all shapes and sizes were lined up. Aney the Ox was represented as was Rose O'Flannery and so was Crooked Billy. All had had previous success and were hoping that this was once again their year.

P.J. and Owl had placed their bets; both had put a pound each way on Sandy. However, on the way back Owl made an excuse, and slipped back to put a further ten bob to win on Diablo.

Before the start Mary went over and whispered something in Gloria's ear. She had positioned herself alongside The Kid, on the other side was the camel like donkey Foncy, who was chatting telling Sandy a tale about his mother. Diablo was sullen as was The Kid, both steely-eyed primed and ready to go. Gloria too had on her game face, firmly concentrating on the race ahead.

After a few minutes there was a semblance of order with most facing forwards. A shot rang out, as did a roar from the crowd, and they were off. About twenty showed willing, others were being kicked and cajoled to join the race, among them was Sandy. Despite being warned by Foncy, the sound of the starting pistol had frightened him. A sharp kick from Gloria re-focused his mind and away they went and soon were up towards the front-runners. Within a couple of hundred yards, the field was beginning to spread. At the front as expected was Diablo, The Kid poised upright in his stirrups, looking every inch the winner.

Mary clasped her hands to her breast quietly repeating Hail Mary's. P.J. had his hands plunged deep into his pockets with fingers crossed.

Owl, his eyesight was not the best was squinting. He nudged P.J., "How's she doing?"

P.J. looked nervous, he didn't respond, and was making quick jerks, as if in the race himself.

"How's she doing?" Owl called out this time to Mary.

Mary interrupted her Hail Mary's, "About tenth."

Owl bit down on his lip.

As they completed their first circuit, Diablo was still out in front. Owners dashed to the rails, shouting advice as the riders went by.

Gloria could feel the sweat building up on Sandy shoulders, and tightened her grip. A dig of heels into his belly moved him up a gear and they began to move up the field passing one donkey then another and another. Soon all Gloria could see were four donkeys in front. Diablo was still showing a clean pair of heels followed by Big Red of the MacSween's, Casper with Sammy Kincaid in the saddle was third and.... *Jesus,* she could not believe her eyes it was Foncy, *What in God's name was Foncy doing there.* She gave Sandy another kick, he picked up his pace.

As they passed Foncy, Liam smiled over, calling out, "Go on Gloria, go on, go on!"

Gloria had now levelled with Sammy, who looked over shaking his head in resignation, Casper was failing quickly and pulled up after a few more strides. Gloria was now on the tail of Big Red.

Mary increased her rate of Hail Mary's; in that she was now annoying the Virgin, who for sure had more important matters to deal with than a donkey race. P.J.'s fingers had turned to claws as the sweat dripped off his neck, damp patches showing on his Sunday shirt.

There was perhaps a furlong left in the race. Gloria was making good progress, cajoling and begging Sandy for a final spurt. But Sandy's strength was failing, he knew he was on his last legs, he thought of how his mother would be looking down. He pushed harder, going past Big Red in the next few strides. All that was between himself and the rosette was Diablo. Stride after stride they were gaining on Diablo's black rump. The Kid glanced back and grinned dismissively as he bobbed up and down encouraging Diablo forward. Gloria was leaning, pushing, pushing, inch by inch until both donkeys were neck and neck. The Kid looked confident, he winked, then urged Diablo on in one last almighty push. Suddenly Gloria felt Sandy stumble and then on again. In her heels went into Sandy's ribcage, he mustered all that was left but was floundering; his strength collapsing beneath her. There was only one thing left. She reached for the needle, pulled to the inside and dug it sharply into Sandy's rump. Sandy again showed willing, his heart was about to burst, matching Diablo stride for stride. The sound of the crowd was deafening, the finish only yards away. Again, Sandy stumbled, Gloria could feel he had nothing left, he was going backwards. The Kid glanced over, he smirked with a look of self-satisfaction. Not fully knowing why, she reached as far forward as she could in the saddle and plunged the needle deep into Diablo's rump. Diablo let out a loud bray and shot off to the left. It was all The Kid could do to turn him from running through the hedge.

Liam and Foncy both looked in shock as they passed Gloria and Sandy on their way to the finish line.

Foncy looked so proud of herself as the rosette was attached to her halter. Mick the bookie was happy enough as although she was two hundred to one, no one had backed her.

Mary's rose won second place and all her cakes and buns were sold, so all was not lost. P.J. didn't buy his pigs, but there'll be another time for pigs.

Although disappointed Sandy had enjoyed the day and was pleased for Foncy.

They never entered Sandy in another race again. P.J. said the stress was too much, Mary agreed. The years sailed by one by one. Sandy was now a mature donkey with a thick grey coat. Gloria would call by now and again and saddle him up for a spin. With the wind against their faces and every stride a force of nature, they were in their element. Gloria would occasionally land a kick to his belly, but Sandy didn't mind, because this time they raced to victory……. Of course!

The Tale that Never Was

This here story was in a time before humans turned up. They were about but just swinging around the trees, squealing and howling, they was nothing but monkeys back then. Well, before they did turn up, it was animals that ran things. Some worked on their power, agility and strength, lions, deer, elephants, snakes and such, but one particular species worked on their intellect, that species was foxes, that's why they're so smart now.

Mr Hightail proudly stood at the front of the class, glasses perched on the end of his snout. Standing next to him was an old grey fox, wiry and withered. "Boy's," said Mr Hightail, "We have a guest with us today." He glanced to his side and grinned. "He's an old acquaintance and I have to say, a bit of a rascal. He and me go way back. Way, way back! You wouldn't believe the scrapes we got into!" His eyes lit up, and laughed out loud as the old grey fox shrugged and scratched the side of his neck. Hightail went on, "He's kindly come here today to tell you young cubs a story, a story that provides a warning." He lowered his tone, "We call such a story, a cautionary tale. I want all you young fox cubs to give him a warm welcome. Hightail looked to his side, "I'll let him introduce himself."

The class clapped with soft applause.

"Thank you Mr Hightail," the old fox smiled, bowed and nodded to his companion, as if dismissing him. He picked up a bit of chalk, licked the end and put it back, "Nice place you got here, mighty fine indeed."

Mr Hightail seemed unsure whether to stay or leave. After an awkward silence, he bowed and left the classroom.

With Hightail out of the way, the old fox seemed more at ease, he selected another piece of chalk and tasted the end of that too, nodded approval and slipped it into his pocket. Turning his attention to the cubs, he announced himself. "My name is Pritchard Cantaloupe III," he pulled out a chair and rested one leg, scratched the back of his neck and leaned forward. "And have I got a story for you." He was about to whistle when his attention was drawn to the back of the room to a cub who was gazing out of the window.

It was Felix Scratchbone, a scrawny little thing who was renowned for daydreaming. Felix just could not concentrate, always watching what was going on somewhere other than where he should be watching. He certainly was not taking any notice of that old grey fox at the front of the class; as outside were a couple of blackbirds merrily dancing along the branch of a tree.

"Hey, you!" Pritchard called.

Felix's hadn't heard a word, his head went over to one side, a paw to his chin, his thoughts were miles away, daydream in full flow. *He was in long grass, chasing a cricket into the undergrowth. A butterfly floated by, its bright red wings fluttering back and forth, so mesmerizingly beautiful.*

"Will someone knock some sense into that young cub's head," shouted Pritchard. The cub alongside Felix gave his dreamy friend a solid slap to the side of his head, which brought the young Felix back to reality. Pritchard waited until he had Felix's attention. "You think I travelled all this way just to waggle my tail in the air? Sit up and listen now."

Felix looked a little shocked but managed a smile, whilst his friend sniggered.

"Now the rest of you look this way too," said Pritchard. "This here's a story," he wiped a dribble from his grey whiskers and once again kissed his teeth. "Yes, siree Bob, one hell of a tale!" He was wearing a pair of baggy worn-out overalls, no shoes, and a straw hat perched to the side on his furry head. "A story my grandaddy told me, and now I'm telling it to you." He looked out at his now captivated audience. "It's about a cat that made herself a fool." Pritchard lifted his foot off the chair and pushed it forward a little, shuffling until he found a comfortable spot. "Let me tell you, cats have always been dumb. That's why the good Lord gave them nine lives." He pushed the chair another inch, "But this cat was about as dumb as the best of them." He chuckled, then grinned, "You ever hear of a cat going to school?" Pritchard looked around the class, "Anybody hear of a cat going to school… anybody?

All the fox cubs shook their heads.

"You, Little Miss Daydream, you ever hear of that?"

Felix looked embarrassed; his snout redder than usual. He too shook his head, "No sir, I heard once of a cat that swam, but I ain't never heard of a cat going to school.

Pritchard Cantaloupe III smiled, "Damn right, you ain't never heard of a cat going to school. That's because?" He looked to the class for the answer.

"Because they're dumb!" they answered in unison.

"Good." Pritchard, grinned, satisfied. "This cat's name was Jennifer J Winterton. A tabby cat by colour but a fool by nature. Jennifer J Winterton, now that name is quite a mouthful, so I'm simply gonna call her Jenny J." Pritchard turned the chair around, sitting on it backwards. "Jenny J was born up at the old mine up by Beaver Dam. Her mamma was pretty friendly with the beavers at the time, they were having problems with rats. There's a hell of a lot of rats up that way, I don't know why, it might have something to do with the apple trees they got up there?" Pritchard Cantaloupe III went on to explain the different types of apples they had and which were the sweetest. When he had finished, he scratched his head, "Now where was I? Oh, I remember. Well, they gave Jenny J's momma the job of rat catcher and she did a mighty fine job of it too. This was before Jenny J was born of course. Any of you ever hear of Big Tom?"

The class was silent.

"Big Tom was Jenny J's daddy, a crazier cat you would not hope to meet. Not just your ordinary crazy. No, Big Tom was plumb senseless crazy." The eyes of the cubs followed Pritchard as he walked between the desks, stopping here and there, picking up the odd pencil and tasting the end. Again, Pritchard went off on a tangent, spending ten minutes telling the class of Big Toms exploits. Of when Big Tom took on a whole pack of wolves and won in a fair fight. The time he tried to jump the creek and damn near drowned. And then when Big Tom got old, how he married a tortoise, saying her pace of life seemed to suit him better. "Oh, that Big Tom was crazy," Pritchard Cantaloupe III laughed out loud, "You won't find a cat as crazy as that old fella today." He looked over the class, a puzzled expression on his face, "Oh yeah! Y'all heard of lucky numbers, right?" he raised a paw and tapped it in the air three times. "Three's a lucky number, and so is seven. I even heard that eight is a lucky number for the Chinese. Mind you, they have a lot of lucky numbers, ain't no such thing as unlucky for Chinese." He chuckled, "Good move eh!"

Felix shouted out, "Thirteen."

Pritchard swung around and smiled, "That's right young'un. Thirteen is… an unlucky number, unlucky throughout the world." He thought for a moment, "Maybe even Chinese… yeah could be... Anyway, never bet on a thirteen in a race, if there's lightning in the sky and it's the thirteenth day of the month, stay indoors. Well, Jenny J was just riddled through with thirteens. It was her momma's thirteenth litter; she was the last and the thirteenth kitten born that day." Shaking his head, he looked around the class, "and I'll be damned if she wasn't born on any other date than the thirteenth of January, way back when." Pritchard raised his voice, "Now I know y'all are taught that there are twelve months in a year, and that is… correct! But times were different then. Folks hadn't figured out what exactly constituted a full year. Sometimes it could be ten months, other times as few as eight. It was more to do with the weather and the seasons than simply counting. And that was a slow year, so another month was added. And if my calculations are right, I'd say she was born in the thirteenth month, if you catch my drift.

Some of the cubs immediately did, whilst others needed Pritchard to re-explain his definition of a thirteenth month year.

"So that cat from the very beginning was cursed," said Pritchard.

Felix put up his hand.

"What you want, Little Miss Daydream?"

Some in the class giggled.

"Do dogs go to school?"

Pritchard flashed a smile, "Good question son." He turned his back and walked to the front of the class. Facing the fox cubs, "Long ago, dogs did go to school, went about the same time as us foxes. Some did ok, but most, well, they just could not settle, playing and fighting all the time. Education wasn't for them. So, the elders made a ruling that school wasn't meant for dogs, and since that day, no dog has ever been to school."

"What about rabbits?" asked Felix.

"Rabbits?" replied Pritchard.

"Yeah, rabbits, did they ever go to school?"

Frustrated and slightly annoyed, Pritchard again sucked on his teeth, "Now listen here son, is it you or me's telling this story?"

The fox cub sitting next to Felix gave him a sharp elbow to the ribs.

"Ouch!" said Felix, "That hurt." He was on his feet and about to strike back when there was the loud slam of a desk lid being shut.

"Settle down, you hear me!" said Pritchard, holding onto the Mr Hightail's open desk, "You're not a pack of dogs."

All the cubs sat up straight and to attention.

Pritchard slowly let the lid fall, and then lifted it again. Something had got his attention, he reached in and helped himself to an apple Mr Hightail was saving for lunch, slipping it into the back pocket of his overalls. His eyes settled on Felix, "No more questions, you hear me. Ok, let's get on with the story." He went to the blackboard and picked up a piece of chalk and drew a quick squiggle, and again licked the end. "You ever eat any of this stuff? Tastes kinda nice." He pushed a handful into his pockets. "Where was I now?" He nodded, "Yeah, I remember, like I said, this here is a story about a cat, a dumb cat that went to school." Pritchard went to the window, "Yes, a dumb cat that went to school. You see Jenny J fell in with a bad crowd, she got to hang out with those crows up yonder, Yeehaw!" he bellowed. There was a cawing in the distance as a group of black crows lifted off the field outside. "Git on!!!" Some of the cubs stood up to see what was the ruckus all about. Pritchard turned, "Them crows is smart, they is almost as smart as us foxes." He pointed to one in particular, "See that one, that one high up in the branches. That's Cornelius, some say he's a hundred years old, maybe even older than that." Pritchard was staring, "You live that long, you're sure to pick up a thing or two." He pointed to another branch, where sat perched a smaller crow, who seemed to be staring directly at Pritchard, "And that there is Corrine, she's even smarter than some foxes. You boys keep an eye out for Corrine, you hear me. She once tricked a cousin of mine who thought he'd killed her. Well, he had a firm grip alright but Corrine said that he should make it quick and that he just needed to move his grip to the side of her neck. That's where you have your jugular," Pritchard touched the side of his neck, Now, if you get hold of the jugular, they're as good as dead. So of course, cousin Wilbert readjusted his grip, and I bet you can guess just what happened next, and you'd be right. Corrine slipped free, and that was the last cousin Wilbert saw of that crow. Yeah, she's smart alright!" He looked off into the field, "And you see that one there...." Pritchard Cantaloupe III went on to tell a story about each and every crow whether perched in a tree or pecking on the ground.

Did crows ever go to school asked one of the cubs sitting near the front?

Pritchard spat onto the classroom floor, rubbing it into the wood with his paw, he seemed unsettled. "No, crows never went to school, they got what you call cunning. We foxes once had it, that was way before the elections. Then it was outlawed," he added wistfully. Going back to Mr Hightails desk, he lifted the lid and poked a paw inside, shuffling through whatever was in there. "I'm not much one for elections. Seems to me that whoever wins does the exact opposite of whatever they promised. You only have to look at the Red Party." He raised his voice, "Now they promised us chicken dinners every second Tuesday, and what did we get? Turkey dinners every other Friday." He shook his head in disgust, "I ask you? Them Silver Fox Party is no better. Promised this, promised that. Tell your daddies they wasting their time voting. Voting is for nothing but sheep and fools.

Felix had his paw in the air, he'd had it up for a while.

"Is that you again?" said Pritchard. "Can't you just settle and listen to the story? Put your paw down!" he snapped. Putting his paws inside his overalls Pritchard proceeded around the class, "Like I was saying, cat's is dumb, always was and always will be."

Suddenly there was a loud noise, it was the ringing of the school bell for end of lessons.

"What in tarnation?" said Pritchard, as the cubs scrambled past, all dashing in the direction of the door. "What in cursed bluebottles is going on," he shouted, "Get back here, I ain't finished my story!"

As the they disappeared, Pritchard turned and was surprised to see one last fox cub still sitting at his desk, it was only Felix.

Pritchard Cantaloupe III smiled, "Little Miss Daydream, you want to hear a story?

"Yes sir."

And that's how a young fox called Felix Scratchbone, eventually, got to know how a dumb cat named Jenny J Winterton got herself an education.

The Auction

With Emily's help, I'd worked out a budget of £450,000, with an emergency last bid of £460,000. We had to take into account buyers commission, the cost of refurbishment, legal fees etc; but at a stretch and with all my fingers and toes crossed it could work out, just.

Reading from the particulars, the property was semi-detached, regency style, four bedrooms, two large reception rooms, two bathrooms, a good-sized cellar, huge kitchen with double doors that opened out into a mature garden of about a quarter of an acre. The guide price was £350,000, which seemed a steal. I didn't for a moment think it would go for under that figure but hoped with all my might that it wouldn't go for a lot more.

As the auction day drew closer, the excitement was getting to me, the night before I didn't get a wink. All night I was tossing and turning with plans and ideas, going through my options. It would probably cost another one hundred thousand to get it up to tip-top condition. But that wasn't my idea. My idea was to spend closer to thirty thousand, tart it up, sell it and make a decent profit. Despite my lack of sleep, I was up bright and breezy, bringing tea to Emily at seven o'clock. She turned her head on the pillow for another ten or so winks. I sat quietly on the edge of the bed, considering my options again.

To say the place was tired was an understatement, to the layman it was bordering on dilapidation. Although not quite Sarah Beeney, I wasn't a complete novice. I'd done up a few in my day and made decent money too. This was a big step up however. The viewings had been an open-day set-up. In a group of six we'd followed the agent, as he did his best to cast his spell. He wasn't having it over on me though, the condition was dreadful, plaster falling, holes in floors, ceiling roses dangling like hangman's nooses. It was off-putting. Straightaway, I knew I was out of my depth, so rather than trust my own opinion, I paid two hundred pounds for a surveyor to go around, not a full survey, just the general condition. Was it safe? Was it solid? He said the gaping cracks in the plaster throughout were only superficial and although it looked bad, it was solid enough, with a decent roof. This was music to my ears. My thoughts being its condition would put off the casual punters. "Just too much to do darling, it could end up being a money pit." Leaving an astute investor like myself sitting pretty.

The auction was to start at 18.00. The weather was miserable, with heavy rain throughout the day, good news, as far as I was concerned. The more obstacles for bidders to attend the better. I took the dogs out and cooked lunch, just a bit of pasta with bacon and cheese, tasty enough. Despite my nerves my appetite had not deserted me. Talking of food, my plan for later, if my bid was successful, was a slap-up meal on the way home, champagne, the works, "Anything on the menu Emily." But I am getting ahead of myself. At four thirty we made a move.

We pulled into a drive on the Gloucester Road, which led up to The Waverly Hotel and Conference Centre, not quite the Ritz but a long chalk from a Wetherspoons. At reception we were directed to a large room with a stage. An attractive looking lady, who I assumed was one of the estate agents, artificial smile, smart blouse, pencil skirt and high heels, handed us a catalogue and a bidding card, number 27.

Where to sit? The room was laid with rows of chairs, at a guess I'd say fifteen deep and probably twenty across. There was already a scattering of people there, a mix of builders and couples. The builders must have known each other as they were sharing jokes and general banter. We chose our seats near the back. My thoughts being, we would have a good view of the competition and still be clearly visible to the auctioneer. Smack bang centre on the front row were what looked like a family of three mature brothers and a father. All were bearded and wore turbans; the dad was in traditional Asian clothing with a long white beard. Knowing how the Asian community pulled together, I thought if they were bidding, I might lose out. A few people had bought themselves alcoholic drinks, and were making a night of it, but most were like me, keeping a clear head with either tea or coffee.

Once settled, I looked once again through the catalogue. It covered all of Gloucestershire, Worcestershire and even as far as Birmingham. Most of the properties were small terrace houses, building society mortgage defaulters. Towards the end of the catalogue were the more individual properties. There it was, Stanhope House, lot number 214. Flicking on, I could see there were a total of 259 lots. I turned to Emily apologetically saying, "We're here for a long night." She smiled in that kind and generous way she has. I personally wasn't too disappointed, hoping by the time we got to Stanhope House, most of the money would be spent. I left Emily with the catalogue and dashed off for coffees. By the time I'd returned there was a buzz of excitement in the air, a bit of a party atmosphere. Another couple of Asians had joined the group at the front, these two were clean shaven and in suits, probably solicitors or accountants. As I looked around, I noticed a Flash Harry type, pinstriped suit, middle-aged, silver-grey hair brushed behind his ears. I wasn't the only one who noticed a beautiful woman by his side, blonde and dressed to the nines, perfect make-up, possibly an ex-model. They made their way into the row directly in front of us. Once seated, Blondie reached into her Gucci bag and took out a set of details. *Bloody hell, they were for Stanhope House,* I nudged Emily, discreetly folded my own set, slipping them into my pocket.

By a quarter to six all the seating was taken, the place was full with people standing. On the side of the stage, huddled together were a group of estate agents, they looked in a self-congratulatory mood.

"Ladies and gentlemen, my name is James Hudson-Brown, from Hudson-Brown and Everett." He was in his mid-forties, film star looks, confident, navy suit and a look of someone who cheats on his wife.

"Thank you for coming along on such a horrible evening. We honestly didn't expect such a great turnout." He looked out at the audience as though sincerely thanking each and every one individually. "We have a range of great properties and parcels of land to auction this evening. I hope you leave with the property of your dreams." He grinned and held up a finger, "And if unsuccessful, all's not lost. We will be holding another auction on the 1st March, next year. Please make a note in your diaries." Like an actor humbly receiving an encore, he raised his hands, a glint of light shone from his cufflinks. "Now I am going to pass you over to my colleague Mr Bennett, who will be conducting tonight's auction." Mr Bennett took a step forward, smiled and bowed. "Once again, thank you all for coming along," said Mr Hudson-Brown, "I'll pass you over now.

Mr Bennett was probably close to retirement but still had a dash of mischief about him. He spoke clearly and concisely. "Ladies and gentleman, we have quite a few lots to get through this evening." He looked up, "Let me draw your attention to lots 29, 54, 112 and 113, as advertised on our website. These lots have been withdrawn from tonight's auction. He repeated, slower this time, "Lots 29, 54, 112 and 113, have been withdrawn." He looked out from over the top of his half-framed glasses allowing for the information to settle. "Please be aware that this evening's auction is held on the conditions published in the front of our catalogue. If you haven't had a chance to read them yet, I suggest you do so now. He nodded to an assistant, a bid spotter, another suit, young and keen-eyed, who was standing to Mr Bennett's right. "Our first lot of the evening," Mr Bennett looked down at his roster, "Lot number one," he paused, "a semi-detached house dating from the turn of the century, it has three bedrooms, a bathroom, generous lounge, kitchen and courtyard garden. Who will start me off?" Looking around the room, "Shall we say one hundred and fifty? Who will give me one hundred and fifty?

I looked down at the black and white photograph in the catalogue, it looked tired, probably ex-rental. I nudged Emily, she grimaced.

Finally, someone raised their hand, the rabbit was out of the trap and the race was on. "One hundred and fifty, can I get one hundred and fifty-five."

I looked over my shoulder in the hope of seeing the bidder.

"One hundred and fifty-five, can I get one hundred and sixty?

Bids came in, and all of a sudden stopped. With a jolt, the gavel hit the podium. It sold for one hundred and ninety thousand pounds. Emily took control of our catalogue and jotted down 190 next to the first lot.

"On to our next lot," Mr Bennett was buoyant and could read the room. He knew his job, a bit of humour, cajoling, coaxing, even a gentle humiliation, anything to squeeze an extra bid or two. He galloped through the early lots and before long we were on lot 50, then 60. I was beginning to feel edgy. At lot 100, Mr Bennett announced a fifteen-minute break. Ignoring my own advice, on the ruse of going to the toilet, I went to the bar and downed a quick pint. One wouldn't do any harm and my nerves were rattling. When I returned, I noticed Blondie was sipping on a chilled white wine, Flash Harry, with a glass of what looked like water, but who knows? I sat down, Emily smiled, then turned away as she caught a whiff of my beer breath.

As people returned to their seats the hum of chatter subsided.

Mr Bennett made his way to his podium, he waited until everyone had settled. "Ladies and gentlemen, can I draw your attention to lot 180," he shook his head with annoyance, "Lot 180 has been withdrawn. Apologies to anyone who has come along tonight specifically for that property." He looked over at Mr Hudson-Brown who smiled apologetically. Mr Bennett continued, "Nevertheless, let us move on. Lot 101." He took off his glasses and looked out over the room, "Now this ladies and gentleman, is a rural idyll. A three bedroomed cottage, kitchen, lounge, bathroom and outbuildings." He leant onto the podium and clasped his hands. "I've personally been around this property. It's absolutely wonderful and would make an ideal place to bring up a young family or... to retire to. It is set in the beautiful Gloucestershire countryside." He smiled warmly as though his mind was strolling through the gardens, then shook himself to life and jerked out an arm. "Who will start me off at one hundred and fifty?

A hand went up from a young guy near the front who was sitting alongside a young girl, almost a woman, she was already biting on her fingernails. Another bidder from the back joined in and in a flash, it was at two hundred. One of the builders had now joined the race, it was between these three bidders. Then it dropped to just the young guy and the builder. With pressure mounting, the young woman covered her face with her hands. On it went, but at two hundred and sixty-five, the builder baulked and the young couple bought themselves a cottage. They embraced; both were crying and laughing through tears of joy. A man sitting nearby leant forward and congratulated them.

"Can we see your number please?" said Mr Bennett.

The young guy immediately shot his hand in the air with his card, "182," he called out a little embarrassed.

Mr Bennett smiled, "You'll love it, a wonderful property."

Unable to contain herself, the young woman still dabbing her eyes with the palms of her hands, called back, "We will, we will. We're getting married next week!"

There was a collective sigh at the couple's unbridled happiness. I nudged Emily and grinned, then glanced to Flash Harry and Blondie. The emotion had passed them by, both stony faced sipping on their drinks. I took a deep breath; my pulse was racing. On it went, lot 176-182, a row of terraced houses, they were all bought by the Asian men at the front, all were rented with occupying tenants. Once their bidding was over they left apart from the suited solicitor type.

We were now on lot number 200, I began to fidget, my armpits felt sweaty, collar too. Emily put her hand on my arm, there is something about that woman that knows when I'm hot and bothered. I smiled; she crossed her fingers. Lot number 210 came and went, so did lots 211 and 212.

"Next lot number is 213, a spacious ground floor apartment, two bedrooms, bathroom, lounge and kitchen. Who will start me off..."?

I haven't the foggiest what it sold for as I was busy getting my bidding card ready. I looked to Emily. Her eyes widened in anticipation, mine with fear.

Finally.

Mr Bennett peered over his bifocals, "Lot number 214. Stanhope House has four bedrooms, two reception rooms, cellar, kitchen, outbuildings and mature well stocked garden." Looking down at his notes, he rubbed his chin, "Now there has been a lot of interest in this property." He looked down at his notes, "We can start the bidding at 480,000 thousand pounds.

I couldn't believe it, *Bastards!* My shoulders dropped, along with my heart, *Fucking hell!* I looked to Emily who smiled sympathetically.

"Who will give me 490? 490 with you sir."

The suited Asian man had his card in the air.

I was still cursing as the bidding continued.

"490, who will give me 500?

It went from 500 to 600 in a flash. Emily gripped my leg, with a smile come grimace. Flash Harry and Blondie who were in my peripheral vision, were yet to join the chase. My eyes were glued. On it went, to 650, then faltered, the suited Asian the last bidder.

"Going once," Mr Bennett looked around the room, "A wonderful property, ladies and gentlemen. Don't miss this one." He raised his gavel, "Going twice."

A movement caught my eye, Flash Harry had raised his card.

"660 to you sir."

Blondie smiled at Flash Harry, whose steely eyes were fixed on Mr Bennett.

Mr Bennett looked to the Asian man, "670 sir?"

The Asian man raised his card, but he was hesitant.

"We have 670. It's on you sir?

Flash Harry immediately spotted the chink in the Asian man's armour. His arm jerked up like a lance.

"680, we have 680," Mr Bennett looked down.

The Asian man glanced over his shoulder to where Flash Harry and Blondie were sitting.

Flash Harry's expression was stone, unyielding, impervious. *Not on my watch, matey.*

"It's on you sir," Mr Bennett repeated, 690?"

The Asian shook his head.

"Are you out sir?"

The Asian nodded.

Flash Harry smiled at Blondie, she grinned.

Mr Bennett raised his gavel above his head, "Going once." Like an owl he scanned the room and very slowly, "Going twice." Again, he scanned his audience.

Blondie was forward in her seat, her hands under her exquisite chin, willing with all her might for the gavel to come down.

"Going twice," Mr Bennett repeated.

Blondie nervously glanced at Flash Harry, whose fists were clenched.

"Going three times," Mr Bennett's arm had begun its arc of descent.

There was movement from the stage, as Mr Bennett's keen-eyed assistant raised his hand, pointing out into the room.

Mr Bennett paused, peering into the distance, "We have a fresh bidder. At 690 sir?" All heads swung in the direction of Mr Bennett's arm. Standing at the back was a grizzled old man holding up a bidding card, number 222. He looked like a tramp; scruffy trilby hat squashed over a mass of grey hair. He was wearing a tweed jacket, which the shoulder had given up on. He nodded.

Flash Harry's hand shot up.

"700! do we have 710?"

The old man kept his card in the air.

"710, to you sir."

Flash Harry raised his card again, the old man didn't take his down. Again, Flash Harry's hand shot, this time with the vigour of a predator. Still no change from the old man. Another ten thousand, then another, it went back and forth. When it got to 780, Flash Harry paused and looked to Blondie. She glared straight ahead. He looked back over his shoulder at the old man and slowly raised his card.

"790....800."

Under pressure, Flash Harry looked to Blondie. Her jaw was fixed like a boxer furious at a slow count, there was no way she was going to budge.

"810, 820, 830, 840," Mr Bennett eyed Flash Harry, he nudged Blondie, who didn't respond. He nudged her again, she turned to face him and whispered in his ear. I don't know what was said but from the look on his face, Blondie could well have been going home with the old man that night. Reinvigorated Flash Harry raised his card.

"850 sir?"

The old boy's hand was in the air. With the look of a condemned man, Flash Harry too raised his, but he was on the ropes. On it went to 890. Even as a spectator, I was sweating.

"890 sir, can we make it 900?"

All eyes were on the old man, his mouth twitched, his tongue appeared, doing a round or two over his lips, he rubbed his nose. Blondie glared straight ahead. Flash Harry's neck was craned, as he wearily stared back. The old man puffed out his cheeks, his tongue doing another round.

"The bid is on you... It would be a shame to lose it, one more bid sir?"

The old man's head went to one side, then the other. With his fingers spread, he held up his hand and mouthed "Five."

"895 sir, is that your bid?

The old man nodded.

Flash Harry put his head in his hands, he glanced up and with the energy of a sloth raised his card. He wanted to be knocked out or for a friend to throw the towel in. But that someone was resolute, Blondie gave him a look that said, "You either win or die."

All eyes shot to the back as a hunched-up man in a trilby hat made his way to the exit.

"Sir, sir," said Mr Bennett as the old man disappeared out the door. He turned his gaze to Flash Harry, "900 thousand pounds. Do we have any other bids?" glancing around the room

The room was silent, all were scanning in the hope the race had yet more to run.

"Once, twice...."

Flash Harry didn't look up as the gavel went down.

Blondie rose from her seat and smiled contentedly as she placed her set of details in her bag. He glanced up at her, dazed and confused; his head went down once more.

Well, what an exciting night and although it wasn't a slap-up meal on the way home, we had a decent enough bite of pub-grub, stopping at the Star and Garter, Emily's choice. I had wanted to go for a curry, which would have kept me up all night. I guess you can't win them all, and at times it's a blessing.

A Frame in Time

"I think you'll agree I was a beautiful baby," Rose laughed as she handed over a photograph to her friend Betty, "That's me with Nanny. It was a black and white photograph Rose was a child of two or even three, staring at the camera, her nanny holding her hand.

Rose now lived in New York and had so for the last thirty years. She leaned forward, as though sharing a secret, "You know I kept that pram… just couldn't bear to let it go." She went on, "I used it for Timmy and Rebecca." Her voice lifted an indignant octave, "Doesn't look if either of them will have any use for it. Everyone is so… caught up in their careers these days."

Rose was now in her autumn years. It would be rude of me to say how old exactly, but if you were to guess fifty, she would have been delighted. She'd always been slim, bright blue eyes, her hair was shoulder-length, auburn apart from a few grey 'on-trend,' highlights.

She took a moment with the next photo before revealing it. A warm smile appeared, "Ah, now, that's Horace with me in Cannes on our honeymoon."

The photo was posed, a professional snap. They were outside a glittering casino. Rose was wearing a long satin evening gown; white fur covered her shoulders and a beautiful diamond necklace sparkled on the nape of her neck. Horace was round-faced, Brylcreemed hair, horn-rimmed spectacles and completely overshadowed by his glamorous wife. She was smiling. He was not. He was grimacing, perhaps telling the photographer to hurry up.

"We only spent three days there, then travelled up to Paris."

Her friend, a brash New Yorker, held the photograph at a distance, "Oh, wow Rose! My god, you look beautiful." She glanced over; a grin turned to a teasing smirk. "That... that was your husband? My god, how long were you married?"

"Don't," Rose giggled, adding, "Too bloody long!"

Betty could hold it in no longer, a raucous giggle burst from her lips, "I mean, talk about beauty and the beast." Going back to the photograph, "He must have had something going for him."

"Well, I'm sure he did, but I just can't remember," said Rose, herself now giggling as she shuffled through the pile of pictures on her lap. "I don't know why I chose him. Money, security? I was a young fool, far too sensible for my years," she added. "I had admirers too."

Rose in fact had been a rare beauty in her day, a head-turner, sort after and fantasied over by many a young blade. A photo slipped onto the floor, she leaned over to pick it up. It was a photo booth shot, stark, cheap and yet beautiful. It was one with Rose when she was sixteen, alongside her was a boy, written on the back was Rico 64, her thoughts drifted.

Against her parents' wishes, Rose Duncan left Calthorpe Ladies college with five O levels and dreams of becoming an actress. Her father, a kindly man, suggested drama school, but she'd had enough of school, drama or otherwise. No, she was going to move in with Uncle Archie, who was dashingly handsome and went to all the right parties. It was even rumoured that he'd had a fling with none other than the infamous Christine Keeler. A fact that Uncle Archie would never confirm or deny. On June 21st 1964 Rose moved to 31 Eaton Mews and into her uncle's spare room. For a day or two she had the place to herself, as the glamour of Marrakech had gripped Uncle Archie by his delicate wrists transporting him to the souks, hashish and free love. So, with the whole of London to discover Rose headed out. The first two days were spent on the usual attractions, Buckingham Palace, the bridges of the Thames, Big Ben, art galleries, museums and monuments. But what really intrigued Rose were the sleazy and immoral back streets of Leicester Square, Piccadilly and Soho. The Windmill Theatre on Great Windmill Street was known to her, one of the girls from college was now one of the dancers. But the Windmill was only the tip of the iceberg of the illicit entertainment available. "Whatever a gentleman desires," she heard a street barker call from outside one of the many clip joints.

It was early evening on her second day of independence. Rose was wearing a pale blue summer dress with a lightweight white cardigan, which because it was so sunny, she had wrapped around her waist. Under the Eros fountain in Piccadilly, she was resting watching the pigeons and passers-by. A boy was wandering up to strangers, it seemed as if he was asking for money, but it was not his lucky day. He made his way over, shooing away the pigeons from his path, and sat close by. From the corner of her eye, she watched as he removed his shoes and socks, rolled up the legs of his trousers then swung around and dipped his feet into the water of the fountain, splashing some of it up onto his face. He was small, sharp-featured; with dark hair, pale, and flamboyantly dressed. His alert eyes had noticed the pretty young girl watching him. When Rose was distracted, he scooped a handful of water in her direction. She jumped and squealed as the cold shock hit her skin. The boy apologized, promising it was a mistake, as he'd only meant to splash his hair. Rose settled but as soon as she looked away, he did it again.

With a grin, he introduced himself. His name was Mick, but everyone called him Rico, originally from Manchester he'd been in London for a year. He said he was seventeen, but looked younger. Pulling a pack of cigarettes from his coat pocket he offered her one. Rose had only smoked once before, which made her feel queasy, regardless she accepted. As they chatted, Rico asked her about her life. Where was she from? How old she was? Did she have a boyfriend? He didn't seem the slightest bit embarrassed, cheekily asking if she was still a virgin. Shocked, Rose blushed and although she still was, she refused to answer.

"I bet you are?" he grinned. "I can tell," he took a drag on his fag, "You posh birds like to hold on to it."

Piqued, Rose replied, "Are you a virgin?"

"Nah, I lost my cherry years ago when I was still at school," Rico laughed. He flicked out a bit of ash, spat on it, then rubbed the mix into the pavement with the sole of his shoe.

"I bet you're still at school though," teased Rose.

Rico gave her a sly sideways glance, they both laughed. "You want some chips?" he said getting to his feet and flicking his cigarette stub for a pigeon to investigate.

Rose thought for a moment wondering what to make of her new friend. She certainly didn't fancy him.

"Come on, I ain't gonna kill you. Chippy is just over there," he pointed across the square.

Although she had two quid in her purse, Rose said that she had no money. Rico laughed, saying it was fine, his treat.

He seemed to know everyone, the chip shop owner, the man on the paper stand, boys and girls hanging around. As they walked, they ate, with Rico pointing out places of interest. That was where the boxer Freddie Mills got shot and killed by the mafia, and that's the brothel where the MP got caught in a raid with a former beauty queen. And over there was a pub where men dressed as women. Rose was loving it, Rico seemed to know all of Soho's secrets. As they passed in front of one of the penny arcades, a ping, ping, ping sounded, someone had won the jackpot, Rico went to investigate. An athletically built boy of about seventeen dressed in denim was scooping up piles of coins.

On recognising him, Rico rushed over, "Fucking hell, giz some."

The boy looked up.

"Come on Figs, giz some."

Figs spoke with a broad Scottish accent, "You gotta be joking," stuffing the money into his pockets. "You still owe me from last week."

"Ah, come on."

"No fucking way."

It was then that Figs noticed Rose, grinning, "Who you got there with yer?"

"Come on Figsie, just a quid."

Figs looked down, there were a few, tanners, (sixpences) left in the tray, he picked up a few and flicked them to Rico. Then went back to feeding his machine.

Rico tried his luck on the slot machine alongside. He pulled down the arm, staring down as the barrel spun.

Figs glanced over, "What's yer name?"

"Rose," she called back, taking in Fig's looks. He was handsome in a rugged ugly sort of way.

There was a moment of silence, Fig's attention was drawn to the spinning fruits. He glanced up, "Rose," he repeated, putting in another coin. Off the barrels went around and around. Eyes fixed, Figs put in another coin, then another, the barrels spun once more. His machine lit up; he'd got a hold. He slapped the button on two cherries and spun again. The machine flashed, *It's your lucky day,* he'd got six nudges.

Knowing the nudges would time out, Rico darted over. He knew the hidden secrets of the fruits of the machine and had to act quick, "You've got a cherry on that one, but you need to bring up the lemons."

Figs looked flustered; Rico slapped the buttons five times and lemons line up. They both smiled at the clunking sound of a pay-out.

"There you go, you wee toe rag," said Figs handing over a stack tanners and thruppenny bits.

Rico wasn't satisfied with his share and seeing a full pack of John Player ciggies on top of Fig's machine, tried his luck, "Give us a couple of fags?"

Figs gave his friend a look and shook his head, "Scrounging wee bastar'," he picked up the pack, took out two and handed them over.

"Cheers mate," Rico grinned.

An older man, spectacles, greasy looking, with a leery smile was watching from a few machines down. Rico looked up, there was a nod of recognition. "I've gotta go," Rico called to Rose. "Stay here, I'll be back in a bit," he shouted over his shoulder.

Where's he going?" Rose asked Figs.

Figs glanced up from his game, "He won't be long, just a wee bit of business."

Rose didn't know if she should stay but decided to wait a while, she'd give him a half-hour, an hour at the most. Figs continued playing as Rose looked on. They chatted a little with Rose asking most of the questions, but Fig's attention was the machine and the fruits going around. After constant losses, he gave her two quid to get change. "Tell him I want tanners."

The change booth was at the far end of the arcade, a sweaty middle-aged man in spectacles, held together with Sellotape sat behind a glass window. Rose handed him the two quid with Figs' request. The man counted out the tanners and wiped his brow. "Anything else I can get for you love?"

By the time Rose had returned, Figs had moved to try his luck on another machine. "Hey," he called out as Rose stood looking around. She handed over the coins.

Ping, ping, ping! went the machine as it paid out. "Fucking right," Figs grinned. "Aye, you m' lucky mascot." He scooped up the money into his fist and held out his hand, "Have a go. G'on fill yer tits."

Rose picked out a few coins, "Thanks." Dithering on which machine to choose, she wandered up and down the aisle. There were all sorts of themes, traditional fruits, cartoon characters, Hollywood Stars, after a lot of hesitation, she finally selected one with colourful selection of jungle animals. The coin went into the slot, she pulled the lever and watched the them spin. It stopped on a zebra, a monkey and a snake, which wasn't going to pay. She tried again, this time she got two monkeys in a line and was flashing for three nudges. She looked over at Figs, who was engrossed. Unsure, she tapped a button three times, a lion arrived, then a rhino, then a giraffe. She tried again, then again and again. The money Figs had giver her was running out, on her last spin, she pictured in her mind's eye three giraffes lined up, a three quid payout. She pulled the lever and around they went, then stopped on a giraffe, a snake and a monkey, she punched the button in frustration. It just wasn't her lucky day. Seeing Figs was still distracted, she changed her own two quid. The cashier winked and wished her luck as he handed over the stack of coins. The next machine she chose were spaceships, and as luck would have it paid out on her first go, but after that initial win, in barely seconds she was down to her last sixpence. This time she willed for three red rockets, she pulled the lever, when someone pinched her bum. She turned around to confront the perpetrator only to see a grinning Rico.

"Come on let's go," he said leading her through the aisles to the exit. Rose glanced back, just in hope, as a blue, a red, and a yellow rocket lined up. "We're off," Rico shouted over to the transfixed Figs, who didn't look or acknowledge their exit. Outside the sun was blazing. Rico raised his hand waving a handful of pound notes in the air. "Come on," he called catching hold of Rose's hand and spinning her around. Rose joined in the merriment as the pair waltzed into the middle of the road. When a car pulled up, they took no notice. The driver honked three sharp blasts of his horn, Rico gave him the V's and kicked out, as it raced by.

From there, they went up to Leicester Square, stopping at a photo booth for a quick snap. In two Rico was trying to stick his tongue in Rose's ear and in the third they were both pulling faces. Next, to the off-licence to buy cider but despite his protests Rico couldn't get served. At the next one, only Rose went in and bought two big bottles of Strongbow and a bag of Fruit Pastels. Rico opened a bottle straightaway and took a long swig before passing it over to Rose, who took a sip before passing it back. Through narrow streets and alleys, he led her to a pretty little park (or more properly described 'gardens') surrounded by a square of handsome houses. They found a spot in the sunshine and sat down.

Once again Rico offering the cider to Rose, she opened it and took another small sip. Rico took it from her, gulping it down. He handed it back, "Come on, have a drink."

Rose matched his slug, followed by a burped, and then another.

Rico laughed, "Yeah."

The cider gave Rose confidence and after a bit of idle chit-chat, she hesitantly asked, "What were you doing with that old man?"

Rico pulled off his coat and t-shirt. His skin was pale. No, paler that pale, as if he'd been whitewashed. After arranging a makeshift blanket, he laid back, "That bloke in the arcade?" He reached for the bottle, took a drink and held it up.

Rose took it, smiled and nodded.

He laid back, his hands covering his eyes. "Just a mate." He stretched over for the sweets, pulled out a fistful and then tossed the bag to Rose. Filling his cheeks he chewed for a while, then back to the cider, finishing the bottle. The last of the sweets he threw into the air, dodging his head to catch it. "He's a decent guy. Sometimes he's got work for me, that's all."

"What sort of work?"

"Just work," Rico looked up, "Hey open that," nodding at the remaining bottle.

As they soaked up the sun, Rose told Rico of her ambition to become an actress. Rico said he wanted to be a singer and sang a very passable *Georgia on My Mind*, by Ray Charles and got up to sing and dance to *Hit the Road Jack*. Ray Charles was his favourite artist, he explained that he was a blind black man who lived in America. Rose hadn't heard of him, but liked Rico's versions anyway.

With some encouragement, Rose performed a rendition of Blanche's death speech from Tennessee Williams' *A Streetcar Named Desire.* Finishing on, "I have always depended on the kindness of strangers."

Rico clapped enthusiastically and asked her to do it again, which she did, but stopped halfway through, as he seemed distracted, throwing sugar remains to a blackbird that had landed close by. Rose sat down taking over the sugar distribution, doing her best to tempt the bird, but sweetness is not for everyone, and after a taste, the blackbird flew off.

As they exchanged stories Rose mentioned Uncle Archies fling with Christine Keeler. Rico then reeled off a list of people he'd met, famous politicians, entertainers and even members of the Royal Family. Rose was dubious as to whether he was telling the truth. She didn't want to call him a liar, but he didn't know much about these famous people and wouldn't explain how he'd met them. *Well, how could he have met Lord Mountbatten for instance?*

"I know this one," said Rose getting to her feet. She picked up a piece of wood as a microphone and began singing Dusty Springfields, *I Only Want to be With You.*

"You stopped and smiled at me,

Asked if I care to dance

I fell into your open arms

And I didn't stand a chance"

Rico joining in,

"Now listen honey...."

"Give us another," Rico clapped and cheered.

Rose tried to think, but the only other song she knew well was, *White Christmas,* which didn't seem appropriate.

Rico opened the cider and between them they soon finished it off. "I knew we should have got another bottle," he said looking over his shoulder, he was contemplating, but after a moments thought, he changed his mind.

The sun was warm and sleepy, the grass soft and inviting. With senses dulled by alcohol, they were asleep in minutes. When Rose awoke, darkness was gently creeping towards them, Rico was still fast asleep. Propping herself up she leant over slowly examining his face, his forehead, the angle of his nose, his lips, his hair, his naked chest. He looked so young, like some street urchin from a postcard. She wanted to draw him, just a simple black and white outline, colour wouldn't have suited Rico.

Quietly getting to her feet Rose went for a stroll. The surrounding houses were art nouveau in style, three and four storeys, with elegant ironwork balconies. Rose wondered who lived there, not just now, but who had lived there? There would have been plenty of famous people no doubt, poets, artists, an actor or two, maybe even a celebrated ballerina. She was about to do a plie when a man called out Season, or it could have been Caesar, both names seemed strange for the little Jack Russell which appeared from nowhere, darting past her towards its master. Rico was still asleep when she returned, she gently kicked his foot. He woke startled, mouth open, eyes alert as though waking from a bad dream.

Seeing his shock, "You alright?" Rose asked.

Rico didn't answer, but sat up, resting his arms a moment on his knees. He looked to his left and right, let out a breath and rubbed and scrubbed the sleep from his head and face. "I need a pee," and wandered off to relieve himself.

Rose glanced at her watch; it was 9.15 pm.

"Come here, look, I've got something to show you," Rico called out from behind a bush.

Rose stepped into a wooded clearing cautiously, thinking he might be about to play a trick and flash his willy.

"Here, look," with a penknife, he was carving into the tree, working the knife with dexterity and ease. It was two R's inside a heart, he looked to Rose and laughed, "Come on, let's head into town. The action will be just picking up."

Rose smiled, unsure what to say.

Before leaving the gardens Rose tidied up the empty cider bottles and was looking around for a bin.

"Leave it," Rico shouted.

She hesitated.

"Fuck em."

But Rose couldn't help herself, tidily tucking the bottles under a bush, Rico shook his head and sniggered.

Dodging between buses and cars and taxis, Rose stuck close to Rico as angry drivers blared their horns, frustrated at a holdup being caused by some protest or other. In the distance police car's sirens were dashing this way and that, off to some emergency, maybe a robbery, an assault or even a shooting.

A young black guy called out to Rico from across the road.

Rico looked over and waved, "Patrick, where will you be later?"

Patrick shouted something, Rose couldn't hear, and Rico probably neither. Regardless, he stuck his thumb in the air and shouted back "Ok, see you there."

Patrick looked nonplussed as the pair vanished into a side street.

Within a few yards the noise level subsided, Rico looked back, he was grinning, "You wanna see a porno?"

Rose's mind skipped a beat. She would have loved to see a porno but didn't want to appear too eager. "What do you mean?"

Rico laughed, "A porno, a blue movie, triple xxx. You know, people shagging?"

Rose checked her watch as though she hadn't already made up her mind. A moment's hesitation over, "Yeah, first time for everything," she laughed.

They walked past quite a few xxx cinemas before Rico approached the entrance of one, *xxx Forbidden Flesh xxx,* flashed from the marquee billboard.

Rose waited as Rico strolled straight up, "My mate works here, we'll be alright," he said looking back.

But things did not go as smoothly as he planned. As they stepped inside, they were met by a burly bouncer, "No way! Not a chance."

Rico looked past him, "Is Frank in?"

The bouncer looked momentarily confused, "Frank ain't in and even if he was, you ain't getting in."

"Frank!" shouted Rico, "Frank!!"

Rose pulled at Rico's sleeve, "Don't worry, we'll do something else."

"Frank, Frank!!!

"Listen, I told you he ain't here."

"He's always here, Frank!" shouted Rico, trying to push past his burly adversary.

The bouncer put his hand on Rico's chest.

Rico looked indignant. Looking the bouncer up and down, "Fuck off!"

The jaw of the man-mountain clenched, his eyes intimidating, as he whispered a threat into Rico's ear. A shove sent Rico sprawling out onto the pavement.

"Now clear off."

In a split-second Rico was on his feet, launching himself at the meat head. It was a lightweight v heavyweight clash; Rico had no chance. Rose screamed, as the bouncer quickly took charge and was pummelling her friend. At the sound of a siren, Rose looked back, waving at the police car which screeched to a halt.

"The bastards stabbed me," shouted the bouncer, "He's just stabbed me. You little…" as he wrestled the knife from Rico. The coppers dashed forward. "The little bastards stabbed me." He had hold of Rico's throat, lifted him into the air and flung Rico out onto the street. Blood was oozing, a stain showing through the bouncer's shirt, he pulled back the waistband on his trousers to examine himself. Whether it was a grunt or a growl, he flung himself once more at Rico. Just in time the police grabbed his arms.

Rico had now gotten to his feet, and was glaring, the glare turned to a smile and the smile a blown kiss.

"Little bastard, and his tart!" The bouncer swung around scowling at Rose.

The shrill of a siren rang out as another cop car pulled up. Rico and Rose were taken to separate police stations. Alone in a cell, Rose wondered what would happen? What would her parents think? Would she have to go to court, a fine, maybe even jail? In the morning her father arrived in his Jaguar to take her home. All he said was that he had sorted things out, neither said another word on the journey home. Her mother looked distraught as she waited on the gravel drive. Rose dashed upstairs and didn't come down for the rest of the day. The following morning her mother brought her breakfast, and watched from the end of the bed as a contrite Rose ate. Once finished, her mother sat on the edge of the bed and calmly but firmly said, that her and Daddy had discussed it and decided Rose should not go back to Uncle Archies, and that Uncle Archie agreed. If she did not want to return to college, it was secretarial school. Rose's heart sank, she sat silently, not looking up, swallowing mouthful after mouthful of humble pie, she agreed to her mother's request.

In the new term, reluctantly Rose went back to college. It was later in the year when on a trip to the Planetarium, she slipped off to the bright lights of Piccadilly. It rained all day, but that didn't bother Rose. Every penny arcade she passed was visited and every side street walked. Someone looked like him on Shaftsbury Avenue, but it wasn't him, it was someone else. At street markets, pubs, she asked. A paperboy said he knew Rico but hadn't seen him for a long while. One guy suggested she look up by Charing Cross, if he wasn't there someone might know. At Charing Cross, she saw boys and girls, all young and eager to be fed. No one knew Rico, or even Mick from Manchester. Exhausted she sat down; her feet were killing her. A smartly dressed man was making his way over, clean shaven, handsome, he reminded her of her father. Rose watched as he approached one of the young girls, after a few moments of negotiation a fiver was exchanged, they disappeared together. Rose now understood a young soul was cheap, rented out by the hour.

The school bus was leaving at 5 pm but Rose didn't care, on and on she walked. Slumped in a crumpled heap outside a pub, she found Figs. Her heart jumped with excitement; Figs would know. But Figs was in a stupor, it was all he could do to raise his head, slobbering some hidden message before his eyelids closed. On she went, passing sex shops, pimps and prostitutes. At the strip club, the same bouncer in the doorway, he looked even bigger now, a mountain of muscle. What was Rico thinking of? A moment of madness.

At eight o'clock she bought a sandwich and sat herself in a corner of an empty shop doorway. It was then the thought came to her.

Yes, this was the square, the same beautiful buildings, the art nouveau ironwork. In moments she had found where they had sat, the tree, the carved heart still looked fresh. The empty bottles were still under the bush where she left them. She knelt and pulled one out. It was covered with tiny creatures, slugs; and dirt. With the hem of her skirt, she wiped the neck clean and after a bit of effort managed to opened it. The strong smell of cider hit her immediately. Pausing for a moment, she drew the mouth of the bottle to her lips, and kissed it.

Maybe a sneeze was on its way when Rose rubbed her nose and eyes, or maybe it was a memory. She took a faltering breath, smiling wistfully as she handed over the small black and white photo, "Now here's one I can tell you a story about."

Betty took the picture, studied it for a while, she looked up, "Gee, that kid looks young."

Change is Gonna Come

Jackson was in his prime but blighted with the curse of being lazy. On the death of his parents, he inherited the farm, all seven hundred acres. Cereal, vegetables, cattle, sheep, pigs, along with a bountiful apple orchard. He was strong and able but lacking energy and focus. Rather than work he would pass the day watching the daily dramas of his chickens, which he considered far more enlightening than Voltaire or Proust. The jobs that needed doing could wait until tomorrow, or the next day at the earliest. Mr Reins, his kindly neighbour, tried his best keeping Jackson motivated and organised, but Mr Reins was getting old and had his own farm to worry about. As the years passed in order to keep going, Jackson was forced to sell a field here, a field there and not having a clue of value was constantly taken advantage of.

Five years after he'd taken it on, all that was left of the original farm was the farmhouse and a smallholding of about twenty acres, maybe twenty-five on a clear day. Years slipped into decades, his once tall athletic body was now bent over, his face shrunken and hard. Understandably life had soured Jackson, he'd become a reclusive skinflint never venturing out unless to buy something that cord or nails would no longer hold together. The once beautiful farmhouse, his father's pride and joy, had become ramshackle. The roof of the parlour was the first to fall, and although he tried to repair it, it was no good. Another roof collapsed, then another and another, until very little of the house was habitable. The crops too were neglected, likewise the livestock which now amounted to two milking cows, a couple of pigs, Delilah the horse and a few chickens.

Regardless of Jackson's lackadaisical attitude the cock was as punctual as ever, at sunrise he would crow to its hearts content, but Jackson didn't stir. Only after a glass or two of cider would he begin his chores. He had now given up on the house and basically lived in his kitchen, it was warm and easy to keep. His day would begin after noon. He'd maybe pick some apples, clean out the animals, collect eggs and then again maybe not. Usually, he would be back in bed by the middle of the afternoon, sometimes up again in the evening for a glass of cider, sometimes not.

It was whilst cleaning out the stable that the idea first hit him and after a week or so of mulling it over, his mind was made up. He was going to become a horse. He'd always admired horses, their grace, their beauty, their instincts, they had it all. He looked over at Delilah, a beautiful tall chestnut mare, she had plenty of succulent pasture and only worked occasionally. He, on the other hand, got by on scraps and in his distorted mind slogged from sunrise to sunset.

In reality Delilah was just skin and bone, hooves unclipped, her coat a tangled mess, scabs and sores covered her body. Her feed was a barren paddock infested with weeds and thorns.

It was a couple of weeks later, he was feeling thirsty and went over to the scum covered trough. Delilah was already there and tried to shoo him away. Quick on his feet Jackson dodged her and returned to the trough on the other side. She however had no intention of giving up her water and chased him halfway down the field. When he returned, she went for him again, trying to bite. He bucked, kicking her firmly with both heels in the belly. That showed her, he thought and it appeared so, for now she accepted him at the trough and also let him choose where he grazed. Initially he found grass tasteless. His favourite feed were dandelions, they were delicious, but they didn't last long as he hoped and after a week of munching, he'd polished them off. After that it was back to grass. He soon got used to it and even learnt to pick out the sweetest blades, whinnying once he'd had his fill.

During the first weeks of transformation, he'd return to his kitchen to forage and rest up, but as time went on he was happy staying outside all day and at night would settle down next to Delilah in what was left of the barn.

It was on waking on a Sunday morning that he first heard her speak. He was having a pee in the corner of the barn, when a deep gruff voice told him to go outside and piss. This surprised him, particularly as it never crossed his mind that Delilah would to use vulgar language. She went on to tell him that if they were to live together then he should do his fair share of the work. He wasn't keen but after further conversation it seemed reasonable. After fitting Delilah's yoke and harness, with some rags and leather he strapped himself alongside her. He was happy for her to take the lead as she had a good eye in keeping the furrows straight. But after a discussion with one of the pigs, he was advised it would be best to create curves because the Earth's gravitational pull was dragging them towards the sun and curves would create better resistance. That certainly made sense but despite explaining this to Delilah and making himself perfectly clear about the importance of creating smooth curves Delilah couldn't quite get it. So, from then on, he took the lead making sure the curves were all of the same circumference as the moon.

One day whilst he was grazing, a car pulled up alongside the fencing, a big white car with red writing. They seemed friendly enough and offered him an apple. As it had been a while since he'd seen visitors Jackson showed them around. The man in the white jacket asked most of the questions whilst the lady wandered about. Delilah called out for him to stay alert, as she wandered to the far end of the field. She was right. The man in the white jacket grabbed hold of him and tried to put him in a halter, but Jackson snorted with fury and reared up as he chased them off. It all began to make sense to Jackson now, planes had been buzzing overhead all through the night, the tractor had probably been planning this for some time. The strange event had thrown him, he went for a trot whinnying at the top of his lungs, until Delilah called out to him to be quiet. Frightened, he didn't sleep at all well and on waking went for another trot, until he picked up the scent of the wolves.

The place was in chaos, fields unploughed, crops gone over. The animals along with himself were mere skin and bone. Although to Jackson everything seemed to be working like clockwork and the farm was thriving. All were happy, even the rebellious pigs revelled in self-determination.

It was Tuesday or maybe Friday when the trucks pulled up. Jackson hid behind the barn as they loaded his friends up and took them away. That evening he wandered around alone. *Where was the farmer? He'd normally have been fed by now.* At the farmhouse he sniffed at the windows and gently kicked the door. He then trotted around to the front and back into the field. The water trough was empty, he licked around the inside edge in the hope to capture some moisture. There was one last dandelion hiding under the hedge, he went over to eat it and nibble some weeds. He let out a lonely whinny and sniffed the air. He felt tired and weary and as the night drew in the cold gnawed at his skin. The best of the summer had gone, slowly he closed his eyes.

Art Lovers

Like a pair of autumn leaves, silently they floated in. She was dressed in black from head to toe, handsome rather than pretty and a little bit thinner than healthy. He was of that flamboyant hipster type, you know the sort, country squire jacket and waistcoat, jeans with a four-inch turn-up, Walter Raleigh beard and waxed moustache. To me he looked a nob, but who am I to judge? At a guess I'd have said they were in their early fifties or late forties, he appeared more confident than she.

The Moreton Gallery is an eighteenth-century building, grade II listed, with lots of history. It is about the size of a good sized three-bedroom house, I live above the shop. Downstairs are the exhibition rooms, four in total. My desk is tucked away towards the rear, allowing the customers to settle in before I approach them. I have a fair view, although there are some blind-spots.

Watching them from the corner of my eye, I pretended to be busy. My initial thoughts were, they were strong potential customers, well dressed, middle class and obviously interested in art. After a few moments they went their separate ways, each working their way around the first room. She slipped out of view but I could clearly see him. He was standing still with arms across his chest, like a worshipper at the altar of art. With his hands under his chin, he was staring intently at a painting of a bouquet of flowers in a plain vase. I watched as he stepped closer to scrutinise the brushstrokes. He took two steps back and waited, thoughtful, with intelligent contemplation. Reaching into his top pocket he pulled out a pair of half framed horn-rimmed glasses to re-examine the details. My hopes of a sale moved up a notch. This was a good time to introduce myself, a tentative strike. Nonchalantly I wondered over, gave them my usual flannel, a jolly welcome and "If there's anything I can do to help," blag. He smiled politely and mouthed, "Thank you." The lady didn't acknowledge the greeting, she was transfixed by a landscape. I returned to my desk, settled on my chair and began fiddling with my laptop, I too must play my part. He was now focused on the information sheet about the artist, roughly half a page, which I keep specifically sparse. I grinned, wondering what pearls he would find. After five minutes of digesting the information he returned to the painting, then once again the literature. Like a vision, she appeared and whispered something in his ear, *it was a secret*. His parson's expression remained apart from a quick glance over his shoulder. Her eyes followed his. He whispered something; *it was a secret*. She returned to her post. My 'Spidey senses' were tingling, maybe they weren't customers after all. What could be their objective? Perhaps they were from another gallery spying? Could they be artists themselves? I felt frustrated. My job is to sell paintings, spies and artists were in the same camp, both a waste of time. I could feel my hackles rising. Onto the next painting and the same procedure, hand on chin in quiet contemplation, five minutes of hypnotic rapture, another five minutes reading from the 'gospel' before moving on to the next.

As I faffed, she appeared before me, only for a split-second, then disappeared from view. Silently he swept in and joined her. Halfway around the second room, they stopped to embrace the intellectual challenges of an abstract piece. For fifteen minutes they contemplated it's worth. From painting to painting, it went on. It was like a religious experience and reminded me of the stations of the cross my mother would insist I do on Sunday after mass.

I wanted to get closer, so wandered over to the ceramic displays. I moved a ceramic pot over a few inches. She watched as I moved off. Perhaps unaware that the eyes in the back of my head were on her, she sniggered, the snigger of cultural superiority. He glanced at my retreating figure, sombre neutrality intact. They moved onto the next painting but only for a moment or two, with the slightest movement of her head she dismissed it. He whispered something; *it was a secret.*

Now I don't know if any of my readers have ever worked in sales? For many years I have. One of the things I've learnt, is to avoid 'dead energy', once it takes over, you are scuppered. At that time the energy was on life support and needed a jolt, so I turned up my music machine, not up to the proverbial 'eleven' that would have been bad manners but up to maybe a seven. It proved to have no effect; they were totally oblivious, neither showed the slightest change. It was like I was in the company of two spectres. I blasted the music up to eight, still nothing. Eight is actually far too loud for a man of my age, so back down it went to a comfortable five as I contemplated my next move.

Busying myself like a bustling housewife from a seaside postcard, I ventured closer again, stretching an ear in the hope of catching a murmur. The next painting was a woodlands scene, blue hues, greens and oranges, with particularly well executed light and shadow. It obviously hit the spot. After a minute or two of quiet reflection, they waited for the 'spirit' of the painting to enter. I too waited. Now I don't know if I was being duped but it did seem as though the spirit moved. Both he and she closed their eyes in tempered ecstasy.

Feeling uncomfortable in the presence of the spirit, I picked up my teacup and wandered into one of the other rooms. I let out a sigh. Over the years I have learnt that the most earnest art lovers are the least likely to purchase. At an educated guess I put their chances of buying in the 'Zilcho' or 'Not a cat in hells' category.

When I returned, they were by my desk, like figures from a Caravaggio painting, dolefully staring up at an oil of a nude female floating in water, deep blues, pale blues and gold. The artist had skilfully picked out a shimmer of light on his subject's body as she emerged to the surface. A beautiful piece. This time it was his turn to whisper a secret. She looked to him with the faintest of nods.

They had now moved into the fourth room, or 'space,' as we call it in the business. Both were enraptured as they engaged with a seascape. It was another oil, a painting with endless depth, ethereal clouds that played and teased the surface of reality, drifting in and out of hidden consciousness. I moved closer in a bid to feel the ripples of their energy.

Breaking the solemnity of the occasion, there was a call from the doorway of the gallery.

"Hello!"

I chose to ignore it, but again it came.

"Hello!"

I gave in, "Hello," I called back, in rather a grumpy manner.

"Hello!"

Huffing, I went to the doorway at front of the gallery. There stood a huge African man, head shaved, his colour blacker than brown. By his side stood an equally large woman. She was dressed in traditional African clothes, bright strong colours. Beside them were a plethora of suitcases.

The man grinned, "We would like to buy this painting please." From outside he pointed to my window display, a country scene in mixed media.

The woman's smile was as warm as a barbeque on a summer's evening, wholesome and appealing.

"Yes, that one," said the man.

By the time I returned to wrap the painting and take a payment, the mysterious couple had gone. For the life of me, I couldn't figure how I missed them. But then again, that's art lovers for you!

God and the Devil

It had been quite a number of years, thousands, some say millions. But however long it was Lucifer was getting weary. He had made many a deal in his day, ten thousand souls here, a million there, so many he'd lost count. But as time passed, he hankered for the simple, less responsible days of his time in Heaven. Yes of course, everybody knows they'd had their fall-outs, that's been well documented, but he still admired the big fellow. Well, who wouldn't? Creating the world in six days is quite a feat!

It niggled and niggled. In the late seventeenth century he shared his thoughts with his trusted allies. Leviathan, Astaroth and Azael were sceptical but Behemoth was more open to the idea. Lucifer pondered and before he realised it a hundred years had passed. Things weren't getting better for the master of evil, and again he pondered. The problem was there seemed to be a desperate lack of wickedness in the world. Despots were now as rare as Harpy eggs, even lawyers and politicians were mostly on the straight and narrow. Life had become boring. Lucifer wasn't so stupid not to see the writing on the wall. He was on a sticky wicket, and before being bowled out, he decided now was the time to negotiate.

He first call was to his old mate Michael the Archangel. They agreed to do lunch the following week, choosing neutral ground, the Vatican.

By the time their starters were served Michael was convinced, he liked the idea. Heaven was just too pleasant these days, too many goody goodies, "It's all rules and regulations now. You're not allowed to smite an evil doer without three lots of paperwork now. Not the job it used to be," Michael lamented. "The crowd we get these days," he grimaced, "Talk about puritans!" And eying the grilled calamari being served by an angelic looking altar boy, "We could do with a bit more fire and brimstone, a few of the old school back to stir things up."

Lucifer bellowed out a huge laugh as they high fived.

They shared stories as they ate the calamari, stories of the good old days. For mains they had steaks in red wine sauce. Lucifer plumped for tiramisu and Michael, panna cotta with strawberries, for pudding.

"What about the time you let loose the lambs and hid his staff," said Lucifer, glancing over his shoulder.

"He still hasn't got over it, very defensive these days," Michael winked.

Late in the afternoon, a not so pious Pope Benedict wandered by. They lowered their voices, waiting until he was out of sight.

Lucifer's eyes drifted to the heavens. "He's a tell-tale. Pfaff! And the favours I've done for him," shaking his head. "I've got to meet him later to discuss the new Bishop of London. Anyway, I've kept you long enough old friend."

They shook hands and embraced. In a blur of light Michael the Archangel left. As he drifted up through cloud after cloud, he pondered, *what was his worth these days?* Saving the planet or issues of oppression just wasn't his thing and not a patch on defending a helpless virgin from a wicked bishop. He hadn't seen real action for centuries. No, he hankered for the return of the likes of Vlad the Impaler, Genghis Khan or Nero, men who didn't mind getting their hands dirty. It was so petty and impersonal now; the fun had gone.

After having his details checked at the gates by Saint Peter, Michael made his way to see Raphael, once a good friend of Lucifer's. In fact, before Lucifer's fall from grace, they'd both led the First House of Heaven.

At the mention of his name Raphael grinned, "How is the old Devil?"

Michael said he didn't seem himself and was a bit worried for him.

On the idea of a possible truce, Raphael's eyes lit up, "Anything for a bit of excitement and if there's one person who would liven up this place," his eyebrows lifted. Raphael said he'd speak to God the Almighty and pass on a message. Weeks and months went by, finally Raphael got back to Michael, saying that God was willing to talk and that Michael should set up a meeting.

Evil doers are most active on Earth on Friday nights, well it's all the drinking and such. Hoping for a swift journey, Michael chose that evening for his descent. At the entrance to Hades he was met by Cerberus the savage three-headed dog, its lips dripping with bloodied drool. From his bow quiver Michael pulled the thighbone of an ass and flung it at the terrible beast, slipping by as Cerberus greedily tucked in. The descent was initially slow, Michael hadn't been there in over a millennium and with a myriad of tunnels to navigate, it seemed more complicated than he remembered. Fortunately, there was fairly good signage. There was one for Limbo, that was where the unbaptised babies were sent, other signs were for Anger, Greed, Lust and Violence. Further on there was one which read Treachery and pointed deeper into the bowels. Michael knew this was where he would find his old friend. The journey was fairly uneventful, the only evil-doers of note were a demon aimlessly roasting a sinner on a spit, and a pair of witches playing hopscotch over a set of tombstones. The rest didn't strike Michael as evil at all, definitely not the Hades of his younger days. There particularly didn't seem to be any young people, everyone was at least three hundred years old, most a lot older than that. After a day of flight, Michael reached the ice-cold centre, pulling his cloak tightly around himself he wandered through.

On recognising Judas Iscariot, he smiled. Judas was hanging naked upside down from a tree limb. He looked in a right state. Lucifer had obviously been chewing him all morning. Michael's heart went out to him but quickly reminded himself, *Well, you've made your bed...*

A little further on he spotted a succubus, she was standing next to a tree hollow with a tangle of branches above. She looked beautiful, slim, dark with cinnamon highlights in her hair, Michael wouldn't deny he was tempted, but realising the evil she possessed he covered his eyes. But temptation is nothing if not a tenacious beast. He risked another glance. She had transformed, even more enticing this time, with blonde hair that flowed passed her shoulders and crystal blue eyes. She smiled and beckoned him forth. Michael clutched his sword tightly, *In another world, maybe, in another world.*

Suddenly a decapitated head flew over his shoulder. The girl scattered in a rainbow of colours as a glow of sparks and flames emerged from the hollowed tree. Two small demons appeared and manically ran in opposite directions into the distance, only to reappear a few seconds later from the same hollow, this time they skipped and danced in circles. A crowd was gathering around Michael, licentious witches admiring his film star looks and golden ringlets. Heaven knows what sort of ruckus he would cause if he revealed himself. Wisely he moved on.

In the middle of 'Treachery' stood a monstrous tree, from its twisted limbs hung millions of souls, all silently screaming in torment. As Michael got closer, he could see below its branches a door painted in a bright shade of fuchsia. Outside, like decorative ornaments, stood cauldrons of various sizes, all filled with human flesh and blood. Above the door was a sign, 'Prince of Darkness,' nailed around and above the doorway at various heights were genitals and ears. *He hasn't lost his sense of humour,* thought Michael as he pushed the door the door open.

Sitting behind a desk of skulls was a clerk who had more than a passing resemblance to Robespierre. Not looking up, the desk clerk asked, "Have you an appointment?"

From his cloak Michael produced a scroll, which was tied with a gold ribbon and passed it over. Fear mixed with ecstasy appeared on the clerk's face as he unfurled the document. He raised a bony finger and pointed "Deeper, deeper."

On golden wings Michael flew, passing desecrated crucifixes, decaying bodies, on past the fornicators of beasts, on over the river of boiling blood where single limbs splashed and thrashed in an effort to be free. After seven days of flight the tunnel opened out into a beautiful palace. Servants were dashing this way and that. All were perfect and naked with shaved heads, a tattoo of a pentagram on each of their skulls.

An extremely tall, blind, spirit, approached, "Follow me."

The spirit led him through a room of silver, where in the centre there was a huge banqueting table. Gathered around it were the gluttons feasting on unbaptised babies, only for later to painfully defecate them whole. They looked up, blood and saliva dripping from their ample chops. The next room was gold. Great pools of it spreading across the floor, with stalagmites dripping with molten metal. Here were the money lenders in twisted ecstasy, each counting days of profit as the glistening boiling metal engulfed them. In the diamond room three huge thrones were aligned, on which sat three giants who gazed out into the world of men. With a sweep of his arm one moved a mountain range, another laughed and raised the waters from the seas. The third plucked up a young boy from his sleep and blew on him sparks of luck, and as quickly as he was stolen, he was returned. Next the boy's sister was chosen, she was sprinkled with envy and she too returned to her slumber.

The final room was dark, a darkness that engulfed all it touched. The blind spirit raised a withered hand.

A voicelessness called out, "Old friend, come and join me."

Michael moved forward. Within a few steps a light appeared, dim at first, but as he ventured on he could see the light was emanating from Lucifer.

"That's some trick."

Lucifer welcomed Michael with smile, "To be honest I'm happiest in darkness. It's a curse from God the Almighty, the light doesn't suit me." A mirror appeared, Lucifer looked at his hideous reflection, raised a hand to cover his eyes and shook his head. "Time has not served me well, old friend." He put an arm over Michael's shoulder, "Come with me, let me get you some sustenance. I have just this moment slaughtered a goat, let us sit together as my servant prepares it."

A beautiful Egyptian woman, who could have been Cleopatra looked up from the spit she was tending. Gracefully she added spices over the roasting flesh, her tears of blood ensuring the meat's succulence. Lucifer led Michael to a table of marble, some may say an altar but regardless it was here they sat. The finest wines were offered as they were served strips of freshly cooked meat.

Once sated, "So, tell me the news?" said Lucifer as he flung a morsel to a goat with the head of a dog. "Is he being reasonable?"

Michael didn't answer but searched in the purse he had slung from his shoulder, from it he pulled out an envelope, which was sealed with wax. Lucifer took it and inspected the seal, with a gentle breath the wax melted. Michael watched as Lucifer scanned the note. He had read to about halfway down, when his eyes squinted and went back to the top.

"Blooming eck! Is Hebrew not good enough for him now?" A long sigh left Lucifer's lips. "Doesn't make it easy, does he?" He flipped the letter over, and with a single claw pointed, look, "*Hereth, pertend, judicious, delation, coil.*" He let out a long slow breath, he seemed wearisome. He called over to a small satyr. "Get me Shakespeare, he's responsible for all this, he's gonna have to sort it out." Shaking his head Lucifer glanced up at the laughing Michael, "I can't make head or tail."

In a second, Shakespeare appeared but not as we would recognise him. He was wearing what looked like a lightweight silver spacesuit, although strangely he still wore a ruff.

Lucifer casually flipped over the letter, "This is your doing. What does it mean?"

Shakespeare bowed, fawningly took the letter and began to read the contents.

Lucifer poured some more wine.

Shakespeare's head dipped; his lips pursed.

Lucifer looked up, "Well?"

Shakespeare's hand went up, signalling he was still reading.

Lucifer shook his head, and mouthed to Michael, "He hasn't got a clue."

"M'lud, tis a quandary that futility hath…"

Whoa, whoa, whoa… just tell me what it means," Lucifer's eyes drifted to the heavens.

Shakespeare looked annoyed, "Well, I'm no lawyer but from what I can gather, The Almighty Father agrees to meet you in purgatory on the eleventh hour, eleven days from now to discuss the current contract of division and responsibilities."

"Does he mention anything about a truce?"

Shakespeare's eyes went back to the letter, his lips tracing out words one more time, slowly he shook his head, "I can't see any specific reference to a truce. Oh, hold on, "The parties thou-eth present shall commence to agreement forthwith on the assumption herein disclosed or undisclosed on the final day of judgement, or…" Shakespeare raised a finger, "that flesh engaged great woes of absent loyalty, that can only be dismissed by your King."

Lucifer looked to Michael, who shrugged.

"I think it means that there may be a possible truce, if you agree to loyalty," said Shakespeare. "But that said… my advice would be to run it past Robespierre, for the final word."

Lucifer clicked his fingers, Shakespeare's arms, legs and torso shot off in opposite directions, his head plopped to the ground. There it lay facing up from the ash and cinders, lips moving but no words could be heard.

Lucifer smiled at the head, "Well, they'll have to come and find you, won't they!" He winked at Michael, "It's the only way I can shut him up."

When it was time to leave, Lucifer walked Michael to a small door marked with a no entry sign, "A short cut," he said as he waved him off.

Eleven days past in a jiffy. On the morning of the meeting, Lucifer was up early, nervous and eager to impress. He was unsure whether to wear his best 'power suit' blood red, with a purple lining or a smart black tuxedo. Behemoth suggested that the 'power suit,' just might give off the wrong impression. Lucifer looked at himself in the mirror, "No, I'm sticking with red, I think it suits my colouring."

"Whatever master," Behemoth smiled, then glanced up to the sun, "We better be making a move."

A long black chariot led by twelve black stallions swooped down and in seconds they were gone. Behind them followed another six chariots carrying a mix of witches, tyrants and demons.

Now, I don't know if you have ever been to purgatory, but it is not an attractive place. It has neither the serenity of heaven or the warmth and colour of hell, very dull. Imagine an open-air hospital or a doctor's waiting room, the weather is mostly drizzle, but not enough to get you really wet. You can't see where it starts, or finishes. On arrival, you take your place in a queue, a long queue. A decade or two goes by before you get to the front. You pull out your ticket from the dispenser, and its number is in the billions, you take a seat, and wait, and wait…and wait. So, as you can imagine, with delegations from both heaven and hell that day, there was quite a lot of consternation and queue jumping for that matter.

Purgatory palace, where the assembly was to take place was impressive however. It had four turrets of shiny bronze; the walls were made from gleaming white sandstone with a bronze roof. At the entrance, Lucifer's delegation dismounted from the left, God's chosen angels, saints and theological scholars from the right. As they filed in, the two sides passed each other. A few of the old school waved with friendly banter, whilst it was obscenities and unwanted blessings from the younger crowd. The inside wasn't as big as you might imagine. A fair-sized theatre, bowl-shaped, around a central platform where two thrones were placed. One on the right was reserved for God the Almighty, larger and more opulently painted than Lucifer's plainer functional piece.

After everyone had settled into their seats, a trumpet sounded, followed by Elvis Presley's Jailhouse Rock, which as we all know is 'The Devil's Music.' From behind a curtain Lucifer appeared. He was right about the red, he looked fantastic, erect and proud. Behind him followed Behemoth, who held up Lucifer's cloak. Behind them trooped Genghis Khan, doing his best at rebel rousing, to get the crowd going. Behind him was an assembly of various dastardly demons and sinners. Whilst Lucifer's supporters shouted and whooped it up, the saintly kept their eyes fixed to their bibles, repeatedly making the sign of the cross.

Once on stage, Behemoth removed Lucifer's cloak. Like in a boxing match Lucifer trotted this way and that, thrusting out a wing here, a claw there, as though warming up. It was plain to see he was enjoying himself. Whilst dancing about he would change form. A huge cheer went up when he appeared as Salome, he danced a couple of veils, then slowly ran a finger across his own throat, and pulled a face of mock terror. With a wink and a click of his fingers Lucifer turned into one of the Popes, which got an even bigger cheer. He walked towards God's exquisite throne and pretended to sit. A roar of outrage went up from the saints, a chorus of laughter from his own quarter. Lucifer innocently put a claw to his mouth in mock apology, cartwheeled to the centre, then like a genie spun at amazing speed to the ceiling, only to return to the floor as himself. With a grin and a long low graceful bow, he took his seat.

The trumpet sounded again; this time followed by the sanctimonious tones of Cliff Richard's 'Lord's Prayer.' Lucifer stood and cupped his ear. With a dismissive wave of his arm and a shake of his head, he sat back down.

From the side of the stage, a light shone, a blinding light, brighter than the brightest jewel, brighter than the brightest star. The music changed from Cliff to a sacred symphony that filled the room. In fear of destruction, Lucifer's followers scrambled, hiding below their seats as God the Almighty appeared. He was dressed in a simple gown. His long white hair hung from his noble brow, over his shoulder he wore a red cloak and, on his head, a jewel encrusted crown. Amazed at its beauty, Lucifer bent forward for a better view.

God the Almighty made his way forward, in the centre of the stage he stopped, graciously bowing to all sides. With a serene smile he waited for the room to settle, then implored the evil-doers from the shadows into the light. Only after all were seated did he take his place on his throne, high on high.

The debate began with the sinners. Lenin made an impassioned speech on the relevance of good and bad in a complex modern society, which seemed to make sense to the hoi-polloi, although the saints and bishops seemed less impressed. He passed the mic over to St Paul who shared his undoubted knowledge of the Bible, quoting chapter and verse. For his letter to The Corinthians on the subject of love, he got a rousing applause. Even Lucifer was moved, and ever the gentleman, helped the old man off the stage.

After thirty days and thirty nights of discussion they called a recess. The saints fasted and prayed, the sinners feasted and fornicated with abandon whilst the Purgatoreans enviously looked on.

It was now time for Lucifer and God the Almighty to speak. The rules were that they didn't have to speak in person but could choose a champion. To howls of amusement from his own side and gasps of outrage from the other, Lucifer asked Michael the Archangel to speak on his behalf. God the Almighty smiled knowingly. Shocked, Michael looked up, God smiled and moved a reassuring arm in a guiding fashion imploring Michael to the stage. Michael hesitantly stepped forward. From his awkward gait it was evident he was unaware that he would be playing a part, especially on the side of The Prince of Darkness.

Michael bowed to his master, then made his way over to Lucifer. Lucifer put an arm around Michael's shoulder drawing him closer and whispered in his ear. God the Almighty who could obviously hear looked puzzled, before a wry smile appeared.

"Now you all know me," Michael raised his arms and turned full circle as he greeted the audience.

There was some booing from Lucifer's supporters but most looked on respectfully.

"You all know me," he repeated. I am not here to bewray, or assay on behalf of this…" he glanced over at Lucifer, "this… fallen angel."

Lucifer smiled.

Raising his voice, Michael went on, "I think eternal damnation is too good for one as such as ye. For ye are truly lewd, immoral, filthy and have both conducted and encouraged drunkenness, rioting, wantonness and of course chambering.

Lucifer's eyes searched out Shakespeare in the audience, and shook his head at the bard.

"And yet! Now that he hath wrought to espouse ten thousand and again ten thousand."

"Plain English please!" An exasperated Lucifer stood, his shoulders went up, and gesturing, his hands went out, "What the..?".

God nodded, as Michael looked over.

"Thank you!" said Lucifer.

"The long and short of it is this," Michael's hand swept to The Prince of Darkness. "This fiend, this devil, this fallen angel asks for mercy. Yes, we all know him as the beast, the serpent, the seducer of the pure, destroyer of good, angel of the bottomless pit. But now he accepts his wickedness is ultimately fruitless and wants once again to follow the path of righteousness." He looked to Lucifer, "Not as a saint, not as an apostle but as an advisor. Someone who is able to bring balance, assurance and insight to those who stray. Who better at understanding the ways of evil? For his eternal allegiance to God the Almighty, all he asks is eight hours. Just eight hours in every full week to be allowed to return to his lair to tend to the fallen and their needs.

A murmur went up from the saints. Frantic chatter from the evil doers. In a hushed silence God the Almighty rose from his throne. He bowed to Michael, and gave Lucifer an adversarial gaze. From the centre of the stage, he looked out. Witches and demons quivered in fear and averted their eyes. The godly looked on enraptured.

"Look up, look up my friends," God the Almighty paused, waiting. "All I see before me are one and the same, two sides of the same coin. It has been a long time since we have been divided. We have fought and battled hard since the beginning of time. Good versus evil. Once..." he looked over to Lucifer, "My friend was loyal, trusted, a worthy ally. But he strayed from the path, his deeds caused the fall of man, war, the degradation of spirit. He now comes before us to ask for a way back. A way to the true light. He asks for time to tend to his brethren, which I am sure will cause many of you to faulter. But what is your God but a God of mercy? I will agree one hour out of twenty-four to attend to his flock. As long as the remaining twenty-three are spent in the pursuit of truth and holiness."

A grin appeared on Lucifer's face, he walked over, joining God in the centre. The audience were silent, the saints wary of Lucifer's deceitful ways, witches and demons unsure whether they wanted to embrace goodness and virtue. A smiling Michael returned to the stage, under his arm was a parchment. Miraculously the terms of the agreement were already set out. Over a tablet of stone, the former adversaries faced each other. Lucifer withdrew from his pocket a beautiful quill pen, it was decorated with scrolls of gold, a plume of rich golden feathers and a diamond head. He raised his index finger, a drop of blood instantly appeared. With the most delicate of touches, he signed his name, Lucifer, Prince of Darkness. God the Almighty took the quill and he too signed the document. It was done, a truce of good and evil. A return to the fold for Lucifer.

It would be a lie to say there was tumultuous applause. There was muted clapping from the newest additions of the saintly but that was about it.

With a new leaf turned, Lucifer thought better than to try and arrange a feast. With a humble bow, he left the stage. From there he went to the tiny chapel and for the first time in over a million years, he knelt and prayed. Yes, he would be the first to admit he had initially liked the lifestyle, and the title, Prince of Darkness certainly had a ring to it, a weight, a gravitas. But in truth to go back to the fold was all he ever wanted.

On the way out he spotted a visitors' book and humbled, he took his place in the back of the queue to sign. As he got close to the front, he reached into his inside pocket. It was only then he realised that God the Almighty had 'coveted' his favourite quill.

Bradley

The story is set way back in the olden days, not quite 'Ye olde days,' probably the late 1950's or early 1960's at the latest.

Bradley smiled and as a way of thanks he tapped the dashboard of his Austin Morris Traveller van. It hadn't let him down yet and today was no different. Yes, it had seen better days. Every tyre was as bald as Bradley himself. It was held together with string and wire, but if Flannery the mechanic was right, it still had plenty of life. He had travelled down from Falcarragh, a tricky road at the best of times but as it was mid-winter, doubly so.

No sooner was he out of the van when a lumbering figure dressed in a black cassock and threadbare grey overcoat appeared through the cold misty air.

"You're late Bradley," said Father O'Malley. "What the hell kept you?" The priest was a lump of a man, thick grey hair with the face of a fighter who, on his best night had struggled to come second. "You should have been here an hour ago. That gang's going crazy." His thumb stabbing in the direction of the church hall.

It was New Year's Eve, a hum of chatter along with cackles of laughter could be heard from the small white-painted building.

"Sorry, I know," Bradley stooped apologetically. "I was held up in Bucranna dropping out a telly set to one of Paddy O'Donnell's," he said as way of excuse.

Bradley was in his early thirties, as thin as a rake and at five foot ten was tall for the times. He was ambitious and going places. His television and radio business had taken off and at the weekends he ran a travelling picture show, he was raking it in.

O'Malley shook his head; he didn't want to hear excuses. "Well get a move on," he said, tramping back towards the warmth.

Tonight's show needed to be an epic, and Bradley had decided on *Gone with the Wind*, which although had been shown only eight weeks earlier, still managed to fill the house. The crowd surmounted to fifty-eight, fifty-nine if you included O'Malley, which Bradley did not, as the tight-arsed priest didn't pay. Josie Breslin arrived to help carry the projection equipment inside.

As they entered, Mrs Dugan from The Legion of Mary was pouring cups of tea from a huge black teapot and handing out tea to all and sundry. The thickset farming men would politely take a few sips from the pretty China cups, but as she moved on the whiskey bottles emerged.

Waving off help from the interfering Mr Dugan, Josie set up the big screen on the stage. Bradley checked the projector and turned on the power. Everything was fine. From an old leather bag he pulled out a selection of film reels resting them in the crook of his arm. As he flicked through them a panic spread from his stomach to his head and back again. He opened a battered suitcase, glancing inside, then slamming it closed again. Biting down on his lip, he cursed himself. *Ya fucking idiot.*

Big Tommy clapped his hands and shouted, "C'mon Bradley where's the fil'm." followed by a chorus of whistles and jeers from the crowd.

Bradley smiled nervously.

After a few more seconds the seated O'Malley roared from the front row, "Will you not roll the fil'm!"

Bradley did not respond. Without a word, he walked to the door and out.

Mrs Dugan's eyes followed him. "Is everything ok with Bradley?" she asked with gleeful concern.

"Everything's ok," shouted Josey getting to his feet trying to calm the situation. "Give him a minute."

Bradley opened the back doors of the van and peered inside. Then with distant hope he went to the front door and opened it, his heart sunk. With his mind racing he mentally followed his footsteps, lifting a finger at each conclusion. *Yes, definitely loaded them.... they were in the basket with the valves.* His thumb and forefinger were in the air when it struck him.

Bradley had a roving eye and despite his lack of success, fancied himself as a ladies' man. Annie O'Donnell was a fine looking woman and in that tight-fitting sweater, she'd kept him talking long after he should have. *Ah Jaysus, young Mickey O'Donnell was hanging around the back of the van.* He bit his bottom lip again. *The thieving ejit! What use is a reel of fil'm to him.* Bradley pictured young Mickey running at top speed with the reel of film trailing in his wake. *The wee bastard will make fun enough. Oh yes, he'll have fun alright.*

Buncrana was at least a half-hour drive away. Knowing O'Malley would string him up from the pulpit Bradley came up with an idea. He had the middle and the end of the film, along with a couple of Laurel and Hardy reels and an Abbott and Costello too. He decided that he would chance his arm and start with the comedy and maybe they would have had their fill with just laughing and leave to get home. So, on went *The Trail of the Lonesome Pine*. He nodded at Josie and the lights went out. With a flicker of life on came the screen, the crowd whistled and stamped their feet.

A few moments later from the front row a dark shadow rose, it was O'Malley. A haze of smoke billowed behind him as he made his way to the back. Bradley hadn't noticed, his eyes had settled on Nora Boyle, and was confused at her expression of blind panic. Bradley looked up; his jaw dropped, his stomach tightened, as about a foot away stood O'Malley.

O'Malley whispered, if a shout could ever be described as a whisper. "What the hell's going on? You came here to show me *Gone with the Wind*. Why am I watching those two clowns?" His finger stabbed through the darkness as Laurel and Hardy were making their way down a dusty road.

Bradley took a deep breath. Like the rest of the crowd, Bradley was Catholic, and whilst a tall tale in the interest of making a bob or two was one thing, but to tell one to a priest was as sure as booking a seat in Beelzebub's parlour. He nodded in the direction of the doorway. O'Malley fixed him with a stony glare. Bradley leant towards the priest "I'll explain outside."

O'Malley nodded, turned and marched towards the door; Bradley followed, focusing on the priest's calloused hands clasped behind his back, as they made their way outside. In the cold air Bradley paced back and forth, trying to explain his dilemma. O'Malley listened intently, head over to one side. With the mention of the glamourous Annie O'Donnell, the priest's demeanour changed.

"Stand still will ya." He grabbed Bradley by the shoulders; "What the hell are yer talking about?".

"Well while she was paying me, that's when the reel went missing."

"Paying yer!" said O'Malley leaning forward to hear Bradley's response

"Only a down payment," said Bradley confidently, "I've put her on the never-never".

O'Malley did a cartoon-style double take as he registered what had been said and subconsciously glanced down at Bradley's flies. "What do you mean the never-never?"

"Well, you know…. she pays me every month."

"Jeezus Almighty," O'Malley drew in a breath, "and what does O'Donnell think of that?" he cupped an ear eager not to miss a word.

"Well, he's fine." Bradley glanced over O'Malley's shoulder. Lowering his voice, "To tell you the truth, he didn't have much to say about the matter Father." Feeling himself and O'Malley had the measure of each other, he smiled, before noticing the priest's demeanour. "What's the matter, Father?"

O'Malley was looking with the eye of a detective, searching Bradley for the carnal sin he was sure he'd find. He scratched his grey beard, intrigued but confused. He wanted to ask more but thought it could wait until Bradley was next at confession. "So how do you propose we sort out the little matter of tonight's fil'm?"

Bradley squinted as he deliberated his course. "I won't disappoint you Father, not at all. If it wasn't for that rascal Mickey O'Donnell, we'd all be transported back tonight to the Colonial South, to days of romance and intrigue." This was his usual introduction to the film. "Oh, it's a powerful fil'm alright, not one to be missed." Hesitantly, he went on, "Could we perhaps show the fil'm on a different night, Father? I'll be more than happy to return another day and do a special performance for yourself." His head empathetically to the side, waiting for O'Malley's response.

O'Malley reached into his cassock and scratched himself, then without a word turned towards the hall. Bradley meekly followed. Once inside the priest marched to the front. All eyes were on him, apart from wee Peter O'Toole who despite the racket had completely dropped off to sleep.

"Lights please," O'Malley bellowed, pausing for the room to be lit. "The fil'm will not be shown tonight but tomorrow instead." He nodded in Bradley's direction for confirmation. Bradley smiled agreeably.

Big Tommy Boyle who apart from his son Wee Tommy, was the biggest man in the room, stood up. Respectfully he held his hat to his chest. "Excuse me Father, why can't we watch it tonight?" His arms went out, the shoulders of his jacket almost bursting at the seams, "Bradley's here, we're…"

Before he could finish O'Malley cut in "You're right Mr Boyle. Right on both of those statements. But they'll be no fil'm…. Bradley!" the priest called out.

Bradley reacted instantly; marching soldier-like to the front.

"Please explain to the ladies and gentleman why they won't be watching *Gone with the Wind* tonight," the priest's arm encompassing his flock.

Bradley coughed and started, "Fellas……Ladies and gentleman, I have to apologise…." He went on to explain.

Once he'd finished, Tommy got to his feet once more. "Can we not have a vote?"

O'Malley responded, "What about?"

"Well, I don't know about the rest of you's," Tommy paused slowly shaking his head, "but I can't come back tomorrow night and would like to see the fil'm tonight." Nods of agreement came from around the room. Tommy went on "Buncrana is only a half an hour away. Surely, Bradley could get the fil'm and be back in no time at all."

A feeble grey-haired man wearing fingerless gloves struggled to his feet, turned and aimed a salute at Big

Tommy and sat back down. Bradley wasn't expecting this and began to pray to his mother that the film reel was still intact and that his fears were unfounded. The crowd looked to the priest.

As he deliberated O'Malley marched back and forth. He didn't like this challenge to his authority, but Big Tommy Boyle, a former volunteer, a commander to boot, held as much respect as himself, and for drinking men of Republican persuasion, a hell of a lot more.

Big Tommy was still standing.

O'Malley had made his decision. "Thank you, Mr Boyle, for your eloquent thoughts on the matter of tonight's entertainment. I am more than happy to open this out to the audience to have their say with a vote."

A show of hands went overwhelmingly in favour of Bradley going for the missing reel. The crowd came out to see him off.

Tommy's daughter, Nora Boyle was standing with her brother Wee Tommy. They were laughing and giggling as O'Malley berated Bradley through the open window of his car, who was nodding like a naughty schoolboy keenly taking instructions. At the sound of laughter Bradley looked up and caught Nora's his eye, she smiled and winked.

....

Bradley's face was red and greasy from the booze and the heat, he was still in his overcoat. Deep snuffles and snores wriggled and popped as drool dribbled down onto his chin. He was in his Sunday best which he often wore on Saturday. He'd been to the Finbarr's for an afternoon session and was sleeping it off in his armchair until the club reopened at six.

Nora was watching the end of the wrestling. As usual Mick McManus in black trunks was up to his old trick of twisting his knuckle into another wresters eye socket when the referee couldn't see. Mick threw a vicious forearm smash which sent the fella crashing to the canvas. A kick between the shoulder blades made sure he stayed there. An old lady in a fur coat was beating her bag on the side of the ring. Belligerently Mick waved her away and casually slung an arm over the top rope. Nora's fists were clenched in frustration, eyes fixed on the black and white picture.

"You're nothin' but a durty cheat," she muttered under her breath.

Bradley stirred, his forehead furrowed, the waxy eyelids opened to a squint, left eye slightly wider than the right.

Nora glanced at him then shouted at the TV, "Blatherskite."

Bradley's eyes closed.

Nora's hair was almost white. She had dyed it for a few years to the auburn of her youth, and then a glossy mid brown but as the years went by she'd let it slip. Her eyes were clear blue, her face pale, pretty with childlike vulnerability. She was wearing a floral apron over a colourful summer dress which didn't quite match but she was past caring about anything matching.

It looked like the end of the fight, the fella was flat out, dazed and confused, the count was up to eight. Nora got to her feet and was about to head towards the kitchen when the camera spun to the back of the auditorium. Rushing down to the edge of the ring bounded Gentleman Bert Royal. White trunks, whiter than white, Bert's muscles looked flabby but with an agility which belied his years. He hopped over the top rope poleaxing McManus with a dropkick. The blatherskite went flying up into the air, another kick from Bert saw McManus outside the ring.

Nora stopped in her tracks; her eyes lit up. "G'on, give it to him Bert."

And that's exactly what Bert did for a couple of minutes, flinging McManus around like a rag doll. Finally, McManus was getting his comeuppance, the beating he thoroughly deserved. Nora's eyes widened; head craned forwards, hands on hips. She was about to clap in delight when McManus sidestepped a flying dropkick and Bert's groin was on course for a painful collision with the corner post. Nora squinted, her face a picture of discomfort, as Bert thrashed in agony on the canvas. It was all over, the referee concluded the formalities, counting our hero out. McManus sneered at the crowd before turning and stamping on the two men lying spread-eagle on the canvas. Stretchers were called but Nora didn't wait to see the blatherskite gloat over his ill-gotten victory. She looked to Bradley for a moment then to the TV screen and switched it off.

From the kitchen, she heard his voice.

"Tea," shouted Bradley.

Nora didn't respond but filled the kettle and lit the grease-stained stove. Her thoughts were on the bingo later that evening. Last week her sister Mary had won fifteen pounds of which she shared five with Nora. She was planning on buying herself a new hat, so hid the fiver it in her corner so Bradley wouldn't find it. She leant down and opened up the oven door removing the blackened chip pan and a frying pan. She lit the burner on the front of the stove and placed the frying pan on the heat. From the fridge, she pulled out a bloodied roll of paper, inside was a pound of mincemeat. On her work surface she started to make up the burgers. With the heat now up, she carefully placed them onto the pan. Potato's next, the scullery was always cold, she didn't hang around whilst selecting the big ones from a brown sack. Back in the kitchen she washed the mud off, peeled them, dropping each spud into a large pan filled with water. Once finished, she switched to her big knife for chipping. The smell of fried beef burger was warming up the room.

Bradley appeared in the doorway, he smiled. "Isn't she the lovely one," he said as he playfully wrestled for a kiss.

Get away from me, you're a smelly old clown," said Nora, and watched as he wandered out of the kitchen to the toilet.

Before closing the back door, he turned, "Dem burgers smell good."

The kettle had boiled so she filled the pot and prepared two cups. Before Bradley was back, she'd poured the tea.

"Take this with yer," she said as she handed him a cup.

When she returned to the living room, Bradley was watching the news and waiting for the football results. Manchester United was his favourite team.

In a couple of minutes, she had set the table and cut up some bread buns, then sat herself down into her chair. Her hand went down into her corner, she picked two toffees from her stash and threw one at Bradley, who nodded, unwrapped it and popped it into his mouth. Whilst waiting for the burgers to cook she picked up her knitting, she'd get another few rows done.

They'd been married now for close on thirty years, to be exact thirty years that October. Like most, they'd had their ups and downs, well, maybe a few more downs than most. Drink is a powerful friend until it becomes your master. Throughout her life she had seen it happen, how it destroyed people, good people, bad people, even the indifferent. Bradley was like his father and most of his family for that matter, all well versed in promises and lies. But then again wasn't it the drunk she'd fallen in love with. The fun and mischief they'd had together, they were good times. In fact, he was always in better humour with a few inside him. Her thoughts drifted to a time, it seemed like a lifetime ago, when she would have left him, taken the kids and return home to Ireland. But not now, she couldn't go back. No, England was her home now. She held up the piece of knitting, pushed the wool along the needles and began, it was going to be a cardigan, green with a mustard fleck.

…………………………..

It was Christmas Eve, and over two years since Nora had died. Bradley was now in a care home; he'd suffered a stroke which affected his left side. His left leg dragged; his arm frozen apart from his index finger which stuck out like a beacon.

He sat trance-like staring off into the distance. Where once there was life there was only structure and empty memories. His spirit had left him, hope had left him, even the pain had left him, he was hollow. His eyes glazed over as he tried to remember, remember all the things, all the things...

Doherty, his old friend was by his side, impotent to help, how could he help? No words could alleviate his friend's pain, no tear could bring her back. This was the curse of life.

Little Mick, Doherty's son, a simple lump of a lad of maybe fifteen or sixteen saw it as a challenge and sat himself on the edge of Bradley's worn-out armchair. With the confidence of youth, he grinned as he shared a joke, but he was on a hiding to nothing.

Bradley turned and stared blankly at the boy's face. *Why is this boy sitting on the arm of my chair? Why is his mouth moving?* Bradley looked to Doherty for an answer.

Little Mick too looked to his father, searching for support. Doherty was a sensitive man, and with a smile released his son. But Little Mick did not possess his father's sensitivity, after all, he was only a boy. Not recognising his cue, he tried again, this time the one about the three Irishmen.

Doherty gently admonished his son, "He's not listening to you son."

Little Mick didn't understand, *Wasn't he the class clown? The jester of the family? He could get a laugh from anyone.* He wasn't about to give up that easy.

Suddenly his father snapped, "Shut the fuck up. Can't you see the man is in no mood for your nonsense."

At the raising of Doherty's voice, Bradley glanced between father and son. His head tilted, he looked puzzled. It could have been two dumb animals he was watching or two timber posts. Whatever energy they represented meant nothing to him. She was gone.

The carer was kind with a friendly face, she chatted about her plans for Christmas day whilst feeding him a breakfast of porridge. He enjoyed her company, her simple innocence appealed to Bradley. He took a few sips of tea from his beaker.

"Are your family coming over tomorrow?" she asked.

Bradley nodded.

Before dressing him, she asked if he needed to go to the toilet, again he nodded. Hauling him from his chair she steadied his frame as he grabbed on. He relished her touch, so infrequent now. Slowly they made their way down the corridor passing staff and patients on their way. Everyone was in a good mood; some already wearing their Christmas hats. She checked the toilet was free and helped him inside. Self-consciousness, as with his body had withered, he waited patiently as she prepared him. She left and returned in a short while, cleaned him and helped him dress. Back in his room she turned on the TV.

"Now this is one of the all-time Christmas favourites," she said smiling, *"Gone with the Wind."*

His mind drifted back to a night long ago, "Days of romance and intrigue," he murmured. A smile appeared and then a hearty chuckle.

Jimmy the Dash

I had a day off and rather than waste my time at home thought a trip to Oxford would be a better waste of time. The train journey was uneventful, apart from witnessing a couple of young girls spitting on the ground at the station, disgusting behaviour, particularly from girls. But like I said, uneventful. First port of call was the Ashmolean, *feed the mind, feed the mind,* after an hour of listening to educated whispers on the work of the great and good, my back started to play up, giving me gip. So, I passed up the Pharaohs, the defaced fruity statues of Greece and headed out into the fresh air.

It was the tail end of summer, still warm but rain had started to fall, not so bad as to sound the retreat, but enough to send me closer to the buildings for shelter. The town was busy, a mix of beautiful students and tourists. I have to admit I am now at the age where everyone under thirty, as long as they are not horribly disfigured, looks either pretty or handsome, so maybe my perception of beauty may be off kilter somewhat.

After passing one or two shops, I decided I might buy myself a coat or a jacket. Nothing too heavy, I had loads of those already earmarked for the charity shop. Something between summer and winter weight would fit the bill. Now I am not made of money, and even if I was, the charity shops would be my first port of call. At Oxfam and The British Heart Foundation, there was nothing. At the Cat's Protection League, I eyed up an Afghan coat: I lingered, dithering, just as I plucked up enough courage, it was snatched up by a very pretty girl, as thin as a stick and wearing very dark eyeshadow. As the saying goes, the mirror does not lie, she looked beautiful, panache, style, she had it all. What could I say, and what on earth was I thinking?

Giving up on the charity shops, I ventured into the shopping mall, or, 'Palaces of Vice and Capitalism,' as my trendy friend calls them. It was busy, *Busy and Dangerous,* I thought smiling as a group of youths debated the ethics of social media outside Blackwell's book shop. As I wandered through the centre, one couldn't help but become entranced by the shops and their displays. It was like a wonderland with the pleasant scent of perfume in the air, windows that sparkled with light, all mingled with the enticing smells of something delicious to eat.

Venturing into one of the upmarket boutiques I tried on a coat, aided by a rather camp young man with blond hair and perfect skin. As soon as he saw me check the price tag, his face dropped from smooth salesman, to sympathetic auntie, smiling pleasantly as he showed me the door.

I'd never previously shopped at the likes of Primark, my thoughts being it was full of cheap tat, but surprisingly it has some wonderful items at a fraction of the cost of the more established brands. They had a beautiful checked coat in various shades of brown. I don't think it was wool, but it looked like it and at thirty pounds, it was a steal. But as luck would have it, they didn't have my size, the small didn't give enough room and the large looked like a comedy coat. It was the medium I needed. The Asian member of staff was so helpful, checking the store cupboard and even the window displays, but I was out of luck, she then offered to put in an order request. But as I was only there for a day, I told her not to worry.

Zara is another shop I'd never previously been to, but intoxicated with the wonderful fare at Primark, I was in that kind of mood, 'adventurous.' From the entrance it looked like the type of shop that would cater for people of a more mature age. I walked straight in. The prices were more expensive than Primark but the quality was up a notch or two.

Two minutes later, I'd spotted a purple and orange jacket, which I know sounds ridiculous but somehow it worked. I had to give it a go.

It was whilst admiring myself in the mirror I first saw him. Close to seventy, neck and arms covered in tattoos, metal studs in the upper part of his ears and big ugly dangling loops for earlobes. I smiled merrily to myself, watching him from the corner of my eye as he tried on a yellow satin blouse over a string vest and ample gut. His hair was a gingery colour, more punk rocker than a Rod Stewart style. He was wearing drainpipe black jeans, baseball boots, and braces. Now I'm as open minded as the next but there was no doubt about it, he looked a mess. As he glanced up, I caught his eye, he grinned, a gold tooth flashed, I looked away and to disguise my embarrassment nonchalantly picked up something, I can't remember what. When next I looked up, to my astonishment, he was heading out of the door, yellow blouse wrapped around his waist. I half expected the alarms to go off and a chase to ensue, but nothing.

I wasn't going to grass him up, that's not my style, but out of curiosity I watched and waited to see what would happen. A black security guard was on his radio, perhaps an urgent message about the thief or maybe something about his lunch break. I'll never know as the vagrant successfully made haste without as much as an 'Excuse me sir.'

Slightly disappointed at the lack of a scene I returned to the purple and orange jacket and after a bit of deliberation decided no. A bit more wandering and seeing nothing remotely like the sort of thing I was looking for, I left Zara, returning to Primark to try on the small again, just maybe? But it was no good, as soon as I let out a breath, it held me as tight as a clingy lover. I was beginning to give up on my errand.

Needing a break, I left the mall. It was nearing lunchtime, my stomach was grumbling. I wondered whether to plump for a Kentucky fried chicken or maybe a Subway. I'd had neither in a year, maybe even eighteen months, so why not? At KFC, I was shocked, the queue was almost out of the door but the smell was enticing, so I joined it. Ordering from KFC has changed, it's all computerised now with groups of youngsters tapping away at screens and phones. I tried one of the machines but didn't have a clue. After ten minutes and a long queue behind me, I gave up. Subway was only a few minutes' walk, hopefully they still treated their customers as human beings. It was on the way that I noticed an 'A' board outside a nice-looking traditional pub. It read, 'Lunch, 2 courses - £12, 3 courses - £16. As I'm not one to dine alone, I stood for a moment to consider. All of a sudden, the rain returned with gusto. It's a sign I thought, treat yourself, so popped my head around the door. From the entrance it didn't look like the place that charged prosecco at eight pounds a glass and a 12% service charge on the bill, so I delved deeper. The solid looking barmaid was the only staff member front of house. After being served my drink, I found a table. A moment later she arrived with a leather-bound menu and a sheet with the lunchtime specials. Although having no intention to order from the *a la carte* menu I checked it out to get a feel of the general prices. The sirloin steak was £27, which seemed very steep, hopefully the quality matched the price and I was in for a rare treat.

At the sound of a cackle, I looked up.

Sitting at a table or two away was the strange man from the clothes shop. He was now wearing the yellow blouse and sharing a bit of banter with a character, who looked like a wizard, so we'll call him that. Once the joking was done, he picked up his drink, took a sup and began looking around. I kept him in my peripheral vision. His eyes settled in my direction, he grinned and to my horror came over.

"Do you mind if I join you?"

Without waiting for a response, he pulled out a chair and sat down. "Jimmy," he stretched a tattooed arm across the table. The yellow blouse was fastened with a couple of buttons over his gut. His chest was covered with a myriad of tattoos, which if my eyesight didn't fail me were mostly of a religious theme. I took the outstretched hand and shook it. I didn't give him my name but could see from his expression, he was waiting for one.

I smiled nervously.

"And who have I the pleasure of meeting?" he asked.

My mind stumbled, "Rose…Rose…Emily Rose," I finally blurted.

Jimmy looked sceptical, but as the gold tooth reappeared, "Pleased to meet you, Emily Rose."

"Likewise."

Jimmy was on the dregs of his drink and with a quick swill, downed the remainder.

"Can I offer you a drink?" he asked, knowing full well that I'd hardly had a sip. I refused.

"A small one?"

Again, I refused. He headed to the bar. It was only after he'd gone, I noticed the smell, a ripe blend of sweat, alcohol, stale tobacco and lingering farts. It was overwhelming, there was no polite way of avoiding it. I wafted my hand and blew out a few sharp breaths under my nose.

At the bar Jimmy's cider was served. The barmaid waited, he reached into his pockets. A well-rehearsed look of alarm appeared on his face, he patted his chest, then a moment of contemplation. He turned to me, his brow furrowed, then turned to the Wizard and made his way over to him. With an apologetic gesture, Jimmy lent forward and whispered into the Wizard's ear. The Wizard dipped into his pocket and handed over some coins to the fawning Jimmy.

"He'll be here in a minute," came the promise.

The Wizard smiled.

My heart was pounding, what was I supposed to do? I knew as plain as the nose on my face what was going to happen. Unless I got up and left immediately, I was going to be put in an awkward situation at best. At worst, God knows. But despite knowing, I sat like a proud dolt, waiting for my executioner.

Jimmy paid, waved a thanks to the Wizard, but aimed in my direction.

"Just a bit short, you know how it is." He nodded sincerely towards the doorway, "My mate will be in in a bit; owes me two hundred quid."

I smiled politely, not believing a word he was saying.

Jimmy's accent was broad Black Country, warm with cheerful sing song notes.

I took a sip of wine, wiped my thumb across my lip, and discreetly pinched my nose.

Jimmy went on to tell me about his life. He'd grown up just outside Dudley in a place called Kingswinford. Left school at fourteen and hit the road, "Richman, Poor-man, Beggarman, Thief," he laughed. Every finger on his hands, including his thumbs had rings, some with two. Most were of the rock and roll type, skulls, crucifixes, but alongside them were pretty delicate rings with a variety of stones in various colours, turquoise, amethyst, agate, an emerald or two. He'd led quite an eventful life and had travelled throughout. As he talked, I was finding it hard to concentrate, I was transfixed by the gaping holes in his earlobes, which hung loose like an old man's ball-sack, flapping around as he moved his head.

The solid barmaid who had shown me my seat approached, order pad in hand. She smiled, "Did you want to order food?"

"Oh, yes!" I said, and picked up the menu.

Jimmy looked up, she smiled, he leant back on his chair, gazing off into the mid-distance. As yet I hadn't a chance to have a good look, I hurriedly scanned through. I had decided on two courses, and was making my mind up between the soup or fishcake for starter, along with fish and chips or maybe a burger for mains.

"The faggots are nice here," Jimmy offered, as way of recommendation, arms folded across his chest,

"I'll leave you for a minute," the barmaid said, as a pair of legal types in tweeds had arrived and were calling for service from the bar.

Jimmy leant forward onto the table, "The faggots are good, homemade on the premises."

I smiled nervously and looked down the menu, *'Homemade Faggots, West Country recipe, served with garden peas. Choose between mash potatoes or chips,'* - £8.99.

Jimmy read my thoughts, "They're good."

So, despite my intentions of a 2-course lunch, I ordered faggots, along with chips. My eyebrows raised as Jimmy ordered a chicken curry. When the waitress left, he explained he'd had the faggots the previous day and didn't fancy them two days on the trot. "They do tend to give you a bit of wind," he laughed, as if I needed reminding. In seconds Jimmy swilled down the remainder of his pint, let out a burp, then waved the empty glass at the barmaid. I turned down his offer of a top-up.

Ten minutes later, the food arrived. Jimmy looked apologetic. The faggots looked like two undercooked testicles. Not quite the hearty dish I was expecting. His curry wasn't much better, a bowl of glistening red gravy, one or two lumps of chicken, with a single poppadom and a measly portion of rice.

Over lunch more of his life was revealed. He had spent ten years in India on the hippy trail, travelled all around the Far East and South America. He ended up in Spain giving out flyers for bars and nightclubs but after being badly beaten up trying to defend a stranger, he returned to 'Dear ol' Blighty' as he put it. "London first, then Oxford." He didn't seem particularly interested in me, in fact, I can't recall a single question. As he talked, he barely ate, I had finished the faggots, whilst he was yet to take a serious bite. He had four sons and six daughters, but only kept in contact with his eldest daughter. He'd even met Mick Jagger at a party in France and didn't have a very high opinion of him, "Small man complex," is the way he put it.

After taking a mouthful of food he pointed to my near empty glass. Despite my protestations, with a click of his fingers befitting a Mughal emperor, he ordered me another, the Wizard one too, who raised his glass in appreciation.

He checked his watch, "He'll be here in a few minutes," referring to his 'money laden friend,' I didn't feel reassured. He turned away from our table and began taking notice of the men in tweeds chatting at the bar, watched them for a few moments, then with a snigger returned his attention to me.

His eye was enquiring, "I think I've seen you somewhere before?" he said as he smashed, then sprinkled his poppadom over the remainder of his curry.

"I don't think so."

"Hmmm' you look familiar," he scrutinised my face. With hooded eyelids, "Yeah, I know you." He scooped up some rice.

There wasn't a cat in hells chance that he really did know me, but we both understood the game.

He took one more bite, then pushed his plate into the middle of the table, "Disgusting," he looked to the bar, "That's bloody horrible! We're not paying for that!"

The barmaid looked over, the men in tweeds looked over, the Wizard looked over.

"That's disgusting, that too," he pointed to my plate, which apart from a few peas left, I'd polished off. "We're not paying."

The solid looking barmaid didn't respond, but dipped back into her service area.

"Come on," said Jimmy rising with intention, "We better be off!"

As he was nearing the exit, with a mix of panic and glee I followed. Outside he pointed in one direction and shot off in the opposite. With my heart pumping I dashed after him. For an old man he could shift and after the second corner, I lost him.

I walked around for about a half hour, but didn't see him again. I didn't dare go back to the pub to settle up. Good god, no, and the coat would have to wait.

On the train home I wondered about Jimmy and the madness that came over me.

Jimmy… Jimmy the Dash, that's what I'll call him.

A Wedding Suit

Norma would describe herself as naturally confident, others might say pushy. She was seventeen, plain'ish, slim with straight mousey hair, which she'd cut into a Twiggy bob, the fashion of the day. After leaving school she went to work in Denson's Hairdressing Salon as a trainee stylist, which basically meant washing hair, making tea and sweeping up. The pay was eight pounds a week, just enough to keep her in fags and the odd Babycham on a night out with the girls. Not that she was out that often with the girls, as most evenings she spent with her man, Victor or Vic to his friends. She didn't really care much for the job or boyfriends for that matter, her sole ambition in life was to get married and have kids. Kids, kids, kids, everybody knew. As a little girl she didn't go in for kiss-chase, hopscotch or skipping, instead she would be seen pushing a pram loaded up with dolls and teddy bears, all had names and characters. When she found Vic, she found her soul mate.

Vic was eighteen and easy going. To say he wasn't the brightest might be an understatement. He left school at fifteen to work as trainee mechanic at Barrett's Garage and Service. Despite his poor school reports however, he proved to be a quick learner, and now was paid the going rate of twenty-two pounds a week. He was tall, fair-haired, gangly, with a bit of a stoop. Norma was his first and only girlfriend.

They met at a local disco, snogging to a slow smooch. It was the typical love at first sight. Two dates later, Vic proposed, Norma eagerly accepted. They planned the wedding for the following spring, Saturday 31st of March 1966. Norma drew a big heart around it on her calendar. Although young by modern standards, people got hitched a lot younger in those days, and with both families blessings, everyone was happy. Coming from a family of five sisters and three brothers, Norma wanted a big family, five kids at least. Vic was happy to go along with that, as far as he was concerned, more kids meant more shagging.

Norma spotted her wedding ring in Ratners Jewellers window, a gold band with a blue stone. A week later Vic's mate dropped it off to him, no questions asked, if you catch my drift.

The plan was to live with Vic's mum and dad for the first few months and hopefully they wouldn't have to wait too long for a place of their own.

Norma and Vic's mum were sharing responsibility for the organising of the wedding. It was going to be a registry office affair, so no need for the vicar to get involved and just family and a few select friends at the reception, a buffet seemed the sensible option. It was going to being held at The Axe and Shovel; Norma's dad's local. Fifty-nine guests were invited, forty-eight had already RSVP'd. She'd booked the flowers, her dress and the car. All Vic had to do was sort out the best man, and a suit for himself. The best man was easy enough, he chose Frank his brother. Frank was two years older than Vic, good looking, trendy, a ducker and diver. He knew everyone and everyone loved Frank. His advice for the suit was to get one handmade and he couldn't do much better than the 'Polak' up on Grenville Street. He was as cheap as the shops in town and his suits fitted well. Norma really liked the idea, something individual for her man. Before going ahead, Frank asked Norma for guidance on style, colour etc. She suggested a Beatles suit, but not black, something brighter. Frank winked knowingly and the following day made an appointment with the 'Polak'.

Grenville Street was a road of Victorian terraced houses, all typical two up two down. In the window of number 19 was a handwritten sign, Kowalski Alteration Tailor. Frank knocked the door, Vic stood back and lit up a fag. Mr Kowalski answered, a small man, late sixties or maybe early seventies. He was wearing a grey cardigan, checked shirt and loose baggy trousers, a measuring tape hung over his shoulders. He rarely smiled but shook hands with the pair. "Come in, come in boys," he said with a strong accent. As he followed them through, he was sizing up Vic, shoulders, height, waist, approximate weight, leg length etc. Of course, he would run a tape over him, but that was for show, Mr Kowalski already knew exactly Vic's size, what fabric and style would best suit him.

The work-room was a converted front room with a singer sewing machine positioned under the window and an old wooden stool in front. A cutting table ran the length of the back wall. Tucked into an alcove hung a selection of patterns of various shapes and sizes, along with a few garments. A black and white photo of a man and woman in peasants clothing hung on the chimney breast, possibly Mr Kowalski's parents.

Not one for small talk, Mr Kowalski began by taking down Vic's requirements. With a stubby pencil, he made his notes. Did Vic want a three piece, or two? Vents in the jacket? turn-ups? pleats or flat front? How many jacket buttons? how many on the cuffs? ticket pocket, yes or no? etc, etc. As he made his notes, he would glance up at Vic with a sharpness of movements and keen eye. There was plenty of years still left in this 'Polak.'

Vic had no idea that ordering a suit was going to be so complicated and was beginning to wish they had chosen one off the peg. He felt intimidated by Mr Kowalski, it was all too much, so he stepped aside, letting Frank decide on the details on his behalf.

Notes taken; Mr Kowalski reached under his work table where a pile of menswear magazines were stacked along with a selection of fabric books. Mr Kowalski flipped through one of the magazines and opened a page. With a sturdy finger, he thumped it, "This suit I make for you." It was a picture of a handsome square jawed model looking out from the page. He was posing with one hand in his pocket, the other on his hip exposing the shirt and trouser waistline. Mr Kowalski glanced up at Vic, "You like this one?"

Vic looked to Frank.

"Where's the one you made for me?" asked Frank.

Mr Kowalski shrugged and squinted, "What suit I make for you?" Flipping the page back and forth, "This one, is good," he turned another few pages but came back to the first picture. "This is the suit for you!" He gazed at Vic's blank face, then with a gruff huff to Frank. "What suit I make for you?"

"It was really nice, a bit more modern," Frank's eyes lit up as he took the magazine. Letting the pages fall, he stopped midway, then flicked back, "This one here." It was a very slim fitting mod suit in a powder blue flannel.

Mr Kowalski took off his glasses, held the magazine at arm's length, then put them back on to take a closer look. He nodded slowly, "Yes, I make a suit." He looked Vic up and down, frowned, then stood square in front of him. He firmly put his hands on Vic's shoulders, turned him around and ran his hand down Vic's spine. Then to Vic's shoulders, pulling, tugging him back and forth. Mr Kowalski stood back and shook his head. With a movement of his hand he dismissed Franks suggestion, "No, this is not good suit..." he paused, then turned to his original choice. "This good suit. This, this man," forefinger thumping the page twice.

Frank too was feeling intimidated. The suit that Mr Kowalski was recommending was nothing like a Beatles suit. It was like an old man's, more your Spencer Tracy than Paul McCartney. He wanted to stand his ground but felt he was on a sticky wicket. He realised that his brother didn't give a monkey's but didn't want a fall out with Norma, who could be a handful if upset. Frank glanced to his brother, then the magazine, "What do you think?"

Vic shrugged.

Frank turned the pages to the mod suit, "This is a good suit, I like it," he pushed it in front of Vic.

Vic nodded.

"Ok, ok," said Mr Kowalski with a shrug, he muttered under his breath. "You want this one, I give you this one."

Victory achieved, Frank smiled, relieved.

Mr Kowalski suggested a lightweight herringbone wool, which Frank reluctantly approved. Vic's measurements were taken, lining, buttons etc, all agreed by Frank. The price was one hundred and thirty pounds for a two piece. Vic handed over fifty quid deposit, the balance to be paid on completion. Vic's first fitting was in three weeks time.

When they got home, it was to a grilling from Norma, "How much was it? What colour, style? And most importantly, "When would it be ready? Frank was a bit vague about it all and made a quick exit. Vic smiled rubbing his nose, as if to say, you'll find out soon enough.

That night it was down to the Axe and Shovel with Norma's mum and dad to go over and pay for the reception meal. The landlord explained the menu, three pound a head included sandwiches of salmon, cheese and ham. They would also get chicken drumsticks, vol-au-vents, and salad. For pudding it was chocolate gateaux. Norma's aunty was providing the cake, which the landlord didn't have a problem with. A whisky or sherry toast would cost an extra pound a head. Fred, Norma's dad said he'd push the boat out and to include the toast with the buffet. After all was agreed, they sat and had a drink. Relieved Norma ticked 'meal' off her list.

Three weeks later when Vic turned up for his fitting, he was told that Mr Kowalski was ill and expected to be in hospital for six weeks. A shocked Vic calculated at best that would take them up until the end of February. Mrs Kowalski suggested that he might be better finding another tailor. Vic thought about his deposit but didn't have the heart to ask for his fifty quid back. On the way home he went through his options, he couldn't really afford another tailor and was scuppered for time. He had to come up with a plan. When he arrived, Norma was already there, she was being consoled by Vic's mum. Left alone, she explained that her dad had lost a bet on a horse. They were skint, she needed thirty quid for the flowers and another thirty for the bridesmaid dresses. Vic kissed her gently, *he certainly couldn't afford another suit now.* He went up to his bedroom, dipped under his bed and pulled out a cigar box, which contained a bundle of ten-pound notes, money he'd saved for a surprise honeymoon. *Ah well, they would have to make do.* He peeled off six and gave them to Norma.

Panic over, Norma cheered and Vic's mum made them tea. When Frank arrived, Norma asked if he had sorted out his speech.

Frank hadn't but he was a natural, so, "Yeah, no problem."

A couple of days later Vic skipped into town during his lunch hour and headed straight into Burtons. After two minutes of looking, he tried on a dark grey suit, it was eighty-nine pounds. With Vic's unusual shape, it wasn't quite right, but he thought it might do. He left and tried an almost identical one in John Colliers which was no better. But still, if push came to shove, he had a back-up plan.

Norma's hen night was a hoot. Her and the girls dressed up as western floozies, gowns, six shooters, stockings, the lot. Wherever they went, they attracted all the attention they could handle. After a run of pubs, they ended up at the Locarno. She had more than a fair share of last night kisses, and one or two offers of final flings. For the stag night, Vic, Frank, their dad and Mr Barrett his boss went on a pub crawl. At the Rose and Elbow, as the rest of the patrons looked on Vic downed the yard of ale without too much trouble. The regulars gave him a round of applause and chipped in for the next round. After another five pubs, Vic was showing wear and tear, slurring his words and more than a little bit wobbly, his dad thought he'd had enough. On the way home they had fish and chips, but no sooner down Vic puked his up on the roadside.

His dad was smiling as he slapped his son on the back, "You done good lad, get it all up."

Vic didn't remember being put to bed with a bucket at his side, or that Frank had stayed up all night to keep an eye on him.

In the morning he was woken by his mum; Mrs Kowalski had called to say her husband was now out of hospital and could Vic come for a fitting that morning. Feeling extremely hungover, Vic made his way over. Despite his own weary condition, he could immediately see a change in Mr Kowalski. Gone were the keen eyes, quick hands and restrained temper. Everything was slow and laboured. Even striking chalk marks took the old man's breath away. Halfway through the fitting he called to his wife to take over. She finished the fitting, leaving Vic instructions to come back midweek.

As the wedding date closed in, Norma's stress levels were peaking. His mum's too, even Frank's usual confidence had gone.

On the Wednesday evening Vic went for his next fitting. Mr Kowalski answered and to Vic's relief, he seemed to be back to his old self. A swift chalk mark here, a stitch there, a couple of pins around the back. The whole fitting only took fifteen minutes, a fraction of the time of the previous one.

A stern-faced Mr Kowalski stood in front of Vic, "Wedding Saturday?"

Vic nodded.

"You come back, tomorrow, ok!"

Vic nodded.

Thursday was slow at the garage, Norma called three times. Her concern this time was that she wanted confirmation that on the day of the wedding Mr Barrett would be picking her up in his Mercedes. From the office Vic looked out at the gleaming white car which he'd polished three times this week. He handed the phone to his boss, who chatted briefly to Norma, telling her not to worry and confirming everything was set, chuckling as he put down the phone. "That girl of yours." Vic asked if it was ok if he nipped off at four o'clock, "No problem," was Mr Barrett's reply.

Mrs Kowalski answered and brought Vic through. She picked up Vic's suit from the rail. "You try," was all she said before disappearing into her parlour.

A minute later, Mr Kowalski appeared, it was obvious he'd relapsed. He looked like a living ghost. It took him close to a minute with his wife's support to get to his stool. Once seated he let out a long breath and looked up at Vic who was wearing the suit over an old work jumper. "Come, come," and with a weary shake of his head and movement of his fingers, he motioned for Vic to remove the jacket. He said something in Polish to his wife, she disappeared, returning a moment later with a white shirt and tie. Vic tried them on together. Mr Kowalski looked to Vic's stockinged feet and shrugged. His hand punctuated his sentence, "Shirt, tie, new shoes. You must have."

Vic nodded.

Mr Kowalski spoke to his wife in Polish. From behind the door, she fished out a long mirror and held it up. Vic looked into it taking in his own reflection. Mrs Kowalski's eyes lit up, she smiled and said something delightful in her mother tongue. Mr Kowalski gruffly nodded, then reached over his table for a magazine, flicked the pages, stopping at the lantern-jawed model, one hand in his pocket, the other on his hip. He turned the page to Vic, "This man, for you suit.

Vic stared into the mirror, then down to the photo, slowly a wide grin appeared, he nodded.

"You like?

"Yeah," said Vic.

The day of the wedding arrived. Norma was frantic, she'd changed from her original choice of dress into a cream mini dress and bolero jacket. Mr Barrett was spot on time to picked her up in the Mercedes. Neighbours waved as the car pulled off. Frank accompanied Vic as they walked into town to the registry office, arriving half an hour early. When Norma turned up, Vic's heart skipped a beat, she looked beautiful.

She looked at her man, so handsome, like a film star, she cried. The service was short, then it was back to the Axe and Shovel. Everyone enjoyed the day, which went on well into the night. Frank's speech went down a treat but why wouldn't it, that lad could charm the birds from the trees. Norma's dad did her proud too, there wasn't a dry eye in the house. There were calls for a speech from Vic, but embarrassed he just smiled and kissed his wife, well, speaking just wasn't his thing.

No one mentioned anything about Vic's suit, apart from the photographer, who said he looked like a young Spencer Tracy.

The following day Mr Barrett turned up at Vic's early, both himself and Norma were still in bed. They hurriedly got dressed and came down. Mr Barrett had a special surprise for the couple, he'd booked them a week in Skegness. He handed Vic a hundred quid spending money and the keys for the Mercedes, to use for the journey. They were ecstatic, Norma cried with joy.

Although the weather was pretty shoddy, they had a great time. Picnics, days at the fair, candy floss and even a ride on the donkeys. When they got home, Vic's suit went into the wardrobe. Three months later they got their own flat, a low rise on the outskirts of town. As the saying goes, 'Time flies,' His suit would appear for weddings, birthdays, engagements, christenings and any other formal occasions. The trousers kept their crease and the jacket held its shape, as classy as the first time he wore it.

Twenty-five years on, Vic had taken over the garage and was doing very well. They had moved to a beautiful barn conversion in a little village near Stratford, Norma had fallen in love with it at first sight. Vic now employed six mechanics and had opened another garage on the other side of town. His friends suggested he should change the name to Vic's Garage Services, but Vic didn't mind having his old bosses name above the door, so it remained, 'Barrett's Garage and Services.'

Norma never did qualify as a stylist, she now worked with Vic answering the phone and taking care of the paperwork. They didn't quite manage the huge family of Norma's dreams either. Despite their best efforts they only had one child, a beautiful girl they called Julie. Julie was getting married herself in a couple of months, to Kevin, a nice fella who worked for Vic.

With her usual bustling energy, Norma had taken over the arrangements. The church and the venue were booked. It was going to be a magical day at a beautiful hotel in the country. Then there was the honeymoon in the Caribbean, no expense was spared. All had been taken care of, apart from one thing which niggled her. It was to do with Vic, and as the date of the wedding was getting closer, she thought she'd tackle him.

Vic had just finished fitting a new clutch on a BMW, and was washing his hands, pulling off his overalls. Norma began with a gentle hint saying she had just spoken to a friend of hers whose son had opened a menswear designer shop in town, "Very classy, very trendy." She wondered if they should go and have a look around. Vic shrugged saying he was too busy to go shopping. On their way home, Norma tried again, suggesting maybe for the wedding he should treat himself to a new suit, something modern, a Boss, Versace, or even a Ralph Lauren. Something more becoming for a man of his standing.

With a curious expression Vic looked across, his eyes lingered a moment before returning to the road. "Nah, I've got a perfectly good suit hanging in the wardrobe."

The Champ

It was the run up to Christmas of 1959; Mick Daly was finishing off his milk round and on his way home, when Begsy flagged him down.

Plump face alight with excitement Begsy held on to the halter of Mick's donkey. "Have you heard the news?" he said.

"What news? Mick looked down from the cart at his friend.

"The champ is coming to Barleycove," grinned Begsy

Never in a million years, Mick thought to himself. *Never in a million years.* Mick Daly was a slightly built man with a shock of dark hair which hung down over his forehead. One might call him hatchet-faced but the brightness in his eyes managed to give him a softer look. He was a fanatical boxing fan, particularly the heavyweights. He knew all the stats, from John L Sullivan to Jack Dempsey.

He lived alone, not by choice but circumstance. No, Mick and Mary McNeely should have and would have married if Mick had gone to the corner of Old Street instead of Old Road for their first date. He tried to make it up to her but Mary was a stubborn woman and did not take too kindly to his excuse. A year later she ended up marrying Frank 'the fish' Fallon. That was about the height of it.

"Why's he coming here?" Mick asked his friend.

"Well, it seems his great-grandmother was from here. It was on the TV last night. She was one of the Daly's," responded Begsy.

"What?" Mick said, bewildered. "A Daly?"

Begsy nodded and went on to explain. "His great-grandmother, that would be your Hughie's grandmother. She went over to America during the famine. Now, her daughter met a darky over there. I can't remember his name but his grandson is the Champ."

Mick rubbed his unshaved chin as he pondered. "Wait a minute, are you telling me that miserable cousin of mine Hughie is related to the heavyweight champion of the world?" He looked confused as he went over his thoughts. A few more moments of pondering, "So, am I related to the champ too?"

Begsy took off his cap and scratched his freckled filled pate, "Of course you are." A few more scratches, "But I'll be beggared if I know if you really are."

Mick grimaced, his voice short and curt, "What do you mean, if I really am? Either I am, or am not," he said indignantly.

They stood looking at each other for a few seconds.

A light went on inside Begsy's head, "Well, they say we're all related to Genghis Khan in some way or another, but.... so, if you look at it like that, then, so you are," Begsy grinned, delighted with his logic.

"Genghis Khan my arse, I'm a first cousin of Hughie, so I must be a second cousin to the Champ," said Mick.

Begsy scratched his head again and looked up, "Well, there you go Mick, a second cousin you are!" Begsy went on to explain that the Champ would be over in Ireland for a few days around St Patrick's Day. He would be visiting the big wigs in Dublin first and then out into the country, meeting up with folk and long-lost relatives.

Mick was never a verbose man, in fact his nick name in the village was Mick the Mute. But after his meeting with Begsy, the mute had a moment of clarity, by clarity I mean he became a windbag. Not a person he met went by without a conversation. The chat would start with the weather, maybe a few words about the crop that year, then the casual, "You'll be aware that the Champ is giving us a visit in the spring." He had it off pat, a casual glance over his shoulder, "Over from America. Of course, I've followed his career since he was a novice. Well, why wouldn't I, he's a cousin of mine." Some took him up on the invitation, chatting on about the Champ's famous left hook and wonderous head movement. Whilst others couldn't give a fig, with nothing more than, "Is that so?"

Cousins, Mick and Hughie Daly weren't particularly close, in fact, if the truth be known they couldn't stand the sight of each other. But non the less, one afternoon in the new year, Mick made his way up to see his 'favourite' cousin, just to confirm the family connection was good, and strong as ever. The road to Hughie's was never good at the best of times and after a wet winter they'd had it was terrible. It took about half an hour in the cart, Mick steered old Skip, his donkey, as it bumped its way cautiously over every rock and pothole until it reached the cottage. Hughie was a whippet of a man, bad-tempered and miserable. A renowned skinflint, a wheeler and dealer, whether it favoured him or not. It was said he had an appetite of a pig but the pockets of a mouse. The result of which were piles of junk piled up around his cottage. A broken cartwheel here, a pump there, two or three tin baths, a couple of doors, things he'd wangled at the fraction of their true value; in the hope he might resell or use them one day himself. His farm reflected his meanness, he just wouldn't spend any money on the upkeep. The thatch had fallen in parts on his roof, sheds had collapsed, windows boarded up, animals were fending for themselves and the pigs had turned the yard into a mire. If it was not for a bit of whitewash here and there, you would have thought the place completely derelict.

Hughie stepped out to meet his cousin and thinking Mick had something to sell walked straight past him and glanced into the back of the cart. Mick smiled cheerily as he dismounted.

With the tact of a fox proposing to a hen, Mick explained his plan, and with beady eyes fixed, Hughie listened. The plan was for the pair to make some sort of presentation, something the Champ would appreciate. Perhaps an old photo or two was Mick's suggestion, unless of course Hughie had something else in mind? Hughie liked the idea of the photos and said he'd dig some out.

Hughie asked if Mick had a photo of the Champ?

"Of course." Mick pulled a wrinkled magazine from his pocket, slapped it with the back of his hand and flicked through it. Folding back the page he pointed at a huge athletic black man.

Hughie squinted; his face betrayed his distain. "A black-fella... A black-fella" he repeated, shaking his head with absolute certainty, "There's no black-fellas in my family." He turned on his heels, slamming his door shut and disappeared inside.

Standing in the mud and shite Mick pleaded with Hughie for fifteen minutes but all he heard was a repeated, "Bugger off, there's no black-fellas in my family".

The winter was short and St Patrick's day arrived in glorious sunshine. O'Neill's on the High Street was the only pub in town. It'd been converted from a house with double bay-windows, a bench out front and for some reason, a wooden cockerel nailed above the doorway. The gaffer Albi' would usually give it a bit of a spruce up in preparation for St Pat's, but this year, with the visit of an esteemed pugilist, no expense was spared. A fresh coat of blue paint to the outside walls, yellow on the window frames and inside it had been cleaned from head to toe. It looked pretty good, certainly the tidiest it had been for a long time, if not forever.

Mick had gotten up early and given his suit a brush down. With the iron he managed to get a good straight crease in the trousers and then hung the jacket on a chair close to the fire in the hope the wrinkles would drop out. He considered running up to the chemist for cologne but dismissed the idea, after all, *It wasn't some fancy fil'm star he'd be meeting. No, it was the heavyweight champion of the world. Smelling like a bouquet, Jaysus no never!*

It was nine in the morning when he arrived at the pub, which looked splendid, shamrock and flowers festooned throughout. Albi' had managed to get hold of a great selection of boxing photos; some were propped up outside on the windowsills the rest decorated the bar. The pub was already half full with ruddy faced men in threadbare suits, smiling and chatting, caps and hats tilted to whatever was the fashion of the day.

Mick gave Albi' a double thumbs-up as he ordered his Guinness. Molly, Albi's wife, waved across, she was the only women present and already looked well oiled. After a quick chat with Molly, Mick looked around for Begsy, who was leaning up behind the jukebox.

"What the hell have you got there?" Mick said spotting a pair of boxing gloves, each glove stuffed tightly in either of Begsy's jacket pockets.

"I'm gonna get the Champ to sign them," he said.

"Jaysus, yer never know, he might want to go a few rounds with yer," Mick smiled as he supped on his pint.

"I'll be ready," Begsy raised his fists into a boxing stance.

St Paddy's Day is a day for drinking, so drinks were bought and swallowed with unrestrained abandon. Mick and Begsy had sunk at least five apiece by noon. Everyone was in good spirits and the pub was filling up.

"What time will he be here?" followed by "How long will he be staying?" were the questions of the day. By two o'clock the party was in full swing. Nigel the

Englishman had run home to fetch his guitar and was tuning up. In truth that was all he ever did. In the fifteen years since he'd moved into the town, he'd yet to play a full song. Thankfully Molly was a damn good singer and managed to fill the gaps.

At three o'clock to keep his clientele going, and thirsty, Albi' made the call to bring out the sandwiches and crisps. Holding back a plate just in case the Champ was peckish. The pub went quiet for a while as they tucked in. The choice was cheese or cheese and pickle, both flavours went down well. No sooner was the grub over than the deep queue returned to the bar; Albi knew his business alright. A few folk were looking at their watches, and the odd, "Are you sure he's coming?" was heard more than once.

Begsy laughed up a muster, "Yes, he'll be here. They're from America, only arrived in Dublin yesterday. The Champ will be shaking hands with the Taoiseach before he makes his way over."

Mick backed his friend. Raising his glass, "He'll be here alright."

It was decided that to give Nigel the guitarist a rest they would set up a boxing ring outside. With a few chairs strategically placed on the road outside, the second round of entertainment was underway. At first, it was the young toddlers who skipped back and forth, blinking and turning away as the punches flew. Then it was girls against the boys, which didn't seem quite fair so it was decided the boys had to tie one arm behind their backs. This evened things up a little bit, but in all honesty, apart from Millie McKeown who knocked the shite out of little Peter Mangan, the boys had the better of it. Next a few of the older men went through their paces. Most pretending not to be giving their best, red-faced, as they huffed and puffed with grunts and groans that would scare a maiden.

As is the way with early spring, once the sun had dropped, the temperature followed suit. All the grown-ups went back inside the pub, and to continue their pious devotion on this holy day, ordered more drink. With a bellyful of drink and with no kids to keep them awake, it has to be said quite a few had started to fade. The thoroughbred drinkers however were just getting into their stride. A stride that would take them well into the night, the following day and beyond if funds allowed. Mick was definitely in the latter of the two camps. Six o'clock blinked on to seven, and seven then on to eight, but still no sign of the Champ. Begsy got into a quarrel with big Paddy McKeown, a brute of a man, who had the gumption to suggest that Begsy was talking shite and all he ever talked was shite. Now, although only half Paddy's size, Begsy, a fiercely proud man wasn't going to take that sort of talk, especially on a day like today. So he bumped his gums, and with his boxing gloves unsigned and a cheer from the crowd, walked himself up home, only to return ten minutes later to an even bigger cheer. The evening went on, a relief barman arrived, allowing Albi' to 'properly' join the party. Albi' managed a late run to catch up with the rest of the field and was truly pissed as a fart by nine. Towards midnight they thought it best to post a lookout at the edge of the town, for whatever reason I'm not sure. By two o'clock in the morning, most were snoozing in their chairs. Mick, Albi, Molly and big Paddy were the only ones still going. Molly who had never played the guitar in her life, slung it over her shoulder and without too much trouble managed a sound more melodious than anything in the hands of English Nigel, which did make you wonder if the guitar was catholic.

At four o'clock there was a loud bang on the door. A few bleary-eyed heads were raised, as puzzled looks went from one to another.

Mick's face lit up, "That'll be the champ," as he raced, he stumbled over Donnelly's ankles, cursed and gave them a kick before pulling open the door. A long black limousine was parked outside, Mick shouted back, He's here! He's here boys," rubbing his hands together as he waited. The door of the limousine slowly opened, but instead of The Champ, out stepped Hughie. With a blast of the horn, the car roared away. Mick scratched his head as he looked up and down the lane.

With a swagger Hughie made his way up to the bar, a shiny red pair of signed boxing gloves around his neck, he slapped a fifty dollar note on the counter. "The drinks are on the Champ!"

An Unlikely Liaison

Felicity was a young fly, only a few days old, six or seven at the most, small for her age but very pretty. She'd never met her parents but had thousands of brothers and sisters, in fact so many she'd never gotten around to introducing herself to them all. It was her great, great, great Aunt Agatha who looked after her along with all her brothers and sisters. Although not exclusive in the world of flies Aunt Agatha had never married, no she was a confirmed spinster. As far as she was concerned male flies were a nuisance with disgusting habits, no better than humans, buzzing around annoying ladies all day. But there was one thing special about Aunt Agatha, she could tell a good story and managed to entertain and intrigue Felicity and her brothers and sisters whilst they were in nursery. They were wonderous tales, there was one about a murderous wasp who attacked helpless caterpillars and sometimes laid eggs inside them. Then there was a centipede who lived under the henhouse, who would lie in wait for worms, sink its fangs into them and suck them dry. They learnt about ladybirds, who'd always seemed so friendly but were in fact nasty killers, and to keep away from them at all cost. Felicity loved Aunt

Agatha's stories and despite losing sleep, they inspired her to find out more about the world.

As Felicity was daydreaming a patrolling hen on the search for a snack flapped over. Felicity leapt from the dead chicken she lived on, stumbled and almost got stepped on as the hen stabbed out a claw-like foot. In the nick of time, she managed to scramble under a shovel, holding her breath as the hen's beady eye appeared again and again, trying to figure out how to get to the juicy treat. Once the coast was clear Felicity flew up to the rafters and avoiding the large cobweb, settled and looked down. On the ground, a group of hens were squabbling and squawking as only hens know how. There seemed to be some argument about a piece of string, which didn't appear to be getting resolved any time soon. They were pecking at each other, with feet and wings were flying in all directions. Felicity flew to another rafter to get a better view.

Although she had buzzed around the henhouse and knew all its nooks and crannies, Felicity had yet to venture out into the wider world. But today was special, with the enticing smell of fresh cow dung in the air and the sun high in the sky, she flew to the entrance and was off on her maiden voyage. In no time at all she was on the edge of the field, flying faster than she'd ever travelled before, so fast in fact, that even with her vision she could not count the beats of her wings. With butterflies floating below and bees buzzing above she was enjoying her exploration when her eyes were attracted to something moving in the field below, a herd of cattle. The sight was one thing, but smell was intoxicating. There were probably fifty or sixty of them, mostly black and white cows, a few brown, and a huge grey bull. She readjusted her flightpath and aimed for her target, a small Friesian calf who had just had a good clear-out.

Life is about experience; every time you experience something, you learn something. But no-one had warned Felicity about tails, how was she to know? So, for a fly on her maiden voyage, her first experience with a tail came as quite a shock. You don't see it, then bam, you're not where you were a moment ago, and if you are really unlucky, bam, bam, bam, you are not where you thought you were last week. Consequently, despite the delicious offerings available, Felicity found herself in a wet puddle struggling to escape. The Lord giveth and the Lord taketh away. Fortunately, on this occasion he giveth. Just as Felicity thought her short life was over, she hopped and found herself on the calf's snout, but as she was finding her bearings, the calf's long tongue was on the move with Felicity on its radar. Luckily although still damp, her little wings served their purpose, flying her to safety. Panic over, this time she chose an unmanned cowpat so to speak and dived straight in. Humans can never really know how fresh cow muck tastes to a fly. I guess you could describe it, as all the culinary delights of the east, vegetables, herbs and spices, mixed with flavoursome meaty treats of the west, simply moreish. At the feast besides Felicity were a bluebottle, another housefly like herself and two blowflies.

From the moment she landed, it was plain to see the bluebottle's eyes were on her and its thoughts were not totally innocent. He took to the air, circled around once or twice and landed right next to Felicity.

"Hellooo beautiful," he said with an oily charm, "My name is Cuthbert, although my friends call me Bertie." He edged closer, "Buzz, buzz…. I haven't seen you before." He spun on the spot, showing off his blue iridescent abdomen, and as bluebottles go it has to be said, he was a splendid specimen. "Can I offer you a drink?" and before Felicity had a chance to respond he vomited in front of her.

Although secretly impressed, Felicity answered firmly, "No THANK you," and sidled away.

Cuthbert wasn't put off, he was of the old school, philosophy being, if at first you don't succeed, try, try again. "There's nothing to be scared of, I won't harm you." His antennae touched her, she recoiled. "Oh, sorry, I didn't mean anything, I just couldn't help myself. You look so pretty, have you just arrived from the cowshed?"

Felicity paused, "No, I hatched quite a while ago from the henhouse, if you must know."

With intention disguised, Cuthbert grinned, "Hey, let me show you around, follow me," he flew into the air, circling whilst waiting for her to join him.

As she considered, a dark shadow appeared from nowhere. Felicity looked up just as a hoof appeared, looming larger and larger descending towards her. She froze, a flash of blue dashed passed her vision, it was Cuthbert. He'd divebombed and scooped her to safety, lifting her higher than she had ever been in her short life, it felt exhilarating. He was obviously a skilled aviator, turning and swooping as the wind buffeted. "Don't be scared," he called.

Felicity felt a strange tingling in her abdomen, she giggled.

"Enjoying yourself, are you?" Cuthbert called down. He loosened his grip, Felicity slipped a fraction and squealed, he pulled her tight, "Ha, ha, that will teach you." A moment later he called out, "E.T.A in exactly one second," as they landed on the dusty back of a Friesian, only to take off again, as the cows tail chased them, landing this time on the edge of a water trough. They were in a paddock with horse jumps and old beer barrels dotted about. Close by was a grey mare quietly grazing.

"That's Blanche, she won't bother us," said Cuthbert, looking over. He studied Blanche for a moment and smiled, "Notice anything about her?"

Felicity looked, although she had never seen a horse before, nothing seemed outstanding.

Cuthbert shot into the air, "Her tail! Her tail's been cut," he called out, heading straight for poor old

Blanche's bum hole. "Geronimo," he shouted, before disappearing inside.

Blanche didn't appear to notice at first, then raised her head, the stumpy brush impersonating a tail thrashed from side to side. She raised her left hind leg and shot out a kick.

In a second Cuthbert reappeared, "Ha, ha, its great fun. Come on, it's warm, jump in! She loves it."

From the look on Blanche's face, Felicity was not so sure. Cuthbert dipped in again, but a few seconds later returned to join Felicity. Together they flew onto the grass, following Blanche at a discreet distance, waiting for the freshest of the fresh dung to fall.

As Cuthbert slurped up some dung juice, he looked to Felicity and asked, "Have you a boyfriend?" He vomited out some juice and sucked it up again, "Hanging around here you'll need a friend, someone to look out for you."

He had hardly finished his sentence when another housefly landed alongside. It was obviously a lady fly, she looked tired, her face was weary. She hopped closer and smiled, Felicity smiled back, Cuthbert looked sheepish and turned away.

"You're not speaking to me?" she asked looking to Cuthbert, then momentarily changed her focus onto Felicity, who looked to Cuthbert. "Nothing to say to me?" said the fly as she shook her abdomen in temper.

Cuthbert grinned, cleared his proboscis and pretended to eat.

"Oh, there's been plenty before you," she glared at Felicity, "and they'll be more after you've gone." She hopped up on a grass mound, sucked up some dung juice, "Ask him about his family," spitting out a brown speck of dung as a calling card. "Good luck, you'll need it," with a buzz of her wings she took to the air and disappeared.

Everyone knows that horses, mares, in fact all the equestrian animals are terrible gossips. Blanche was no different, she'd been listening and wandered closer, head tilted, studying the pair.

Felicity had her eyes on Cuthbert, who made as if nothing had happened. "Who was that?" she asked.

Cuthbert shrugged his wings.

"You do know, don't you?

Cuthbert raised his antennae in innocence, "I don't know." He spun a quick loop, "Anyway, I'm going to have to go. Catch you later alligator." With a shake of his thorax and a buzz he too disappeared.

Felicity was in shock, but not so much that she didn't recognise the warm horsey breath of Blanche who was looming, her tongue wrapped around a clump of grass. Not wanting to get slurped on, in a second Felicity was airborne. She buzzed around once or twice and landed on Blanche's back and as the mare wandered close to the hedgerow, Felicity hopped onto a rambling rose to take a bit of time to consider. As she took in the warming rays of the sun and feeling sorry for herself, a friendly little aphid crawled over, it looked so cuddly and cute that Felicity couldn't help but stroke its slimy back. A busy little ant, like a ruddy faced farmer was running up the stem to check on his charge, "On my way flower," it called out. Suddenly there was a buzzing sound of wings from above as a huge red and black ladybird landed. In a split second it had seized the tiny aphid and was devouring the poor little creature alive. The ant did its best to defend the little fella but it too ended up in the sharp jaws of the ladybird. Shocked at the brutality, Felicity wanted to do something, but remembering the warning given by Aunt Agatha decided wisely against intervening.

The day was drifting, Felicity hadn't anticipated that her first flight would be so full of drama. Back in the henhouse she took some time to settle, hopping from hen to hen until she found the edge of one of the coops. A few seconds later she was happy to see the friendly face of Aunt Agatha who had flown from a broken egg to join her. As Felicity talked, Aunt Agatha noticed some blue dust on Felicity's thorax and brushed it off.

"You're filthy girl." Aunt Agatha went on, "Where have you been? You need to look after yourself, you hear me?" she said, with one eye on Felicity whilst the other scanned a hen who was getting a bit too close for comfort.

Starry eyed Felicity told Aunt Agatha all about Cuthbert. How handsome he was. How he had saved her from the calf's hoof, and how he'd held her so… close that it made her tingle. She giggled when revealing the tricks Cuthbert played on poor old Blanche. With a hint of guilt, she mentioned a bit about the distressed female fly who had spoken in the field.

On mention of the female, Aunt Agatha's attitude changed, "Where'd you meet him?"

Felicity raised her eyes. "That field over there," she pointed.

Aunt Agatha paused, "You mean farmer Ted's field, out there yonder? The one with all the cows in?"

Felicity nodded.

"What did he do exactly?" Aunt Agatha's eyes narrowed.

Felicity regaled her story once more, followed by twenty questions from Aunt Agatha, who was particularly interested in the part where they flew together.

"You been messing with Bluebottle Bertie," Aunt Agatha huffed, "That crazy bluebottle still shaking his tail?" She let go a dismissive sucking noise from her proboscis, "God, he's gotta be older than the two of us put together." She started examining Felicity, checking her abdomen, tapping her thorax and even her private parts.

Felicity began to weep and the weep became a sob.

"Oh now, come on sugar, you pull yourself together." Aunt Agatha reached over and hugged the young fly, sucking away her tears. "Everything is gonna be ok." She held Felicity at arm's length, and looked into her eyes, "Now if there's one fly you need to forget about is Bluebottle Bertie. That fly's crazy."

It was a hot night and with all that had happened, Felicity didn't sleep so well. On waking the following morning, she felt strange, restless, she just had to move. Taking to the air she buzzed around the open fields and felt a little better. For some reason she didn't feel hungry, food seemed disgusting, even a fresh poop from Goober the farmer's sheep dog could not tempt her, she was feeling snappy, agitated, just could not settle at all. She got so confused bad that in farmer Ted's house, she spent a crazy half hour bumping into a dirty window pane, which isn't a good thing for a bright young fly who should know better. Even when she'd figured it out and in the fresh air, she was still cranky, not herself at all. An hour later it started, a rumble at first, like you get when you skip breakfast, so she paid it no heed, but by the middle of the afternoon, she knew something was wrong. She went to see Aunt Agatha, who shook her head, saying she knew exactly what the problem was and Felicity herself would find out soon enough. By the middle of the afternoon, she found herself next to a dustbin and crept inside. The bin was loaded with scraps, peelings, leftovers and a chicken carcass, a better place to raise a family you could not hope to find. It didn't take long, in minutes it was over, Felicity had laid a cluster of tiny eggs. Now, flies are not renowned for being caring mothers, once they lay their eggs, that's it, they're somebody else's responsibility. Maybe it was her tender age, or maybe there was something in the air that day, but she didn't want to leave, so, like a brooding hen, she sat watching over her clutch. Around the farm word soon spread of the strange occurrence and throughout the day she had many visitors. Flies came and went, bees too, even a hairy spider came to take a peek. 'A broody fly hatching her eggs?' None had ever seen such a sight, it was unheard of and caused that much consternation that by night fall Felicity had an audience of hundreds, even a slug or two had crept in to watch the events.

As you would expect, it was the busy bees who were up first and their buzzing soon stirred the rest. Within a few minutes Felicity was surrounded by every critter that was in that bin, ants, beetles, bees, spiders, flies, you name it and all were astounded.

All I can say is, there wasn't a dry eye among them or a prouder mother as Felicity cradled the cutest, prettiest little maggots you ever did see.

Paedo

Matthew looked at himself in the mirror slapping his generous belly with both hands, lifting the flab he let it drop. He was in his mid-thirties and painfully shy. With a garlic bulb of a nose, and wispy sandy hair you would struggle to call him handsome.

It was an hour since Matthew had turned on the emersion heater, so whilst contemplating the day ahead he poured himself a bath. Before getting undressed he picked up the folder, and although he knew it inside out, he glanced through it again. The preparation was over, it was now or never, today was the day. It had not been easy; he'd struggled with his conscience and knew what he was going to do was the biggest sin he'd ever commit. Every night he would cry himself to sleep asking God for guidance, but every morning that demon was waiting, a demon too strong to ignore.

Once bathed, he stated to dress. From the wardrobe he pulled out a plastic bag. Inside was a set of clothes he'd purchased a year ago, dark blue trousers, short sleeve white shirt, white trainers and a baseball cap. He put an identity card in a plastic sleeve and placed it alongside a clipboard and green rucksack. Like a bear in the zoo, he paced back and forth, waiting, waiting, *why was the time going so slow?* A feeling in his chest was telling him maybe today wasn't right, another day might be better. He went over and picked up a photo, it was one of Matthew and his twin brother Freddy. They were smiling, grinning at the camera. He gently brushed his thumb over the image of his twin. The phot was taken on their fifth birthday, the day of the accident. No one said it was his fault, at that age how was he to know. Matthew had found a screwdriver and in his innocence, he'd opened up a plug socket. Matthew didn't celebrate their birthday anymore.

Enough!

He kissed the silver crucifix from around his neck, picked up the rucksack and left.

The Captain's Table café was opposite the station and afforded him an excellent view of his target. He ordered burger, chips and a coke, a lunchtime special for a fiver and found himself a spot by the window. On the other tables surrounding him were workers on their lunchbreak chatting to each other between mouthfuls. He'd allowed himself thirty minutes for this part of the plan but when the waitress collected his empty plate, he still had twenty minutes, so he asked for another cup of tea. All he could do now was watch as the clock slowly ticked seconds into minutes, and the minutes ticked on.

Finally! Ok, it was time to go.

It was a short walk to the florist, he selected a huge colourful bouquet, chatting pleasantly to the lady who served him. On his way he pulled a clipboard from his rucksack, running through his list of possibilities before dumping the bag in a litter bin.

Five minutes later he was at the playgroup.

He pressed the buzzer. A voice responded, "Hello"

"Delivery," In his arms were the flowers, clipboard under his elbow, he stepped back.

A young fresh-faced girl opened the door; she wore a badge, Alison Smith.

"Hello I've got a delivery for Rebecca Swanson."

On seeing the bouquet Alison's eyes lit up. "Becky, Becky, someone's sent you flowers," she called excitedly.

Matthew stepped inside as she signed for the flowers. Around her children were on tip toes and milling about. An Asian man, broom in his hands was at the back of the hallway, who nonchalantly looked up from his cleaning duties.

"Miss, Miss, can I smell them," asked a pretty blond girl in pigtails.

Alison sniffed the petals, then lowered the bouquet as the children crowded forward.

"Nice! They smell nice Miss," said the little girl.

"Come on, let's give them to Becky," Alison turned Pied Piper like heading down the corridor.

As they moved off one dark-haired boy, possibly aged three or four, did not follow but instead gazed up at the big man who had brought the flowers. Matthew smiled; the boy smiled innocently back. This was not what he'd planned but in a split-second, Matthew had scooped him up and was out of the building. He knew he shouldn't look back but out of the corner of his eye, he could see the confused cleaner standing in the doorway.

He'd gotten halfway down the road; the little boy had been compliant but was beginning to struggle. "It's ok, mummy is here," said Matthew, as he kissed the top of the boy's head.

His route was indirect, cutting through alleys, clear of CCTV surveillance. They were now back in Matthew's flat. The little boy was dressed in a striped blue T-shirt, red shorts, ankle socks and yellow trainers. His angelic face gazed balefully at the large smiling man. Unsure of his next move, Matthew sat watching the boy.

"My name is Matthew, what's your name?" he asked.

The boy took no notice. Matthew reached for some soft toys, a yellow bear and a blue bunny and a giraffe.

"Toys! Toys!" said Matthew.

The boy's bottom lip twisted, tears appearing before the sobs.

"Whoa, whoa, whoa…. Sweeties, sweeties," said Matthew picking up a brightly coloured packet. Down on his haunches Matthew looked closely at his captive, through his tears the boy's face shone with wonder and innocence. Unsure, Matthew stood and rubbed his head, he let out a grunt, *What the fuck have I done now?*

"Mm, Mm," the boy cried, his bottom lip curling down further. He looked toward the window then back at Matthew.

Fuck, fuck, fuck. Matthew steadied himself, *back to the plan, back to the plan.* He opened a pack of chocolate buttons, took one and held it out. The boy instinctively put forward his tiny hand.

"Yum yum. Yum yum yum, chocolate buttons," Matthew said gleefully, offering the whole pack. The boy delicately picked up another single button.

Matthew began dancing, jigging and clapping his hands. Confused, the boy watched. Again, the little face turned to the window tears in his eyes. "No, no, no," Matthew scooped him up holding him to his chest. Just to feel the boy's tiny body, felt comforting to Matthew. He wanted to hold him forever but the boy screamed, his little arms pushing against the barrel chest.

"Nice dance, nice dance. Dance with Matthew, dance with Matthew." Around and around, they went. The boy screamed; Matthew placed him onto the floor. Panicking he snatched the pack of chocolate buttons. "Buttons, buttons…. nice button…nice!" imploring. Matthew picked up the photo of him and Freddy and showed it to the boy, suddenly the tears stopped. That's me, and that's Freddy."

The boy studied the photograph for a second longer, then his hand swiped out at the picture.

"No naughty," said Matthew sharply.

At this the boy's tears began to flow, his cry turned into a scream.

"Fuck!" Matthew called out. looking around he grabbed the bag of chocolate buttons, "Buttons, buttons."

"Weeties," said the little boy distracted from his tears.

"Yes weeties," said Matthew relieved, "Nice weeties". He held out the pack, the boy took it. Matthew watched the boy as he finished the chocolates. When he offered another pack, the boy wasn't interested, instead he wandered off to the window, "Hey back here now little monkey." Matthew scooped up the boy, "Come and play." He gently sat him down on a tiny stool next to a table along with a selection of toy cars, tractors and buses, which had once belonged to him and Freddy. The little boy picked up a blue car, then spotted something, and pointed at a box of Lego on the shelf.

"Egi," the boy said turning towards his captor, a faint smile on his face, "Egi."

"Egi? Egi? Matthew repeated not sure what the boy meant but could see delight in the boy's eyes.

"Egi, egi," the little boy was on his feet, pointing up at a shelf.

"Oh Lego, Lego, you like Lego. Lego's good fun," he reached up for the Lego, took a deep breath trying to relax. Opening up the box he poured the pieces onto the desk. "Shall we build a house?"

The little boy raised his arms watching as Matthew picked up a green oblong shape. "That's the floor and some yellow bricks for the walls." He began to construct the tiny building, piece by piece as the boy looked on. "House looks good," Matthew said, holding up the unfinished Lego house.

The boy stared blankly at Matthew, then the house.

Matthew continued to build explaining as he went on, "These are the walls, we need a roof too." He was beginning to relax.

The boy looked up.

"What do we put on top of the roof? A chimney! Got to let the smoke out, haven't we?" His voice was warm and comforting. He took a deep breath; he was feeling more relaxed. Matthew placed the finished house in front of the boy, waiting for the child's reaction. The little face remained impassive as he studied it, he then looked to Matthew.

"Shall we make another one?... Shall we make another one?" Matthew knelt forward and began to break up the little building handing some of them to the little boy. "Oh, oh, no you don't, that's dangerous." His huge fingers carefully reached in the boy's mouth removing a tiny brick. "Dangerous," his face showing concern, again he repeated "Dangerous."

The little boy tried repeating the word, "Jus," and his fingers went to his mouth.

Matthew had begun to build the second house when an earth-shattering crash filled the room. Matthews's heart jumped with fear, he could not move; he could not think.

"Police. Police. On the floor!" came a shout.

Matthew was pinned down, with two police officers on his back whilst another held his legs. He felt a blow and a numbing pain as one of the officers slapped his head to the floor.

"Suspect down," was called out.

The little boy had frozen, his arms stretched in front of his chest, his fingers wide open. A female officer scooped him up and disappeared.

Matthew felt the cuffs tightening and a sudden jarring pain in his chest as he was roughly stood upright. In front of him, a policeman was saying something, Matthew nodded a response. Moments later he was dragged out on the street.

Confused neighbours were gathering, asking questions. Matthew was shoved into the back of a police car, in seconds it pulled away. At the junction, they stopped, across the road the little boy was being taken into an ambulance, leaning forward he mouthed "Bye bye Freddy"

Look What You Made Me Do

Gabriel said it was too warm to be indoors and with Pauline saying she'd look after the boys, why not? So, off they went arm in arm up the road to wet their whistle.

Five minutes later they were in the Woodbine. Margo had found a seat by the window and was fanning the cool air towards her face. The bright sunlight was beaming into the pub through stained-glass windows giving the room a tropical feel. It was hot, too bloody hot, she let out a long sigh and adjusted a strap of her favourite summer dress, white and blue floral with pretty daisy straps. Gabriel had gone all out wearing a Hawaiian shirt and shorts, with a pair of flipflops.

The 'Rose and Woodbine' was on the Stoney Stanton Road and was their local. Mind you there was plenty to choose from. There was never a need for a man to go thirsty on the Stony Stanton Road. The bar was through the main entrance with a snug to one side and off-licence to the other. It was a working man's pub, no food apart from crisps and a jar of pickled eggs.

Little Michael, the barman, nodded over, and with a wink from Gabriel he began pulling a pint.

A Guinness for himself and a Babycham for the Missus, Michael knew the score.

Up at the bar Gabriel was chatting to a man perched on a barstool. The man was thickset, grey hair in a crewcut style, he'd distinctive jet-black eyebrows and a seventies droopy moustache. As they chatted, the man would occasionally glance back in Margo's direction.

To Margo's left were a group of four leathery skinned navvies playing dominoes, each with a half and a swift one to keep them lively. Despite the heat were still in suits and didn't appear to have much sweat on them either. Searching in her bag for her fags Margo glanced up at a young couple on the next table on the other side. The girl was blonde, voluptuous lips, with a face of an angel. She wore denim cut-off shorts and a tight-fitting t-shirt. Her partner had his hair slicked back; horn-rimmed glasses hung halfway down his nose. Perhaps Margo lingered too long, as the angel faced girl turned with a belligerent smile. Embarrassed, Margo looked away. Dolores Feeney, a geriatric neighbour, along with Old Tom were sitting in the corner next to the fruit machine, Dolores raised a feeble hand and waved over. Margo smiled and waved back.

With a slap on his friend's shoulder, Gabriel turned away and weaved his way across. Once sitting, he explained to Margo that the guy was John Montague who he'd worked with when they were in Liverpool, a great lad. John had arrived in Coventry a couple of weeks ago and was looking for work. Margo looked across, John was sitting with his elbow on the bar, he looked trim in a crisp white shirt, sleeves rolled up exposing tattoos on both forearms. She asked where John was from. Was he married? Any family? The usual stuff. Gabriel didn't have the answers and didn't care.

With throats as dry as the desert, it didn't take long for them to polish off their first drinks.

"Another?" said Gabriel as he jumped up to get the next round in. At the bar he pushed his way in alongside John.

Margo lit up another fag and watched as Gabriel laughed and joked with his friend. They'd been married for ten years. For her it was love at first sight, Gabriel's dark Mediterranean looks along with an air of danger was an intoxicating mix. He certainly stuck out from the average pasty-faced Irishman in Dublin. She smiled remembering Noel, the police cadet with great prospects. All seemed to be on course to an engagement, the wedding and steady family life. Then Gabriel turned up and it all went out the window. She dropped Noel, like the proverbial sack of spuds and ran away with Gabriel to Spain the following Sunday.

But Spain was a shock, the heat unbelievable. Initially she thought it was coming off the engines of the airplane but as they crossed the tarmac it didn't subside. A couple of months later Margo was pregnant and a wedding was hastily arranged. But Spain was not the dream she thought it would be, with pregnancy and the constant heat it all got too much. Margo realised she'd made a mistake and wanted to go home but Gabriel was having none of it. Madrid was now their home, he loved it. She stuck it for another two months, then packed her bags, arriving back in Ireland on her own and pregnant. A week later a sheepish Gabriel turned up at her parents and together they made plans to move to England. That was eight years ago.

The barman had lined up the drinks and was waiting to be paid. Margo smiled as the two men argued about who was paying, with John keeping Gabriel at arm's length whilst the barman took his money. They returned together. Margo pulled a stool out from under the table pushing it to the other side with the heel of her foot. By the way John held out a hand to greet her, she could tell he was shy. They chatted a while, with Margo asking John about his life. He'd travelled a bit, mostly up and down the country and with a spell in Germany. Margo enquired if he was married. Looking embarrassed, he shook his head explaining that he'd lived in sin for five years but she was too much of a handful, with a wandering eye for any fella that showed her the slightest bit of attention. Then he met Gloria, whom he married after a whirlwind romance, but that didn't work out either.

"One of those cases of can't live together, can't live apart," John reminisced, adding, that he was now at the stage in life where he was content enough in his own company.

Margo nudged his elbow with a grin, "Don't give up, they'll be another."

John rolled out his stock line, saying if any pretty lady out there wanted company for an evening, he was very happy to make the breakfast. Whether it was his lack of timing or nervous delivery the joke didn't quite fit. He looked slightly uncomfortable and took a long gulp from his pint.

Margo figured he was older than Gabriel, maybe forty or forty-five. His face had been busted up a bit but he was handsome with brown eyes that fixed on you like a child's. The conversation continued with Gabriel tending to lead with story after story, mostly far-fetched boastings but funny all the same. Occasionally Margo would disagree and set the record straight, which didn't go down too well with her husband. A few more rounds and they were definitely tiddly. It was apparent that John's confidence emerged with a drink and it was now him who was cracking the jokes. The hours passed quickly; they were having great fun. Gabriel checked his watch, rose from his seat, nudged Margo, saying they'd better be off home. John laughed, teasing him and insisted on one more.

Gabriel shook his head, "Nah, we've got to get back." With a wink in Margo's direction, "This one gets rowdy after a few."

Margo was enjoying herself, so glancing to her husband cautiously with a giggle and a wink said that she wouldn't mind another Babycham. A stony-faced Gabriel glared, then quickly controlled himself.

With John at the bar, Gabriel's mood turned serious, saying Margo had had enough drink and was making a fool of herself. She didn't take much notice, mockingly asking who he was trying to impress anyway with his tall stories. John returned and had bought Gabriel a drink anyway.

"And a Babycham for the lady."

"Thank you, kindly sir," said Margo.

Things were getting boisterous and as Margo and John joked, Gabriel was simmering. The blonde on the next table glanced over. Margo burst out laughing.

"Another drink," said John and before anyone had a chance to refuse, he was on his feet.

Gabriel pulled up Margo's dress, she was showing more cleavage than she was aware, "We need to get going," he said, his face like thunder.

Margo shrugged.

Gabriel got to his feet, picking up Margo's bag, "We're off," he called over to John at the bar, "I better get this one home." He was trying to be breezy to his friend. Margo let her shoulders drop like a naughty child and very deliberately, and with a shake of her head, moved out from the table snatching at her bag.

John called over, "Ah come on, just one more," raising his thumb and forefinger, "A wee one? Come on!"

"Not this time but next time we'll make a weekend of it," Gabriel laughed.

John swayed as he crossed the room. With a firm handshake and embrace, he made Gabriel promise that he would be there at the weekend. He leant into Margo as they embraced, and placed a sloppy smacker on her cheek. "He's a lucky man," he said, and kissed her other cheek.

It was a five-minute walk home, Gabriel had sobered up and not waiting on his wife, even in his flipflops was clipping along at a pace. He'd occasionally glance back as Margo was a good twenty yards or so behind and struggled to keep up. He opened the front door and disappeared inside.

Fuck him, she thought. In the kitchen Gabriel was preparing his sandwiches for the following day. "What's wrong with you?" she asked.

He didn't respond.

She pushed past and opened the back door to the garden. In the doorway she lit up a fag, as she hummed a lullaby her mother sang to her as a little girl. "Idiot…It would be a different matter if it was you." Margo mumbled. After a few drags on her cigarette, she wandered down the garden and sat herself down on the lawn. She lay back on the moist grass. Spreading out her arms and legs she looked up gazing at the stars. The sky was so vast, the stars, the planets the and moons. *What was it all about? Surely this cannot be all there is? Heaven, Hell, there had to be something.* She had read somewhere that whether animate or inanimate, we were all the same ingredients but just in different cakes, she smiled. Her eyes felt heavy, after another drag, she stubbed out her fag. John passed through her meanderings, she hoped he would find someone, he seemed such a nice guy. Margo shook her head, *Yeah, I'll flirt to wind him up but I'll never leave him. Both as bad as each other, kindred spirits. What's love without a few ups and downs?*

There was a sound of footsteps, Gabriel appeared asking if she wanted a cup of tea. Margo refused with a dismissive wave; she'd let him stew for a bit longer.

Minutes later he returned, asking if she was coming to bed.

"I'll be there in a while."

Five minutes later he was out again, asking if she was coming to bed.

Slightly exasperated and more than a little bit drunk she raised her voice, "Piss off, I'll come in when I'm was ready."

The kitchen door slammed shut.

Margo giggled, *Serves him right.* The air was warm and comforting, she was tempted to sleep out but she'd go in soon, go in and make up with grumpy. Her hand went to her head, the headache was on its way, she'd feel lousy in the morning, but for now the stars and the lullaby were enough. She heard the door opened; Margo let a breath roll over her lips but didn't bother to look up.

It felt like a dull thud in her stomach followed a sharp pain in her chest.

"Fuck you, fuck you, fuck you!" Gabriel screamed as he plunged the knife in again and again.

Margo tried to stand but fear had gripped her and taken all her strength. Raising her head, she looked around, Gabriel was nowhere to be seen, maybe it was just a dream. A warmth spread between her shoulder blades, there was a strange hissing sound coming from her chest, she reached up, it felt wet.

She called for Patrick and Diego, her children and then for Gabriel, but sound had deserted her.

Red Roses

Beguiling smiles, that said, if you love me the way I love you, we'll be together forever.

He awoke with a shudder and was panting like a dog. His bedclothes were wet, his t-shirt too. It was nothing new, since she had gone, night sweats were the norm. On his bedside cabinet, was a picture of Jane, red lips, her blonde hair cascading over a red wraparound blouse, eyes cool and seductive, brazenly staring out at the camera. It was from a shoot that he had organised for a surprise treat. The photographer said she could model professionally and asked if she would be interested in doing some glamour work, but that wasn't her thing. No, she was far too classy for that. He picked up the photo and kissed her before turning it over. Written on the back was, *'Love You Forever xxx.'*

He pulled back the covers and got out of bed, went to the window and looked out. It was a stormy night. Defying the laws of gravity rain streaked up the windowpane, with the wind pushing and pulling at every crevice. In the garden trees were doing their best to prevent their leafy children being scattered to the wind.

Jane needed space and time on her own. Those were her words, and who could blame her, he could be a bit full on. A little bit of time.

The red digits on the clock glowed and clicked on to 12.14am. He picked up his phone, it was in agreement with the clock. He turned the phone off, then on again, hoping a text would flash up. *Nah nothing.*

It was 2001, Paul was thirty-eight and despite his dashing good looks, for thirty-seven of those years he'd never had a girlfriend. He'd wanted one, wanted one more than words could explain. His work colleagues thought him weird, maybe gay. To be honest more than anything else he was socially awkward, shy followed by a lot of plus signs.

He was nine when his tick developed in his left cheek. It wasn't constant but when he was stressed it would put him in his place. Maybe it was something to do with his mum, who had left home when he was just a nipper. All he had left of her were vague memories, or maybe they were just photographs. She was glamourous and blonde, the last time he saw her was on his fifth birthday, she'd dropped in a present, a little motor boat, red with a white deck. He'd played with it in the bath that night but he smashed it up the following day. But whatever he missed from his mum was made up by his dad. Archie Hepworth was handsome, matinee idol handsome, some said he looked the double of Gregory Peck. A finer man you could not hope to meet. He'd served in the Airforce, Flight Lieutenant Hepworth. Unfortunately, he lost a leg, not in action but when a small wound from a fall became infected. Reluctantly he left the Airforce and despite his handicap he became Chief Engineer at Bennett & Walthorps, and Midlands's area stock car racing champion. He had trophies galore, they were the glory days, great years.

Paul would go everywhere with his dad, to the racing, the pub, fishing, whatever. He particularly remembered their weekend stay in London; a real treat. They visited all the sights, Buckingham Palace, Madam Tussauds, the London Dungeons, they even drove out to Kew Gardens. In The Natural History Museum; he was captivated by the dinosaurs, and still had a model of a brontosaurus tucked away somewhere. *"The deadly duo,"* was what his dad had called them. Paul would respond, "Yeah, the deadly duo, Paul and dad," and they'd slap out a high five. At thirteen he learnt to drive, it was illegal, but as his dad would say, *what were rules if not for bending.* By fourteen he could handle a car around the race track. At fifteen he was competing with the men. Paul loved speed, the sounds, the smells, the vibrations of the engines. And like his dad, he was an excellent mechanic. *The glory years alright.*

But tragedy brought those years to a premature close. At forty-eight his dad had a stroke, then another. Paul became his dad's permanent carer and nursed him for years. It was hard work, but it wasn't a chore; he loved his dad.

Tears would still flow whenever he remembered that day. The British Grand Prix was on the telly. They had plenty of time, there was no need to rushed, but they did. His father fell. An ambulance was called, but he only lasted to the end of the day. Paul was devastated and didn't leave the house for weeks.

Months and years passed, and life got easier. He got a job working for Halfords, *Happy with his engines*. That was until he met Jane.

He slipped on his dressing gown and padded his way through to the front of the house. With the shine from the streetlights, the rain lit up like fairy lights dancing on the breeze. A scrawny fox circled, sniffing the bins. Mr Fox was to be disappointed however; all the bins had been emptied the previous day. On neighbouring drives executive cars slumbered, content in the knowledge of a lie-in, it was the weekend after all. On Paul's drive was his vintage GTI Ford Cortina, yellow with a black stripe down the side. Yeah, he could have bought a more modern car, but who needs a Jap or a Kraut car. This was classic British; it suited his style and went like shit off a shovel.

Where was she? What was she doing?

He dressed, putting on a smart pair of faun-coloured slacks, a black rollneck sweater and went downstairs. After making coffee, he clicked through the TV and for a while watched a re-run of Kojak. He was a big fan of the bald-headed detective, but on this occasion, Kojak couldn't hold his man. Paul paced nervously back and forth in front of the mirror, his face twisted, a quick twitch, then another, and another, it had started.

He could get away with a five o'clock shadow but his thick black wiry hair was up at all angles. In the bathroom he brushed it back, then forwards, splashing water on the bits that wouldn't comply. He ran a comb through his moustache, put on his black leather jacket and picked up his keys.

He lived in a quiet Cul-de-sac of twenty 1980's semis. Pulling his jacket up over his head, he made his way towards his car. The bleep of the remote shrieked out an alert. It really was a nasty night, with both the wind and rain demanding his attention. Once inside the car, he flattened his barnet back into shape and slipped on his driving gloves. A thought came to him, *What if she asked where he'd been?* Back out again, the rematch with the wind and rain was just as ferocious as he fought his way back into the house. From the faux antique globe drinks cabinet, he selected a bottle of Johnnie Walker Black Label, and splashed a few drops on his face. Not much of a ruse, but hey!

Although not a raconteur like his father, he'd continued with the annual neighbourhood BBQ's, every first Saturday in June. All were welcome and most attended. It was Tim who lived next-door who'd introduced Jane, she was Tim's cousin. It was as if they had known each other for years, two peas in a pod. She had a way about her and recognising Paul's bashful nature she took charge of the conversation. Like him, she was into Formula One and had once met his hero, Jackie Stewart. The afternoon had flashed by as they talked cars and racing. A date was planned, Jane suggested The Black Bear, a pub on the outskirts of town for the following Thursday evening. Paul couldn't wait and struggled to sleep for the next few nights.

Thursday arrived, they were due to meet at 7.30pm, Paul arrived early and sat idling in his car for half an hour. Once inside, he ordered a half of lager and chose a spot overlooking the carpark. The place was quiet, a few couples were sitting at tables and a couple of guys were propping up the bar.

After finishing his drink, he checked his watch, it was now 7.50pm. He was beginning to think he'd been stood up, when a taxi pulled up. She looked like an angel, dressed in white jeans and a peach-coloured blouse. Paul dashed to the entrance to meet her, and led her to the seats. Jane asked for a Bacardi and lemonade, Paul had another half. After a slow start, they quickly picked up where they'd left off. Jane said she'd changed her mind about Mansell, and now favoured Senna for the grand prix, who was Paul's choice anyway. She was an only child, her dad worked in the planning department of the council, her mum was a housewife.

Paul told her about his own life, his words stumbled whilst talking about his dad, she smiled and reached over to hold his hand. After another Bacardi, Jane explained her situation, she'd recently split from her boyfriend, and was currently searching for a new flat.

Paul dropped her home, they kissed in the car, just a peck and she left. On their second date, she said she didn't feel safe, Barry, her ex', had been hassling her and threatening her. It was just as Paul thought, she wasn't safe around Barry, who sounded like a right bastard. Tears flowed, with Jane having to go to the ladies to get herself straight. By the time she returned Paul had come up with a great idea. He had a spare room, which she was welcome to. Jane's eyes lit up, she hugged and kissed him. Paul felt ecstatic, and despite Jane offering to pay rent, Paul was having none of it, she could stay for free. That night they made love; it was the first time for Paul, but he needn't have worried, Jane helped him through. After a tentative start, it didn't take long for him to lose his water wings.

Over the next weeks and months Paul was walking on air, it was a dream come true, the shag every weekday and twice on Sundays. But it wasn't just sex, they were in love. Seriously, they were two peas in a pod. He knew what she was thinking and she knew his thoughts too. She loved to watch soaps, not his cup of tea but as long as they turned over for Top Gear at nine, he was happy. She loved Italian food, he loved steak and chips. Her fashion taste was like her personality, fun, sexy and passionate. His was non-existent but she soon sorted that out.

Very rarely did they argue and only once seriously. She'd applied for a job in marketing which Paul knew wasn't right for her, well, it would involve overnight stays in faraway towns. She wouldn't feel safe. Far better sticking to the beauty counter at Boots, with Paul dropping her in in the morning and collecting her in the evening, it worked well for them both. Although upset, she soon cheered up when the following week he bought her a beautiful Triumph Spitfire, she loved it. It was a few years old and needed a bit of work, which was a doddle for Paul. With only 37,000 miles on the clock, it was a cracking car. He had it sprayed painted yellow to match his Cortina. He even managed to get her a personalised numberplate JA25 SPT, she loved it.

He flicked on the windscreen wipers and waited for the interior light to dim. His plan was to slip away silently but not so silently as to arouse suspicion. Very deliberately he turned the ignition key. Someone appeared at the window next door, it was Pauline, Tim's wife. Her motherly face stared blankly in his direction, he waved but she didn't react. Pressing gently down on the accelerator the engine purred, then growled, as he pulled off his drive.

At that hour in the morning the roads were quiet. He pulled up to a set of traffic lights, an old man and a Labrador stepped out and began to cross the road, going at a snail's pace. The lights had changed to green, the old boy raised a thumb, the dog looked grateful too, Paul waited. Just as he was about to move off the lights changed back to red, frustrated he punched the steering wheel.

It was a forty mile an hour limit, he was doing forty-five but eased up to fifty, *what were rules if not for bending.* His tyres hissed over the wet tarmac, as the car whistled along. On the radio there was a programme about saving the Brazilian rain forest, it didn't interest him. He pushed a tape into the cassette player, Fleetwood Mac's Rumours and turned up the volume. You couldn't fault the Krauts for quality, or Stevie Nicks' vocal for that matter, the sound coming from the Blaupunkt speakers was fantastic. He tapped the steering wheel as he sang along.

And what you lost
And what you had
And what you lost...

Oh thunder...

Jane lived on the other side of the city, a good twenty minutes' drive. He switched tapes, this time slotting in The Carpenters, *Karen Carpenter, another great vocalist.* He felt alert, alive, buzzing on a cocktail of fear and excitement.

He turned into a road of post-war semis and pulled over. From his jacket he pulled out a pack of Embassy Slim Kings and pushed down the cigarette lighter, there he sat for a few minutes. He pulled on his ciggie, *This is stupid, why do I keep doing it?* It was an urge, no it was more than an urge, it was something he couldn't control. He took a couple more drags and flicked the fag out of the window, with a flash of bright sparks it hit the ground. He started up the engine, left and left again. After a hundred yards he pulled up, this was her road, he turned off the headlights and shut down the engine. Once satisfied that he wasn't being observed he adjusted the seat into a comfortable recline position. Flicking through her texts, he read them again and again, every meaning construed then misconstrued, every word twisted, every nuance squeezed. The most recent, apart from one, was five months ago, well just over. She'd promised love, love for eternity.

How could she have changed? She couldn't have changed.

Her downstairs curtains were closed but the bedroom ones were open. He played with this thought as he got out of his car and quietly walked the twenty yards to where a brand-new Fiat Punto was parked. He knew it was hers, *I'tye crap.* The Spitfire was parked in her front garden, propped up on bricks, the yellow paint covered in dirt and grime. Casually he placed his hand on the Fiat's bonnet, it was stone cold. With his finger, he wrote in capital letters LOVE YOU???, on the windscreen.

Back in his car, he returned to her texts. Maybe it was half an hour, it could have been longer, when suddenly from behind a set of headlights lit up the road. He sat up watching his rear-view mirror. As the car drew alongside, he sank back into his seat, turning his head away. A silver Audi A6 pulled up just beyond her house. Paul flicked on his windscreen wipers, just once.

The Audi indicator remained flashing. He felt sure it was her and flicked the wipers again. Whoever was in the passenger seat was leaning over, they were embracing, not just a goodnight peck, no this was sleazy, sordid, base. *How could she?* His heart was racing, beating against his chest. He took a few slow breaths.

Five minutes later the interior of the Audi lit up and the passenger door opened. Long legs appeared, then out she stepped, blonde hair, slim figure, a pencil skirt accentuated her sexy swagger.

Tits out, slut! Paul sneered as Jane adjusted her blouse.

The driver of the Audi tapped on the horn, she smiled and blew a kiss. Pap, pap, the horn went again, she blew another kiss.

It was whilst searching in her bag for her keys, she noticed his yellow Cortina. A look of panic, then anger flashed across her face as she hurried down her path. Before closing the front door, she glared across. "Stay away from me!" she shouted. A moment later the bedroom light went on and the curtains closed.

Paul sat watching his phone, just in the hope. Fifteen minutes later he turned on the engine and pulled away, right at the end of her road and right again, *I'll send her some more flowers tomorrow, red roses.*

Perfect Storm

Miller had finished his chores and was loading up the cart. It was a Tuesday morning in July, the sun was blazing bright in the sky, it was going to be warm. He was heading to McGonigle the baker to deliver milk and wheat. McGonigle paid well but was a stickler for punctuality, you needed to be on time. The cart was piled high, but even so Miller took the chance and added another few gallons of milk in the hope that he could persuade Mrs Hall, the hotel Cook, to take some for her speciality cheeses. He gave Pixie, his mule, a good brushing, knocking the dust off her rump and harnessed her up, then tugged on the strapping, double checking all was secure. He wiped down the paintwork of the cart; well, it wouldn't be good to be seen in town with a dirty wagon. Cassie his wife waved him off with half a chicken pie and a few pickles for the journey, all wrapped in a fresh white tea cloth.

Miller pulled his cap forward over his eyes for shade and focused.

"Away, Pixie, away!"

With a clip clop, Pixie started up the lane. Colourful butterflies fluttered past, as bluetits and sparrows dipped in and out of the hedgerows. Miller glanced up at the sun, it was going to be a hot one alright. He let out a low grunt of encouragement to Pixie, figuring, an hour and a bit they'd be there. Relaxing back he gave the mule her head, she knew the way and was sensible enough. Blacky his sheepdog, tongue lolling, was trotting alongside, Miller whistled and with a sprightly leap the dog hopped up onto the cart, sitting next to her master.

Along the road, Miller stopped to chat to old Tom Cooney who was sitting on his porch taking in the morning. Tom lived alone. He'd been crippled in the war by a loose horse which had stumbled as it galloped through the ranks, crushing Tom's pelvis. He could get around a bit but not enough to work. They chatted, shooting the breeze for a while but Miller was conscious of the time.

"Away now Pixie," a few slaps of the reins and Pixie moved on.

A steep hill rose in front of them, it was known as Boyle's Castle and fabled to have been the burial place of King Boyle, the last king of Donegal. Being too steep to go directly over the road curved around the side, but still it was a mighty hard climb. Pixie was fourteen years old, still in her prime. She was a good size, thirteen or fourteen hands, with a grey wiry coat and a white star on her forehead.

Miller sat up, something was wrong, Pixie could usually manage the journey with twice the weight on board but for some reason her energy today was sapped and halfway up she stopped. With the back of his hand Miller wiped the sweat from his brow, and called out a grunt of encouragement. But it was to no avail, Pixie wasn't moving. Miller dismounted and tried pulling and pushing, she wouldn't budge. With hands on hips, he thought for a while and then went around checking her feet, *maybe she'd caught a stone.* But there was nothing he could see. He stood back and looked at her, raised his hand to his brow and glanced up at the sun, it was too hot to figure it out. Reaching into his overall pocket he retrieved a dirty handkerchief and wiped his brow. From the cart Blacky was looking over with a quizzical expression. Miller smiled to himself, knowing Blacky had the answer. He scratched his head, thinking, *The milk will go off in no time.* He pulled himself back up onto his seat, reached for his whip and reluctantly gave Pixie a crack. It seemed to do the job and she trotted on, but after a few yards she stopped again.

"Come on girl," Miller grunted from the back of his throat, "Not today."

Holding the whip high, he cracked it down sharply, raising a cloud of dust from Pixie's rump. The cart jolted forward a few paces then stopped.

It's the heat, he thought.

Now if you were to ask anyone in town, they

would tell you that Miller was as kind a gentleman as you could hope to meet. But of all days, today was not the day for things to go wrong. With patience wearing thin, Miller seized the whip and brought it down as hard as he could muster. With this Pixie ran on at a pace but the shock had frightened her. This was not the Miller she knew; no this was someone else. After a few strides she began to buck. Up and down she went and the cart followed, crashing in the gravel and dust.

"Whoa, whoa," shouted Miller, the cart was now flying. He scrambled down, grabbing hold of Pixie's halter. But it was to no avail, as he was flung into the air like a misused puppet. With every buck from Pixie, the milk churns were thrown about like empty buckets, wheat sacks too had joined in the fun, all dancing merrily to Pixie's tune. Miller let go of the halter and rushing to the side tried to save his cargo but no sooner had he a hand on one churn than a buck from Pixie would send another flying. One by one each churn crashed heavily to the ground. Anger welled up through Miller's usual calm, the mule was not going to get the better of him. With conviction he grabbed the whip and struck Pixie lash after lash, screaming all the time for her to whoa. Things went from bad to worse, as without the churns and wheat to act as ballast, higher and higher the cart flew. Then with one huge leap it keeled over pulling Pixie with it. She fell with an almighty thud, lying motionless the wind knocked from her sails. Miller froze trying to make sense of what'd happened. Suddenly as though someone had flicked a switch, the fallen beast's legs flailed furiously in her efforts to get free.

Manically Miller began lashing and kicking at the fallen animal. Blacky was running wildly back and forth yelping and barking and suddenly leapt up and clamped her teeth onto the raggedy arm of Miller. He cursed, trying to dislodge the dog but Blacky's jaw was locked and she was not going to let go.

"Get off, get off me," Miller screamed, swinging the whip at Blacky's face, but in his panic, he missed and struck his own arm. With the pad of his fist, he tried to dislodge her but couldn't prise her loose, as Blacky shook her head furiously from side-to-side tugging at Millers flesh for all her might. Miller slipped to the ground dragging the dog with him, still grappling he managed to right himself but only for a second. There was a sound of a loud crack, Miller cursed out loud and stumbled forward. He straightened, touched his forehead then fell backwards raising a cloud of grey dust. Blacky still had a hold of Miller's arm but after a few seconds of no resistance, she cautiously let go. She sat back on her haunches growling and barking as if goading Miller. She then skipped forward, nipping and tugging at his clothing, but the battle was won. Miller was lying, expressionless, eyes wide open, a hoof-print clearly outlined on his balding forehead with crimson dripping from his ears and mouth.

Pixie had worked herself loose and with a bit of a

struggle was on her feet, Blacky had now calmed. There they stood quietly waiting for their master.

La Bête

Year 2138: Bukk Mountains, Hungary

In a clearing in the middle of a forest stands a small timber shack, a plume of smoke is rising from its chimney. We enter, it is dim, the only source of light is a small window. Furniture is sparse, a solid wood table with a single chair takes the centre of the room. To the side is a cupboard, dishes stacked up in the sink, mugs, plates and a single bowl. To the back of the room is a timber-framed bed, on it lies the body of an old man. The emaciated corpse, hollow cheekbones, jutting chin, and fishbone ribcage, do not tell this man's story. For he was no ordinary man, this is all that remains of a monster, a nightmare, a fiend.

Sitting on the edge of the bed and holding his hand is his daughter Monika. She is twenty-nine years old, slim, with blonde wispy hair and the face of a librarian assistant. Reaching over she closes his eyes and tenderly kisses the cold forehead. Turning to her mother, "You spoke to the agent?"

If you live long enough, you may or may not be surprised that in the future a method was developed, a process in which after death, every second of a human's life could be analysed and replayed for investigation, amusement and satiation. Initially, it was by the use of a microchip implanted at birth. This however proved to be blunt and obtuse, missing out on the nuances and randomness of human thought and experience. Science advanced, twenty years later it was found that the brain itself could be downloaded. The minds of great artists, scientists, authors, and politicians could now be used for the education and enlightenment of the population. But due to commercial pressures, laws changed, and the sex lives of the rich and famous could now be used to prick the public's interest. But very soon the moveable feast called morality shifted. Anything, whether written text or film containing any sexual content was now banned. Advertisers and filmmakers were at their wit's end and quickly moved from sex to violence to deliver the ratings. Initially, animation seemed to satisfy, but eventually, people wanted a backstory, something they could connect with. Brains of violent criminals became sought after; the more notorious and atrocious the crime, the higher the price.

Gloria holds herself like a model, she is in her late fifties and just arrived from Paris. Tall and elegant and dressed far too glamorously for the occasion she ignores her daughter's question and walks to the window. In the distance is a mist-filled landscape, pine trees lining the edges of dramatic mountains. "It's beautiful, I can see why he chose to stay here." For five years she shared her life with Marton, her mind drifts back through the years. With a shudder, she is awoken from her memories. Wiping away a tear, "Yes, she has a buyer. They've offered twenty million." She reaches into her pocket for a tissue and dabs her nose, then looks at her dead husband. "An insult. After what we've had to go through."

"There'll be a scramble. All the big shots."

"Double at least," said Monika pushing back a loose strand of her hair. She touched what looked like a dot on the side of her head, "Agent 240 Paris, please. Yes, I'll wait." She's about to speak to her mother when her train of thought is interrupted. "Yes, hello... this is Monika Hegedus, I would like to report the death of my father, Marton Hegedus. Yes, he's just died."

Gloria's eyes widened with anticipation.

Monika, "Yes... The Marton Hegedus... Ok, we'll wait."

Her mother smiled approvingly.

Three minutes later there is a knock at the door.

Year 2062: Budapest, Hungary

After the collapse of the European Community, the Romanian Caliphate became the driving military force in Europe and was waging war across the continent. The caliphate's objective was a drive against technology, and to re-establish traditional values.

Marton Hegedus is now fifteen years old and lives with his twin sister Kati and parents, Laszlo and Eniko in Budapest. Hungary had been under the Caliphate's occupation for two years. A resistance force was fighting fiercely but had lost control of all the major cities. Laszlo Hegedus is in his late fifties; his sympathies lay with the Caliphate. He too, despised the evil that technology had brought to the world and hankered for the simple life of his childhood. But despite his leanings, after a vicious missile assault by the resistance, Laszlo decided to lead his family from the city. April was hotter than comfortable when they loaded up only what they needed and before dawn, they were on their way to the Austrian border. Laszlo knew Budapest like the back of his hand and with the main roads congested, he chose an indirect route.

They had not gone far when they were met by a Romanian army truck blocking the road. A blond soldier, age no more than twenty or twenty-one, approached their car. He was polite, almost apologetic, it's a routine inspection; once done they could be on their way. With feigned cheeriness, they got out of the car and Laszlo produces his papers.

A dark-haired soldier with a scar above his eye has noticed Kati, who at fifteen was developing into a beautiful woman. With a wink to his comrades, he jumped down and wandered over. In perfect Hungarian, he greeted the Hegedus family courteously, then turned his attention to Kati, he begins to fool around, horseplay at first, a tug of her plaits, a compliment on her outfit. He asks if she has a boyfriend, and then reached to kiss her hand; she pulled it back and moved closer to her family. Embarrassed by his rejection and with jeers from his comrades, the soldier grabbed her firmly and pulled her towards him.

"Papa," Kati called.

Laszlo, a bear of a man, has been watching from the corner of his eye. He shouts and with a speed that defied his age shoved the scar-faced soldier, sending him flying backwards.

It was only a shove in defence of his daughter, what's a shove? No one could have expected what would happen next. The blond soldier steps forward, pulled out his revolver and with the callousness of swatting a fly shot Laszlo just below his left eye. A stream of blood spurted from Laszlo's face, a confused expression appeared; he collapsed to the ground, his legs twitch for a moment, then went still. Eniko screamed and fells to her knees. Cradling her husband's head, she pleaded for help. The pleading turns to horror as a terrified Kati was dragged and bundled into the back of the truck.

Year 2068: Paris, France

It was at the refugee centre two years later that they met. Eniko spoke perfect French and had applied for a job as a translator. Henri was a jovial Frenchman who volunteered as a driver. As he drove Eniko home they chatted, Eniko explained that she was looking for a new apartment, as the place they were staying was infested with rats. Henri smiled; he had a spare room which they were welcome to it until they got back on their feet. Eniko accepted and within a month they were lovers. Marton found a place in a local school and was doing very well.

But a story would not be true unless it reflected the ups and downs of life.

Eighteen months down the line, Eniko began to notice a change in her son's behaviour. Gone was the well-mannered boy from Hungary, and in his place, a belligerent youth, who didn't care about his schoolwork, didn't wash and was obsessed with the occult. Friends deserted him, at school there was an incident; a concerned parent reported that he had cast an evil spell on her daughter who became so upset she tried to kill herself. The headmaster spoke to Eniko, Marton laughed and said it was nonsense, but Eniko knew her son.

Alone in his bedroom, Marton learnt the hidden secrets of the Astral Plane, and at night he would project through the heavens, land, desert and sea. In a faraway forest, he found his father, his left eye still hollow from the gunshot wound. He was building a house of wood and showed his son the nature of trees, explaining how all things furthest are true, and closest a lie. He led Marton from the forest to a hill and pointed to a dilapidated house, a hovel with a straw roof, and a tiny doorway.

"She must wait," said Laszlo, "Only as pain."

Marton was confused and turned to his father and was about to ask what he meant, but woke with a start. His mother was facing him, shaking him.

Eniko hadn't allowed herself to believe her son would steal, least of all from her, but while folding a pair of Marton's jeans, a ring tumbled out onto the floor, a simple silver band Henri had bought her.

"Why was this in your pocket?" she asked, holding up the ring.

Still half asleep, Marton looked for a moment, his thoughts jumbled, "I don't know," he shrugged.

Eniko didn't believe him; her eyes fixed on his. He smirked, and something exploded in her. She struck him hard across the face. "You do know."

Marton was shocked, but only for a second, he rubbed his cheek and with a contemptuous sneer, "Yeah, I took it, I took more too. I will take everything. Everything from you and that bastard!" He shouted, "Why did you leave Kati?"

Eniko's eyes filled; she struck him again, "How dare you."

Year 2075-78: Paris, France

Years passed and with the help of counselling Marton's life appeared to have settled. He had filled out, his once fair hair had darkened, he was short but handsome in a geeky sort of way. His course results were enough to get him a place at Bordeaux university, but before going, he explained to his mother that he wanted to return to Hungary to search for his sister. Eniko refused to entertain the issue. It was dangerous for anyone from the West to enter the Caliphate, and the thought of what might have happened to Kati was just too painful. No, he couldn't go. But a mother's control is like the passage of time; it slips by and once lost, never returns.

Marton's mind was set. He packed a small bag and a notebook of semi undecipherable messages. Five months later, Eniko had a phone call; he was at the airport and could she collect him? Marton was alone and looked ghostly thin. As they walked to the car, he didn't respond to her small talk or hesitant questions and stared silently out of the window as they drove home. The following day Eniko plucked up courage and asked if he had managed to contact Kati.

Marton's reply was abrupt. "The real Kati's gone."

Eniko was confused, *The real Kati? What did he mean?*

It was six months later that they packed the car and; it was the start day for university. They set off early, Henri waved them off. After an hour of driving, she wished that Henri was there. Marton was morose and silent throughout the journey. As soon as they arrived, he took his bags, leaving his mother in the car park. That night Eniko cried as never before; all she had truly loved was gone.

Year 2078: Bordeaux, France

It was on a Friday morning two weeks later, that a distraught Henri turned up unexpectedly. Marton left him standing in his apartment doorway as the pitiful Frenchman stuttered between tears explaining that Eniko had committed suicide. Marton didn't ask how or why as he closed the door, nor did he attend his mother's funeral or speak of her again.

The following week Marton organised a séance and invited five students to take part. Although most were too drunk to take it seriously, Marton was deadly serious. Anna was a friend of a friend and an art historian from Munich. She was pretty with dark hair, a devotee of mysticism, and very much a free thinker. As Marton began questioning the spirit guide, one of the students began to laugh. Marton tried again; the laugh turned into a fit of giggling. Enraged

Marton pushed the table over and began laying into the guy. It took three to separate them, but Marton wasn't finished, still furious, he wanted to fight the peacekeepers. It was this intensity that attracted Anna; within a week she'd moved in with him. For the first few months, it was a burning passionate affair, that only youth truly experience, with suffering and blessings in equal measure. But the relationship was doomed, Anna was popular, confident and a flirt, he was a loner, insular and unsociable. There is a thought that you can only know your true self when put under stress. Anna stayed away for a night. On her return, Marton went crazy, threatening to kill her and then kill himself. It all got too much for Anna; she needed time, so went home to Germany.

For weeks Marton didn't leave his flat, he covered his windows and would not take any calls. He studied love spells and created a love altar for Anna, but followed up with a curse. One Saturday morning, out of the blue, she returned. Marton was shocked and confused, his emotions a tangle of ecstasy, pain and righteous conviction. That night they smothered each other with kisses and made love like it was their first time. In the morning the questions began and after a lot of shouting, Anna admitted that while in Germany, she'd had a fling with an old friend, it meant nothing and she truly loved Marton.

He was right all along; just another fake.

Year 2079: Bordeaux, France

AtlaS T1 had originally been developed for dogs that pined when left alone. It worked through nerve transmitters creating a hallucinatory effect, in that the pet believed its master was constantly present, as far as the animal was concerned, they were mentally and metaphysically as one. In 2079 an updated version was introduced for the use of humans. Scientists explained that violent and anti-social behaviour was predominantly a result of repressed anxiety. AtlaS T2 relieved this by providing users with a reality of choice, whether a jungle adventure, a science fiction fantasy, or an innocent return to your childhood, you could now release your innermost thoughts and emotions. Wherever your mind went, your metaphorical body followed. Trials were initially conducted on prisoners and emotional institutions; the preliminary results were excellent. It then went to volunteers and after passing all necessary efficacy tests, it was rolled out to the general population. The result was a dramatic improvement in societal behaviour; violence was now considered a problem of the past.

Marton had always been wary of drugs but after a night out and once back at his flat Anna persuaded him to try out AtlaS T2, the new legal high. Despite it being considered harmless, something happened to Marton. A half-hour into his trip he became confused and was convinced Anna was his sister Kati. They were in Hungary, he wanted her to leave before the soldiers arrived. When Anna tried to calm him, he flipped out and in blinding fear ran from the apartment.

Her body was discovered the following day, a tangled mass of blood and sinew. Limbs had been removed and rearranged into a macabre body jigsaw left on the kitchen floor. The sight was monstrous. Neighbours had reported hearing screams, someone noticed smears of blood outside. Marton was still asleep when the cops broke the door down, he was dragged from his bed and taken to the police station and left to stew. Soon after a specialist team of investigators turned up. DNA was recovered and bloodied handprints were found. After tests were taken it was thought that Anna had been killed close to midnight, 01.00 am at the latest.

A lawyer was assigned, Marton was advised to remain silent until officially charged; he ignored that advice.

Where did he go when he left the apartment? Could he explain why his PN, 'personal navigation had been switched off? What did the occult pictures that decorated his apartment mean? The questions went on and on. Marton's answers were vague and didn't add up. He said after leaving Anna he went into the forest, turning off his PN because he was contemplating suicide, but his mood changed. He'd walked for an hour, maybe two, found a comfortable spot and had fallen asleep. He wasn't sure what time he awoke but got back to his apartment just before 8 am and thinking Anna had gone to work he went straight to bed. It was only when the cops turned up that he had any clue of what had happened. The occult pictures, well, they were hers; he didn't understand their meaning or particularly care for them. Shown an image of Anna's mutilated corpse, he appeared repulsed, but there was something in the way his eyes lingered.

The following morning, he was re-interviewed; mind scopes taken and blood tests performed. Step by step he was taken through his life. Every report was analysed and event studied. Photographs of his mother and father were introduced and their lives discussed; hypothetical scenarios were explored. His answers were detached and clinical. Next they discussed his school life, his college life, his friends, interests, and fears. What did Marton think about religion? What were his fantasies? Who were the people he admired? Who were the people he detested? His answers were the same, vague and controlled. It was only at the mention of his sister Kati that he showed the slightest hint of emotion, but somehow even that seemed unnatural, as though he was playing a game.

After four days, the test results were available. The DNA was Anna's, the bloodied prints were too. Marton's blood tests, however, showed abnormally high levels of testosterone along with the hormone HT207, an indicator of psychopathy.

The investigating Detectives were unsure, but in the hope of gathering further evidence in the coming days, Marton was charged with murder.

****

The news media went into a frenzy. La Monde christened Marton, 'La Bête, The Beast, the name stuck. Able Universal signed a deal for the TV rights; Al Sinema Arab the film rights. It was to be prime time viewing, '*A cause celebre*'.

On the opening day of the trial, Marton pleaded not guilty. The lawyers weren't the only ones to sigh in relief.

The prosecution opened their case by coolly outlining the tragic events and their proposal of the night's events. Next, there were a series of witnesses, one claimed to have spoken to Marton close to the apartments when the crime was thought to have taken place. Another said she saw him leave the area early in the morning, he appeared panicked and confused. The defence said both witnesses were either mistaken or lying and showed a blurry CCTV film. It was of a man of Marton's height and weight leaving the apartments at 11.38 pm heading towards the forest area and possibly the same man returning to the apartments. The time on the video showed 07.47 am. If it was him, it would have tied in with Marton's statement. The problem was, that the image wasn't clear. It could have been him, but not everyone was convinced.

One thing that the prosecution was struggling with was despite the brutality of the crime, only a few flecks of Anna's blood could be connected to Marton, on his t-shirt. The defence suggested they were as a result of the previous day, Anna had a nosebleed and sneezed. Adding that if Marton had been involved, surely there would have been more evidence of blood than a few specks. Marton spoke in his defence, repeating that when he left the apartment he went straight into the forest, and when he awoke, he went back to their apartment. Yes, in his confused state he had intended to commit suicide, but as he walked the confusion left. The prosecutor didn't agree and suggested he had returned much earlier or even, not left the apartment at all.

There was a question regarding AtlaS T2. Could it have played a part? A scientist from Evercare, the manufacturer explained that AtlaS T2 had passed all government regulations. It had been tested and retested. Over five hundred thousand subjects had volunteered for trials and only twelve had any kind of reaction, all extremely mild. "It is one of the safest society drugs available," he announced. There was no circumstance where it could have caused an aggressive reaction, never mind the horror that befell the victim. Asked by the magistrate, what if the psychosis produced by the drug could stimulate the subject into committing murder? The expert firmly clarified, "That would be impossible," stating that none of the test subjects had ever experienced a negative psychosis, full stop.

The prosecution suggested Marton's testosterone levels were an indicator of aggressive behaviour and queried whether his high levels of the hormone HT207 could also have been a factor. The expert from Evercare agreed. The defence countered and produced their expert, who said Marton's high testosterone levels were most likely as a result of the incident, 'trip,' and their current understanding of hormones, particularly HT207, was very much in its infancy. A psychologist was next on the stand to give an opinion on the trauma that Marton suffered when leaving Hungary, particularly witnessing the death of his father and the abduction of his sister Kati. Before the psychologist could speak, the magistrate interjected, asking if Kati was ever traced or found?

Marton, who was sitting with his lawyer, shook his head and coldly answered no. He closed his eyes, then slowly opened them again.

Over the years, this moment was to be played and replayed, in slow motion and at every angle. As Marton's eyes opened, a flash of darkness came over him. Maybe it was a shift in light, a camera reaction, but whatever, it appeared that through his eyes a demon had emerged.

He was found guilty and sentenced to forty years of imprisonment.

Year 2114: Regina Prison, Italy

Regina Prison was where Marton had spent the last thirty-five years. During that time La Bête had become a celebrity. Books had been written, plays performed and even a film made. Pen-pals had become visitors and visitors' friends. He'd received eight proposals of marriage and one young lady even wanted to become his adopted child.

His once thick dark hair was now grey and receding; his trim physique had spread; he was fifty-five. Marton's day began with a form of yoga, which would usually take an hour. Yoga complete, he approached a screen on the wall of his cell, placing his palm on the surface.

"Good morning, Marton," the voice was robotic but pleasant, "I hope you slept well."

Marton answered, "My medication please." A small hatch opened and two pills were deposited along with a carton of juice. He didn't trust the juice; no one in prison did, it was rumoured to be contaminated with a sedative. At the sink, he pressed the steel button; a sprout of water appeared; he gulped at the stream and swallowed the pills, then splashed some water onto his face.

"What would you like for breakfast Marton?" There was a pause, "I can recommend the scrambled eggs and salmon?"

Marton wiped a hand across his face, "Yes, that's fine."

"I will arrange that for you."

In Regina prison as with any civilized penal system, the rehabilitation of inmates was considered paramount. Prisoners were treated with care and respect. It had excellent educational, sports, and social facilities. Intimate relationships were encouraged, wives, husbands, boyfriends or girlfriends were all allowed occasional overnight stays. If an inmate was not in a relationship, they could have access to one of the love androids.

Tall, athletic, with dark hair and brown eyes, Gloria was the mindfulness teacher for the prison. As Marton was segregated, he was allowed one-on-one lessons. They struck up a friendship that became a romance. A year later they discussed it, and with permission from the prison authorities, they tried for a child. Monika was born on Christmas day.

During his final year, and in preparation for his release, Gloria and Monika were allowed to stay for one week every month, and a secured bungalow on the prison grounds was made available. These were Marton's happiest times. No one would bother them. They could eat together, play together and sleep together. For those weeks' life seemed normal.

On the morning of his release, to avoid the reporters, Gloria picked him up just after midnight and drove to the small fishing village where she lived.

Despite doubts, Marton managed to get a job at a furniture manufacturer. He had a great eye for detail and his work was excellent. For the first few months, everything was fine. It was summer, most evenings were spent at the water's edge, Marton taught Monika how to swim. Gloria had a little sailing boat, she was an excellent sailor. At the weekends they would take trips to other little towns and villages along the coast.

But word of La Bête soon spread, reporters turned up daily at their house and workplace. To Marton it didn't matter if it was on or off the record, his response was always the same, "No comment," any photograph had either his or Gloria's hand raised to the camera. While his boss was sympathetic, he couldn't run his business with camera lenses pointing at every entrance or exit of his building. He explained to Marton his predicament, Marton collected his wages and explained to Gloria. The reporters followed them to Lyon, and again to Toulouse. The constant chase was wearing, they began to argue and fight. Three years later, Gloria decided she couldn't take anymore and left, taking Monika with her.

On his own, Marton moved back to Hungary and time slipped by.

Year 2138: Bukk Mountains, Hungary

Monika straightened herself and zipped up her black one-piece suit, checking herself in the mirror, before opening the door. Marton's body was laid on the bed with a sheet pulled up over his face. A tall nurse with a handsome face and hair in a bun politely asked Monika and her mother to leave the room. Two minutes later, Marton's corpse was removed on a trolley; Monika cried, the nurse followed a moment later with a capsule containing his brain.

There had been an approach, a true-crime author had offered twenty-five million. The agent's advice was to wait and allow news of La Bête's demise to spread. Monika and Gloria agreed. The next few days went by and a few more days after that, nervous and frustrated Monika made contact.

The agent broke off from their conversation but a moment later was back, "Sixty-five million from Transom Tusk. It will go higher," she said dismissively.

Bids went up and up and up. The final bid was a world record, it was from a Saudi/US conglomerate that agreed to pay two hundred and seventy-five million. The deal was for exclusive rights to Marton's image, his brain, and name in conjunction with the term, La Bête. Gloria and Monika quickly accepted.

'L'Esprit Si La Bête.'

The First Night

The studio set is a subtle white, with hints of cream and red furniture, a small table and three chairs. On a backdrop screen, are images of Marton, a good v evil scenario. Good, he is smiling, a picture of wholesomeness, the other is the still from his court appearance, demonic eyes boring into the audience.

"Good evening, ladies and gentlemen. My name is Francois Rolhein." He is the presenter of the show, he's dressed in a blue suit, mid-thirties, handsome and tanned. "In this series of three shows, we will explore the case of one of France's most horrific crimes. The brutal murder of Anna Liszt. A murder so horrific that it still leaves a scar on the nation to this day." He looks into the camera, he looks solemn, "I have no doubt most of you will be familiar with the name La Bête. Who has not heard of La Bête the monster, La Bête the demon, the fiend and yes, perhaps even, La Bête the legend!" A faint smile, his eyes shine, "After being found guilty Marton Hegedus spent forty years confined for that horrific crime. Ladies and gentlemen, in this series we will get to know the truth behind the legend… of La Bête." He introduced his guests. Alongside sits a woman in her mid-thirties, she is suited, elegant, blonde and beautiful, she is a criminal psychologist. Beside her is a detective, older, a bit heavy around the middle but still good looking. With one leg casually crossed over the other he looks disarming. The presenter sits at an angle between the two.

For the first half-hour, they discuss the history and barbarity of the crime. They show a clip of Anna. She is at a party, music is playing, and people are milling around. The camera focuses, the cameraman calls her name; Anna turns, eyes wide and a beaming smile. The presenter briefs the audience on Anna's life, where she grew up and how she met Marton. We get an impression of her as an individual, hopes and dreams cut short. We see images of her parents, there is an interview with Anna's father. There is some original film of the crime scene with police milling back and forth. A detective is seen discussing the case with a reporter; a few clips of the court case and then Marton being led away to prison. The presenter turns to the detective, asking if he believes that Marton Hegedus was guilty.

The detective raises his hands, blows out his cheeks and sits back, "That's the million-dollar question." He suggests that the original evidence was very scant, "Would it hold up under modern scrutiny?" He shrugs, "I don't know; Marton Hegedus may not have even been charged today."

This surprises the presenter, who questions him. As they are talking, the psychologist interjects saying she feels that guilt is a man-made construction that should no longer apply in modern society. She goes on to say she is looking forward to understanding more about Marton, particularly his early life.

"You will have to wait a little while longer," says the presenter smiling, "Ladies and gentlemen, please re-join us after a word from our sponsors Evercare and AtlaS T2."

The show returns with extracts from Marton's early life. These clips are from scans taken directly from Marton's brain. Every clip is viewed from his perspective; and only in reflections do we see his face.

Laszlo Hegedus is smiling and gently rolls a ball to Marton; who screams with glee and runs into his father's arms. Another clip shows Laszlo teaching Marton how to fix his games console, a simple trick of turning it off and then on again. Next, we see Marton in a playground; it is not at school but in a public park. He is approached by a stocky dark-haired boy who asks about the toy in Marton's hand, a small metal spaceship. The bully shoves him and tries to take the toy, Marton resists but is easily pushed to the ground. Kati arrives, she picks up something, we are not quite sure what and hits the bully, who touches his nose. She hits him again, and he falls to the floor crying, his face pouring with blood.

The psychologist raises an eyebrow as the camera pans to her, the presenter and detective are smiling. The next clip is shown.

Marton is home, Kati is explaining to their mother what had happened in the park. Eniko, scoffs at Marton, telling him he needs to stick up for himself.

Next, they are at the dinner table. Eniko is scolding Marton for not eating his food, a bowl of vegetable soup. He stares at her, then the bowl, his hand swipes across knocking the soup off the table. His mother slaps him, Marton cries and runs to his bedroom, moments later it is Kati who arrives to comfort him.

The panel go over this incident, the psychologist remarking on how negative emotions and particularly humiliation imprint onto the psyche.

Marton is being spoon-fed by Kati, who is wearing make-up and looks much older than her years.

The presenter reveals that in the scene Marton and Kati are only ten years old. The psychologist looks confused, as she considers the scene.

Kati picks up a blunt knife and pretends to cut off each of Marton's fingers one by one. Marton is giggling and reaches out his arm; then the other, the knife passes over each arm.

The camera cuts to the psychologist, who is sitting bolt upright, absorbed by the images on the screen.

Marton's legs go out, and again the knife passes over. Kati is grinning as the knife is drawn across Marton's throat. Marton squeals with delight. Kati is laughing too.

The clip finishes and we return to the panel, both are spellbound. It is the detective who is first to speak. "Did I just witness the primer?"

The Second Night

The show opens with a clip of Anna, she is about seventeen and looks stunning; surrounded by bright, wholesome laughing faces, they are modelling for a photoshoot on the beach. The scene cuts to an interview recorded at the time of her murder; her parents are visiting from Munich to attend the trial; they bravely manage to control themselves as they face the press.

****

Marton and his family are by the edge of a lake. Kati is about thirteen and developing as a woman, she is changing into a red swimming costume. Marton is staring, Kati glares, embarrassed, he turns away. Marton's father is packing their car as they prepare to leave Hungary; reaching into a suitcase he holds up a snow globe, showing it to Marton, who smiles. Soldiers are waving them down; they get out of their car. Marton is distracted by a plane flying overhead. Raised voices are heard, and a shot rings out, Marton shudders, his father is on the ground. Kati is screaming as she is being dragged away.

The film stops as the psychologist theorises that this event could be the root and trigger of the horrific crime. Her opinion was that the flirting between the soldier and Kati, then the horrific barbaric death of his father had somehow twisted Marton's mind in connecting both love and horror.

The presenter interrupts, "Assuming that you are right, why would he have mutilated the victim in such a manner?"

"It is the existential affirmation to the horrors of war," replied the psychologist, "Don't you see, he was making a statement."

The detective looks confused and shakes his head, "I am not convinced, I believe this sort of crime is purely for wanton deviant pleasure."

The psychologist rolled her eyes to the ceiling.

"Ladies and gentlemen, that winds up the programme for tonight." The presenter smiled, "Please join us for the concluding part tomorrow."

****

Monika and Gloria are watching the show from a hideaway, a hotel room in Norway. She is crying and looks at her mother; "He never told me about leaving Hungary. Why didn't he tell me?"

"Your father was a man. Lies, more lies and secrets" replied Gloria.

The Third Night

"Good evening, ladies and gentlemen. Welcome back to our third and final part of L'Esprit de la Bête. On the first night, we discovered..." The presenter backtracks over the previous night's events before cutting to advertising. When they return, he chats briefly with his guests before introducing the clips.

Marton is walking through a city; he looks to his left; at a scene of destruction, rubble and dust. He scans over a river, trees, then Hungary's famous parliament building. It looks different, the dome is gleaming in gold; the towers, now minarets, each topped with a golden crescent. It is his home town of Budapest; the caliphate has control. He leans on some railings gazing a moment or two, then continues his walk. In the doorway of a dilapidated house, sits a man, a set of prayer beads in his hands. Speaking Hungarian, Marton whispers, "Sir, I am looking for my sister. She was lost in the war."

The man looks up, nods and fingers his beads.

"Is there somewhere that records missing people?" Marton glances away, then back.

The man speaks, but Marton only catches parts of what is said, "If she was lost, she is lost?" Marton repeats. The man nods and without adding another word gets to his feet and disappears inside. Marton trudges on, he enters a small café and orders a coffee, taking it outside. He is peering into the distance when the owner of the cafe takes a seat alongside. He is an old, unwieldy looking man, with a weathered face and watery eyes. Marton glances over.

The café owner smiles, "Where are you from?

"Naphegy," replies Marton.

The cafe owner looks confused.

Marton lowers his voice, "I live in Paris now but my family were from Naphegy, Fem Utca, we left during the war."

The cafe looks away, with an inquisitive smile, he repeats, "Fem Utca?"

"Yes. My father's name is Laszlo Hegedus."

The cafe owner rubbed the crown of his head; "I once knew a Laszlo Hegedus from Fem Utca…A good man, but…he is dead.

"Yes, my father, he is now dead."

"The university administrator was your father?"

Marton hesitated for a moment; he never really knew what his father did for a living. "Yes, Laszlo Hegedus."

The cafe owner smiled and reached out his hand, "Nadia, Nadia," he called back through the cafe, "Nadia, come, come."

A few moments later a broad babushka of a lady appeared, her face severe and unemotional.

"Nadia, this is the son of the administrator from the university. You remember the administrator, Laszlo?"

Nadia's face is impassive and despite her husband's prompts, she seems unimpressed, she mumbles something inaudible.

Bemused The cafe owner shakes his head and turns to Marton, "She knows but she doesn't know! What can I say?" He looks to his wife, "The administrator's son!" His hands point in Marton's direction.

Nadia stares intently at Marton for a moment, shrugs, once again mumbles something inaudible and goes back inside.

The café owner smiles, "Let me get you another coffee."

On his return, Marton explained that he was looking for his sister. The café owner looks nervously around, before going on to say there was indeed a department for the missing, but advised him against going there. "In all likelihood, if she is not dead, they would have been taken to the IIV District, the red-light area." Taking a sip of coffee, he raised his eyes to the heavens, "It is there but it is not there,". He warned Marton to be careful, as the country was a web of spies and informers. "Do not trust anyone in government, your father was a man from an educated background, which is not good in Budapest today." He wrote down the name of a contact who now worked in IIV District, "His name is Ivan, but ask for Chips, he can be found here," he said, scribbling down an address.

"Another short break ladies and gentlemen, and we will be right back," said the presenter. After the break, the experts discussed whether something could have happened to Marton in his search for Kati, something that distorted his mind?

The presenter smiled.

"From what I see, Marton is showing great courage in his search for his sister," said the psychologist. "But yet, in putting himself in such immense danger, undoubtedly reflects a strong link to psychopathic behaviour."

"The next clip, I think will prove to be enlightening," said the presenter.

Marton arrives at the entrance to a concrete block of apartments. A small man in a long Arab style robe arrives and introduces himself as Chips. They greet each other and begin to walk with Chips leading the way. Eyes alert, Chips takes Marton up a busy road. As the noisy traffic races by, they start with small talk, weather, the cost of fuel and a short conversation about the small man's pet dog. Further along at an area of heavy tree cover, Chips slows his pace and asks Marton for details on his sister. Marton describes Kati and her abduction. They continue and loop back to where they started from. Chips enters the block and returns five minutes later, he discreetly slips Marton a piece of paper, along with a small loaf of bread. Chips shakes hands with Marton and kisses the side of his face, as though saying farewell to an old friend.

Marton is in a narrow alley; there is a mattress propped up on one side, an old shop sign and some broken furniture on the other. Arriving at a doorway, he knocks. There's a sound; a spyhole flips open, then the door. Facing Marton is a big ugly bald guy, with thick lips and a stoop. Marton smiles, but the big guy doesn't respond. Marton hands him the scrap of paper. The guy examines it, grunts, and with a nod leads Marton inside. It is dark, the only source of light are fairy lights. They pass through into another room, the guy nods in the direction of a bar, grunts again, and turns back in the direction from where he had come from. Marton joins a group of men perched on stools drinking. One of the other customers looks up, his face is pockmarked, he grins, and a row of gold teeth shine. Marton orders a beer and moves away to find himself a seat. A few moments later, a dark-skinned woman in a gold sequinned dress appears. She walks onto a small empty dancefloor, on the wall is an ancient jukebox, she selects a tune; slow and sexy and begins to perform. Her hips swaying to the rhythm of the music. One or two of the men at the bar turned to watch; Marton too.

A woman dressed in a white loose-fitting gown, with a shaved head is walking toward Marton; it looks like Kati.

The scene cuts and the presenter shows the audience a picture of Kati at fifteen. She looks almost identical to the woman, apart from the young Kati has a fuller face and figure. This woman's features are fine, and maybe because she is so thin, her eyes look bigger.

She nods at Marton, turns and walks towards a doorway, He follows, his hand reaches for her shoulder; she takes it and leads the way.

They are in a room, it is small, the double bed dominating the floor space, a few photos are pinned to the wall. She smiles seductively and reaches for his waistband, asking, "What do you want?"

Marton holds her back at arm's length, "I have come to take you home."

Confused, her mind stutters, she laughs, "Sorry, I cannot, I cannot, I only work from the club."

"I don't mean that, I've come to take you home. I'm your brother Marton… Marton, you remember me?"

She stares intensely, examining his features. Her hand reaches to her face, a look of horror, her mind stutters again, "You don't know me? You think you know me…but you don't." she turns and briskly walks towards the door. Marton takes a few steps but doesn't follow as he watches her run down the hallway and disappears. A few moments later the big ugly guy returns, he eyes Marton suspiciously. Marton meekly returns to the bar and orders a drink, then another. The dark-skinned girl has now finished dancing, she sits beside him.

"I think from here we should move to the night of the murder," said the presenter. He paused and looked into the camera with an earnest expression, "The scene which we are about to witness is truly harrowing. We only show it as they are pivotal to uncovering the truth about this horrific crime. Please do not watch if you are sensitive or under the age of twenty-five."

Marton is exiting his apartment in Bordeaux; he looks back at an empty doorway. His breathing is short, almost panting. At the edge of the forest, he slows. He looks down at his hands, examining them, "No! No! No!" and stumbles on. Pushing through branches he enters deeper, "Kati, Kati, help me,

Kati!" he calls. There is a sound of breaking twigs and a rustle of leaves. Grunting like an animal; his mind is scrabbling through a myriad of images and thoughts. We see his father on the ground after being shot; his mother kissing Henri, Kati as a young girl playing, and then being dragged away by the soldiers. There is a woman in a white gown; Marton has a large knife and is slashing at her throat, her arms, her legs, her wrists. He screams again, "Kati." The white gown is torn; her pale naked body exposed. With bloodied hands, he removes her limbs. He is panting as he places a leg where once the arm had been, the bloody head he puts down between the stumps of her thighs. He falls to his knees, then onto his chest. His words are undecipherable, guttural words of anguish and pain.

The Dinner Party

The Rich man boasts with a laugh
The Poor man with a swagger
Only the Beggarman knows his worth

Lanigan gazed: haunting memories, things he couldn't quite remember, memories of beauty and hell. Her pale iridescent skin, her flaxen hair flowing in gentle ripples, every ripple creating a beautiful swirl. Unblinking eyes stared up at the stars. Did they register? Could she see? Was she there? Or rather, was some part of her present? An essence? Of course, scientist said it was impossible. But with every generation, what was once conceived as impossible became possible. It was cold, Lanigan looked across the river and blew onto his hands to warm them. To the west golden tipped clouds hung loosely over the horizon, bowing at the moon's ascent.

How many songs and sweet nothings had they shared?

Reaching out he touched her forehead, slowly tracing the outline of her nose and down to her watery lips. In fear, he pulled back.

But what could he do? She would give him trouble, trouble that he didn't need. A dark winged angel cawed out a warning as two young lovers walked by. Lanigan rose, casually looking off into the distance, the corner of his eye restless. He waited, waited until they were out of sight. With the toe of his boot, he pushed. The wind lifted the current towards the bridge, silently she disappeared.

....

"Berti, Berti, are you ready?" shouted Paddy.

Berti drew in a breath, he'd been daydreaming. He finished off the spliff he'd been smoking and threw the stub down the loo. Looking into the mirror, he examined himself. Blue eyes with saggy halos stared back at him. His colour was golden brown, thanks to the solarium. He lifted his fringe to scrutinize his retreating hairline and made a face. *Oh, daddy, why?*

"Coming," he called out.

They were off to a dinner party. Paddy was Berti's wife of the last eight years. She was elegant, beautiful, and twelve years younger. Quite a catch for a man in his autumn years.

"Have you got the wine?" he asked, slipping on a blue velvet jacket.

"Oh darling, I do like that ensemble. Cream and blue work well on you." Paddy remarked. "Sets off you're colouring."

Berti stood back from the hallway mirror. *Ok not quite the athlete I once was. Perhaps a little more out front than I would like, but after thirty years of debauchery, not too bad.* He swept his hair over to one side, stood up straight and pulled a James Bond pose, *I've still got it.*

Paddy laughed.

"Would you help me with these?" he smiled and held out his hands, each containing a gold cufflink studded in rubies. Paddy placed a warm kiss on his lips, took the cufflinks and fixed them in place.

"What time are we expected?" asked Berti.

"We're supposed to be there for seven, but you know what it's like with Charles and Julia."

Berti raised his eyebrows knowingly.

Charles and Julia were scientists, experts in their respective fields. Like his father before him Charles was on the board of ICI, a huge British chemical company. He'd met Julia on a holiday in Morocco at a party for Yves St Laurent. At the time, Julia was a student studying biochemistry at the National University of Medical Science in Madrid. That was twenty-five years ago. Charles took her under his wing and sponsored her studies in London. They'd had years of excess on Charles' expense account but recently they'd settled into a more domestic setting. Very rarely did they agree on anything whilst sober, although shitfaced, they were as one.

"What about a swift one sweetie?" Berti asked.

Paddy glanced up at the old grandfather clock. With a mischievous smile, "Ok, a quick one." She unbuttoned her blouse, reaching into her bra and pulled out a small plastic bag of white powder. On the surface of the glass console table, she chopped two lines with her credit card

With a ten-pound note tube at the ready, Berti's eyes widened, "After you dear," he offered politely.

Paddy took the rolled-up tenner, lowered her head towards the coke lines and in a second there was one.

As she wiped her nose, Berti looked to her, "Darling did I mention that Lucy has asked if I would enter the dads race this year." He dipped down to the single line and in a second there was none. Letting out a smack from his lips. "Can you speak to her?"

Lucy was Paddy's daughter from a previous relationship. She was thirteen and a serious swat.

"Oh Berti, that's so sweet, when is it?" Paddy asked as she buttoned herself up.

"I don't know, she didn't say," Berti stepped forward to help her with her jacket. He paused for a moment before cautiously going on. "I mean I... I don't think it's such a good idea. I haven't run a race for thirty years, and even then I was disqualified for cheating."

Paddy laughed, "What a surprise!"

Berti shook his head as he remembered. "Cross country, and I would have won anyway," delighted with himself, he chuckled. "I was a fine runner in those days, always on the podium." He paused. "But legacy is a demanding taskmaster. I wanted to smash the school record, and being a belt and braces type of fellow, I instructed my friend Fleming to secrete a bike in the bushes on Cadlin Corner." His mind followed his eyes to the ceiling, *I wonder where old Flem is these days?* Recognising Paddy's annoyance, he shook himself back into reality. "I couldn't fault him. The plan was for me to dash out a mile in double quick time. No one could keep pace with me in those days. Hop on the bike for the middle of the race, dump it at the boundary of the school fields. Come home to a rousing ovation." He shrugged and let out a breath, "Trust my luck, Spotty Hall, head of biology was in the bushes with his camera. Supposedly doing field research," he gave Paddy a knowing look. "Yeah! Schoolboys in tight fitting shorts. Well, anyway, he saw me dump the bike. I was miles ahead, never mind the school record, I was up for the bloody national record," Berti chuckled. "I can still hear those cheers. *Hurrah! Hurrah! Come on! Come on Berti!"* he bellowed. "Even Batesy, our headmaster's face was beaming. "I was the hero for an hour. I thought when he sent for me, I was to be given a medal. Not six of the best which I received," he winked, "But as luck would have it, Old Batesy had a thing for mummy. If it wasn't for her, I'd definitely..."

Paddy laughed. "I bet your mother had him around her little finger."

"I don't think that was the only place," quipped Berti.

With her forefinger Paddy tapped Berti's nose, "Another layer revealed." A quick kiss, "I do like a bad boy. Come on, we better get going. Those two will be semi unconscious by now."

Half an hour later they stepped out of a taxi on Cheyne Walk, Chelsea, Charles and Julia's house. It was regency in style and faced out onto the Thames, white frontage with iron railings and a black door.

"Come in come in," Charles' face shone with a warm alcoholic glow. "You both look f...fabulous." He greeted them with double kisses, before taking their coats. Charles called upstairs, "Julia, Julia, Paddy and Berti are here." Charles was in his late sixties, he had grey hair and a thin delicate body. He was as straight as a dye but as camp as a Christmas tree fairy. He was wearing light grey trousers with a yellow sweater, his wore his hair swept back and looked very distinguished. He looked back as he led them through. "She's had a rough day."

The hallway was filled perhaps cluttered would be a better description. Antique antlers lined the wall, a full-sized bronze boar next to an over ladened hat stand, chairs, console tables, lamps, stuffed birds in glass cases, they were obviously in a transition. The drawing-room in contrast was light and expansive, minimalist furniture with modern art on the walls, two identical tan leather couches dominated the middle. To one side there was a state-of-the-art stereo playing Ella Fitzgerald. Double doors led out into the gardens.

Two other guests were already there. "Everybody, this is Paddy and Berti," said Charles with an exaggerated wink, as they all knew each other. There were the usual rounds of kisses and handshakes. Charles waited patiently, as the greetings concluded. "Now what can I get you to drink?" waving his hand towards a table full of bottles of various shapes and colours. "White, red, cognac, whisky, vodka?"

Paddy paused, taking in what was on offer.

"Scotch and ginger for me please Charles," answered Berti.

"White for me. Is that a Louis Jadot?" said Paddy as she eyed the labels.

Charles smiled and poured her a huge glass, "For the lady," he announced.

He selected a bottle of Glenlivet, showing it to Berti, who nodded approvingly. "Say when."

Before Berti had a chance to speak the glass was full. "Any chance of a drop of ginger in that?"

Charles grinned, "Not unless you take a sip first." Then, "Fuck, we haven't got ginger." Before changing his mind, "No, what am I thinking, we have got ginger." He took a slug out of Berti's glass himself, "Ginger beer, ok?"

"Fine," Berti nodded.

Charles did the rounds, and when he was sure everyone was topped up, he headed into the hall. At the bottom of the stairs he swung round the balustrade, "Julia," and cupping his ear, "Julia dear," but with no response he headed upstairs to investigate.

Berti and Paddy were chatting to Melissa. She'd just got back from the Cayman Islands and was regaling an event at the airport.

Melissa was in her early forties but still very much a teenager. Blonde, suntanned with an excellent figure. Her father was a bigwig in mining and chemicals, he'd made a fortune, which on his death, Melissa had inherited. She was married to Philip, who was Berti's stepbrother. Melissa didn't get on with her husband. Apart from gatherings they led separate lives. In fact, but for an expensive divorce she'd have got shot of him a long time ago.

Philip was a stock broker and dabbled in property development. Quite a success in his own right but compared to his wife's squillions, he was small fry. He was standing purposefully with his back to the three, feigning interest in a piece of art, hoping to earwig some secret to his advantage. He was wearing chinos and a sweater draped over his shoulders. He turned to Berti, "Beautiful, don't you agree? On the wall was a painting, completely white apart from some scratches which revealed a darker colour beneath.

Berti looked up, glass in hand, other hand on his hip. He blew out his cheeks as he took in the picture. He frowned, a quick glance towards the hall, to make sure Charles or Julia weren't in earshot and shook his head. "I just don't understand it? I really don't... I'm struggling to flog real art, works of real masters. And people pay tens of thousands for.... THAT!"

With the smile of a fox Philip went on, "How is the antique business going?" Knowing full well that Berti was bordering on bankruptcy.

Berti sipped his whisky.

His antiques shop in Chelsea was at one time the go-to place for the rich and famous. He even knew Lord Snowdon as Tony. But business had nosedived. People just weren't buying quality antiques. Nowadays, it was all this Scandinavian tat. He'd placed too much trust in his Swedish connection Allana. Only to find out *'This year's hot product in Stockholm,'* was London's dead duck. If it wasn't for Paddy's income, he'd have closed.

"Busy!" said Berti with good humour. "If only the fuckers would pay." He let out a raucous laugh, "It's a nightmare getting money from people these days."

Philip grinned as Berti's tell-tale eyebrow twitched, which said he was lying. "Oh, that reminds me, I still owe you five hundred quid for that jewellery box."

The box had slipped Berti's mind. Its mention sent him in a spin. Yes, he remembered it now, a nineteenth century piece, tortoise shell with mother of pearl inlay. Funny, he thought he'd sold it to a Korean couple. *Bastard, and I let him have it at cost.* He smiled, thinking, *Tight arsed bugger.* But as Melissa was one of his best customers, he laughed, "Oh, don't worry. I hope she liked it."

Philip called to his wife, "Darling, I was just saying how much you enjoyed that little jewellery box I bought from Berti."

Hearing her name, Melissa momentarily glanced up, then returned to her conversation with Paddy without comment.

Philip and Berti looked at each other, both grinning.

"She loved it," Philip answered. "Can I get you another?" he shook his wine glass by the stem.

Whilst Philip was sorting out the drinks, Berti rejoined Paddy and Melissa.

"Hi everyone." A tall swarthy bearded man entered the room. It was Roberto, Julia's brother. Roberto was a tennis coach, perhaps thirty-five, but looked younger.

"Ahh, just at the right time. What can I get you?" said Philip glancing up from the drinks table.

Roberto hovered over Philip's shoulder. Speaking with a thick Spanish accent, "A pineapple juice would be great, thank you." He turned towards the ladies, smiling with a perfect set of gleaming white teeth, "Hello Paddy, long time no see," he kissed her on both cheeks, then stood back. "You looking younger, every time. Yes?" He winked at Berti, who was standing proudly alongside. "And sweet Melissa, you look so good, so tanned. You have been away in sunshine, I can tell."

Melissa smiled weakly, unimpressed with Roberto's oily Latin charm. Philip handed out the drinks.

"You might as well top us up," Melissa said, purring with distain. She glanced to Paddy, who forwarded her glass.

There was a clatter from the kitchen, a moment later Charles appeared with a tray of canapes. "Can I interest you in some nibbles." He held out a tray as the contents raced towards the edge.

Berti was first to hand, taking it, he offered them around. "Vol-au-vent, anyone?"

With a flamboyant wave of his hand Charles turned. From the bottom of the stairs, he called, "Darling, come on, people are waiting," then disappeared into the kitchen.

Roberto, "I better go see how he's doing." Popping his head through the doorway, "Everything under control maestro?" Another crash. Roberto looked back to the group with a grimace come smirk.

"Everything is under control. Perhaps you could persuade your wonderful sister to join us," said Charles sarcastically.

Back in the drawing room, Paddy was proudly explaining a business deal Berti was working on. "He's supplying props for a new period drama series, 'The Officer.' It's one of Freddie's. They've submitted it to the BBC but it's one of those American channels that have picked it up...."

Berti knew the deal was on thin ice to say the least. So, before Paddy had finished, he butted in with a roaring laugh. "You know what these fuckers are like, I'm not taking it too seriously. It might come to nothing. It's been on the go for quite a while now."

"Freddie Malden?" asked Philip.

"The very man," replied Berti.

Melissa was taking an interest and was in Berti's peripheral vision. He feared he'd been rumbled, so repeated the tenuous probability, much to Paddy's confusion. To his relief and rescue, Julia arrived.

"Welcome, welcome, welcome!" Julia called, beaming as she entered the room. She was wearing a pale blue sequinned dress, which Paddy enthused over. Julia embraced her guests, with a positive word for each. Her looks were dark and exotic, unmistakably Mediterranean and like her brother she did not look her years.

On hearing his partners voice, Charles appeared, "Oh, you've decided to honour us with your presence." He was half cut and well on the way to three quarters. Julia leant over and gave him an exaggerated sloppy kiss on the cheek. Charles swooned in comical ecstasy.

Philip spoke, "Berti was telling us about a deal he's working on for a movie." He turned to Paddy, "It is a movie, isn't it?"

Paddy glanced to Berti. "I don't know?"

Berti cleared his throat; his voice a little raspy, "I don't think there's a hope in hell but stranger things have happened." Changing the subject, he went on, "Anyway how are things with you Julia, have you managed to secure that patent you mentioned last time we spoke?"

Julia shook her head wistfully; her accent was softer than the guttural tones of her younger brother. "No, nothing yet." Her voice went up a tone, "The red tape in this country is ridiculous. In Spain I could speak to a government advisor and things would be settled. Here I have to submit paper after paper, month after month." Her eyes went to the ceiling. "To be honest I am no further." She quickly downed her glass of scotch, holding it out for a top-up. "I tell you one thing. This country will become paralysed. It is like being sent from pot to pot to piss only to find a stinking turd in each one." Her anger was real but tempered.

"She'll get it through soon, I'm sure," volunteered Charles reassuringly. "I do sympathise however. This Labour government has tied us in red tape. Anything that makes a profit..." He let out a long-drawn-out breath. Once handsome, and often compared to a young Peter O'Toole, Charles' best years had passed him by, a cloud of alcohol his respite. "I daren't go to the club these days. It's protest this, protest that. Only last week I got stopped by one of that pro vegetable gang wanting me to sign something. Won't eat meat... Potatoes have mothers too," he laughed out loud. "I told them to fuck off... as if life has got some sort of sliding scale of value." If it's not them, it's CND, or those bloody Irish terrorist sympathisers." He shook his head and poured himself a large scotch, topping it up with soda.

Melissa looked up, "Don't you think we are due a bit of a shake-up, some new ideas?

"At my age dear, no thank you," replied Charles.

Melissa smiled, "Sometime or other, the chickens have got to come home..." She took a sip of wine, "Things change."

Paddy nodded in agreement. Charles' smirk, didn't go unnoticed.

"Oh, come on," said Melissa, "For fuck's sake we can't expect the rest of the world to kow tow forever, can we? Queen and country and all that." She raised her voice, "Actually, I don't think this government goes far enough. We should be forced to return whatever we've stolen from wherever. And... withdraw our military from these far-flung places." She paused, "What are we doing in these countries?"

"Bloody hell, I didn't have you down as a communist," said Charles.

Philip's head dropped from side to side, weighing up the options. Morals weren't his thing but he prided himself on his knowledge of world politics. "I... don't think it's quite that simple darling. If we were to withdraw our influence, a lot of those countries would return to barbaric savagery." His voice was clipped in comparison to his wife's soft mid-Atlantic drawl.

Paddy wanted to speak, but feared confrontation, so stood quietly, arms folded across her chest.

Berti spoke up, "I understand exactly how you feel Mellie but I do think Philip's got a point. We were in Goa a couple of years ago, apart from the resort, it was just squalor and filth. I know the natives live with it, but, come on. Isn't that right Paddy?" Paddy looked unsure of herself but nodded. Berti went on, "It was the same in Kenya, once out of Mombasa, you needed security. These people don't live like we do. I mean I love their sense of exuberance, but for the life of me... no. If we withdrew it would be a bloodbath. A big mistake."

Charles let loose a boozy laugh. Suddenly his eyes turned to panic, "Oh Jesus," as wisps of grey smoke crept into the room.

"I've got it," came a shout from the kitchen. It was Roberto.

"Where's your maid this evening? asked Melissa.

"Her bloody father's ill," annoyed, Charles shook his head and let out a drawn-out breath.

Roberto appeared holding an oven tray with a tea towel, with what looked like a collection of crisp black fingers. "I think the piglets in blankets have, erm…. A little cremated, perhaps even more."

The ladies pulled back from the still smoking offerings.

"Don't worry, I'm not offended," said Charles. He placed a hand on Roberto's shoulder. "Would you be a dear and pop the Beef Wellington in, I think it should take about an h'our."

Roberto placed the burnt offering alongside the vol-au-vents. Helping himself to some more pineapple juice, he tried a sausage. "Not too bad," he said grinning.

The conversation continued on Britain's influence on the world. Charles pointed out that Melissa's family had made their money mining in Africa. Melissa's defence was that she could not change history and didn't know too much about the mining business. Charles explained that she didn't have to, her father was wise enough to have all their funds in offshore trusts so that the greedy socialists could not get hold of it.

"Well, I don't see any of it," insisted Melissa.

Roberto returned from the kitchen. The debate went back and forth like a well-rehearsed tennis rally, eyes darting one way and then the other, the odd "excellent point" thrown in.

Slipping away from the discussion, Paddy and Roberto stepped outside into the gardens which were lit up with discreet lighting. It was quite chilly; spring colour was in its infancy, with a promise of more to come. A full-sized bronze of a Greek athlete, spear raised and muscles rippling, dominated the lawned area. Moss-covered urns were dotted along the lilac edged borders. Roberto plucked a few buds and offered them to Paddy. She squeezed them between her fingers and took in the scent. Further along they passed an early magnolia; Paddy stretched up to the open petals.

"It is beautiful, yes?" said Roberto smiling.

"I love magnolia, that mix of sweet and spice, I find it so attractive," replied Paddy.

Roberto pulled a branch towards her and held it invitingly.

She took in the fragrance, "Ummm, beautiful."

Roberto let go, the branch flicked skywards, showering them with pollen. "I am so sorry," he gently brushed the pollen off Paddy's clothing and hair. But his attempt was simply spreading it further. With a smirk, "I am making it worse."

Paddy smiled, reassuring him and tried herself. "Oh, we're both making a mess."

"Ahh, there you are." It was Berti, making his way towards them. "Politics... I thought it best to leave them to it."

All three continued down the garden, with Roberto pointing out various plants in their Latin and common names. His knowledge was impressive. He stopped at an acacia tree and grinned, "This is beautiful, it is the Caragana Arborescens, the Acacia. Let me tell you a story about this particular one." He smiled, "Charles brought it back from Mexico for Julia, I think ten years ago." He stood back admiring.

Berti and Paddy waited in anticipation.

Roberto raised a finger and went on, "It should not grow well here, in this country. It is too cold. In the first year nothing, second year nothing. But my father back home in Spain, he recommend... to piss on it." Laughing he pretended to piss. "So, Julia, she pissed, every week, just one time...every week." With his forefinger he pointed up. "Now see how it blooms." He snapped off a stem and handed it to Paddy. "This tree, it is for love too." With a wink he put a hand on Berti's shoulder. "Maybe you get lucky tonight?"

Berti took the stem from Paddy, then grinning he sunk to his knees, presenting the bloom to his wife. "Darling."

Paddy raised an eyebrow, embarrassed she smiled at Roberto.

"No, not him you fool. Me, me," Berti laughed.

"Get up, for goodness sake." Paddy held on to Berti as he stiffly straightened himself. "You know you shouldn't be doing that; you'll end up in that corset again."

Berti laughed, "She's right, my back's buggered." He leant forward to ease himself.

The first course was now ready and as Charles and Julia had forgotten to set the placings, Melissa volunteered. Knowing Philip was borderline obsessive compulsive, for fun she mixed up his order of cutlery. Once satisfied, she marched into the drawing-room, struck a fork against a glass, "Ladies and Gentlemen. Can we have you seated?"

The dining room walls were painted a maroon colour, dark oak panelled, a huge crystal chandelier hung over the walnut dining table. Portraits of military men stared out at the guests.

Charles smiled and looked to Melissa, "Where am I to sit?"

"At the head of course Charles," pulling out his chair.

He followed her guidance, falling into his chair with a thump.

"You can sit here Berti," said Melissa. She had reserved adjoining seats for herself and Paddy. After directing each to their place, and with a nod of satisfaction, she disappeared into the kitchen.

Charles poured the wine, both white and red were offered, whatever suited. He sat back in his chair, smiling as a panicked Philip rearranged his setting. Paddy too was enjoying Philip's dilemma, she whispered and giggled something in Roberto's ear.

"That woman of yours has got a sense of humour," said Charles raising his glass.

Philip looked up, "I should know better." He'd finally sorted out his soldiers and took a sip of wine.

"Like her mother, headstrong," said Charles. He turned to his left, "How's business Berti?" Not waiting for an answer, he called through to Melissa in the kitchen, "How's your mother Mellie? Is she planning a trip to Ascot this year?"

"Oh, she'll be there," Melissa shouted, "Wild horses couldn't stop her.

Charles let out a throaty laugh and slapped his thigh. "Now there's a woman. She'll have a bet no doubt?"

"If she can find a bookie who'll take it," came the reply.

"Yes, there's a woman," again he slapped his thigh.

Melissa's mother was a renowned high stakes gambler. If not on the race course she could be found at Aspinall's casino.

There was a rumble of footsteps across the wooden floor. Julia appeared, holding a silver tray, followed by Melissa with a gravy boat containing extra sauce.

"Moules Mariniere," Julia called out.

There were smiles all round as the tray was placed in the centre of the table. Julia stood with hands on hips contemplating, making sure all that was required was present. Just as she was about to take her seat, Charles called for salt. She disappeared, returning a few seconds later with both salt and pepper. The mussels were passed around to the usual dinner table chatter. Once all were served, they began to eat.

After one bite, Melissa put down her cutlery, "How long have you cooked these, Julia?"

Hesitantly, Julia looked up, "Are they ok?"

"Well, they're perfect if you are partial to salty galoshes," Melissa raised her napkin to her mouth and spat out the remains.

Tentatively, "Seem ok to me," offered Paddy politely.

With eyes upon him, Charles worked loose a mussel, gave it a quick chew and quickly swallowed. "Perfect," With a nod in Julia's direction. "Ladies, don't chew, swallow.". He winked at his wife, who smiled.

Roberto followed, "It is good, but yes, perhaps a minute earlier from the pan. Maybe perhaps?"

"Nonsense," was Charles' brusque reply, as he eked out another, "They're first class, fresh from the fish monger today… and cooked to perfection. Now can we get on?" He turned to Berti, "I'm looking for a bit of advice, you might be able to help?"

Berti placed his cutlery down, dabbing the sides of his mouth with his napkin.

Charles took a sip of wine. "Could you pass me the salt?" he looked towards Paddy.

She passed the salt to Melissa, who in turn passed it to Charles. He tossed a couple of spoonsfuls onto the side of his plate and returned to Berti, "I've been thinking of getting rid of a piece or two and wondered what I could expect."

Julia nodded.

In his mind Berti was wondering why Charles was selling. He was usually a prolific buyer, a hoarder in fact. It seemed against his nature to sell. "Well, I would be delighted to give you a valuation. Do you know what in particular?"

Julia called over, "We are full. We have rooms crammed to bursting, maybe if you could look through?"

Melissa spoke, "Can we have first dibs?"

Philip flashed her a look.

"What? Charles and Julia have impeccable taste," Melissa said abruptly dismissing her husband with a shake of her head.

Charles looked down the table, "Yes, we have far too much, we need to scale back. So, if you do have a free day, I would very much appreciate it.

"Absolutely," said Berti, debating in his mind what commission rate he could work on. Charles and Julia had an Aladdin's cave of a collection. The paintings alone were certainly in the millions, possibly tens of millions, add to that any furniture. This was just the sort of job to get him back on his feet. He didn't want to sound too eager but knew that he'd not be the only valuer Charles would use. "I will double check my diary but should be able to pop over one afternoon next week. Obviously if that works with you?" He glanced across to Paddy, "Darling we haven't anything particular going on next week, have we?"

Before Paddy could respond, Charles cut in, "Splendid, anytime next week is fine. If I or Julia are not around, I will leave instructions with Martha.

Martha was their housekeeper.

"How's the property market these days?" Julia asked Philip.

"Very good thank you," he paused, "and if these proposed planning measures actually take place, it will certainly swing the pendulum."

Charles' eyes flicked to the foot of the table.

"What do you see happening?" asked Berti.

Philip glanced at his brother, "Well up until now, to do anything with these larger properties is nigh on impossible. But the new legislation will allow for the sub division." Philip scooped out a mussel, pausing. "The effect will be a free for all with landlords, subdividing to gain their best return."

"So, all these beautiful houses will be converted into flats?" asked Paddy.

"In theory, possibly," Philip coolly replied. "The deciding factor of course will be a balance between investment, income and capital growth. Philip was playing a close hand; he was looking for an investment and was aware Charles and Julia's lease was due to expire the following year.

The second course of Beef Wellington was served. Charles picked up his knife and fork, bumping them on the table. "Now you can't do better than a Wellington. Hope you all enjoy it." At the sound of the doorbell, he glanced over his shoulder with a puzzled expression, "Who the devil could that be?"

Melissa jumped up, "I'll get it. A few moments later she returned, followed by a man dressed in old work clothes. He looked about forty, his face was dirty, his dark collar length hair a tangled mess.

Charles eyed him suspiciously, "What have we got here?"

"This is Lanigan. He's asked if you need any jobs doing?" Melissa looked to Charles.

"What can you do Lanigan?" asked Charles.

Lanigan shuffled from side to side.

"Can you cook mussels?" Philip laughed sarcastically.

Lanigan looked confused. He spoke with a broad West Country accent, "No, I don't cook, I do general handyman work. Gardening, gutters, painting, that sort of thing."

Charles wiped his mouth with his napkin. "I don't think we can help you Lanigan." His tone was dismissive. "Melissa, please show him the door."

Julia looked to Charles reproachfully, "Charles!"

"What?" Charles replied. He glanced at Lanigan, then to Julia and shrugged his shoulders. "We don't need anything done, do we?"

Lanigan looked to Julia.

Roberto rose from his seat and made his way around the table. "I am sorry sir; we have no work for you."

Lanigan's eyes dropped to the Beef Wellington.

"Would you like some?" offered Roberto.

"Yes, have some food," said Julia.

Roberto leant over and cut off a slice. He looked to Charles, "Can I use this?

Charles flipped his napkin across, Roberto wrapped the food.

"Now show him the door," said Charles sharply.

Roberto put his hand on Lanigan's shoulder, with a sympathetic shrug he led Lanigan away.

Melissa scrambled to her feet, dodging in front of the pair to her bag. She dipped into it and pulled out a couple of tenners, a handful of change and a pack of cigarettes. She caught up with them at the doorway. "Here, I know it's not much but..." she smiled.

Lanigan looked down at the money and fags, his heart said no, but his head knew better. Digesting his humiliation, he spoke slowly, "That's very kind Miss, I really appreciate it. Very kind, thank you."

He slipped the napkin of food in his pocket and disappeared into the night.

....

Lanigan looked back confused, he was sure this was the house he worked on last week and couldn't understand why they had been so rude. Waiting five minutes, he crept back into the front garden. Yes, he was sure, he had painted the whole front. *But why was all the paint old and dirty? Maybe someone had somehow come in and took off the new paint? It had to be.* He looked up at the top windows. *Someone had changed them, the front door too.* He suspected who the culprits were but didn't want to say until he had more evidence.

....

An hour later the food had gone. They'd skipped desert, instead a box of chocolate was passed around. Cheeses had been nibbled, brandy poured and cigars for anyone who wanted one. Not interested in politics, Paddy, Julia and Roberto had left the dining room leaving Charles, Philip, Berti, and Melissa to argue their case.

Melissa was for dismantling the commonwealth, but with all the boys against her she was up against it,. She puffed her cigar and blew a long trail of blue smoke over the table, another pull, and with a movement from her jaw, perfect smoke rings emerged from her mouth.

"That's quite a trick," said Charles, "What is it you do?"

"It's nothing," said Melissa, sending another volley across the table. "It's all in the jaw." She performed the trick again, showing how it was done.

Charles tried without success. "I bet that's not your only trick?" he asked suggestively.

Melissa giggled, brushed her blonde hair back, then pushed her tongue into her cheek with a knowing wink. Charles grinned and looked down the table towards Philip, who strained a smile. Melissa was spluttering with laughter. She was a first-class tease, particularly after a drink, it was just in her.

Charles had fancied Melissa from the moment he'd set eyes on her. Her mother introduced her at a garden party, she couldn't have been much older than sixteen or seventeen. Even now, he remembered what she was wearing, cut-off denim shorts and a t-shirt, tied just below her bust. Even at that tender age, she held the eye of young and old alike. Charles sat back, puffed on his cigar, brandy glass in hand. Charles was always regarded as a gentleman, although he himself was not so sure. *Well, what is a gentleman? A social grace, a skill? A deceit of nature?* He took a puff of his cigar. With wisdom in the ascendency and charm now waning, his mind drifted, meandering with carnal thoughts.

In the drawing room, Paddy was on the leather couch, next to her was Roberto, who was making gentle inlays. Julia was facing them on the other couch and had put her feet up. Recognising the slippery designs her brother had on her friend; she chose to interrupt the exchange. "Tell me, how are things with Berti, I worry about him?"

Roberto sat back, knowing his intentions had been scuttled, for now.

"He's fine," Paddy said, the truth being he was struggling both financially and mentally.

Julia pushed, "That's good." Then pausing, "I don't know if it was right," her voice was finely balanced between nosy neighbour and trusted councillor. "It's just I heard something about bailiffs." Once again, she paused, "I don't know…" raised her hands, "I know times can be difficult, but if there is anything we can do?"

Berti had not mentioned anything about bailiffs, Paddy thought.

....

Lanigan was sitting on his favourite bench, looking out over the river. A woman, whom he thought he recognised passed by. She was accompanied by a little girl of maybe four or five, innocently skipping as she tagged along.

"Hello mister," she said, her voice uninhibited, confident.

Lanigan's heart glowed with a memory, he smiled and raised a hand.

The little girl skipped on to the next lamppost, then turned, giving Lanigan a goodbye wave.

He was four years old and sleeping next to a woman, a gentle woman, who smelt of alcohol. In her embrace the world was safe and good.

Whether hungry or not, he began to eat. It was his first meal of the day, if you didn't count three cans of cider. Spring had sprung, but winter had yet to loosen its grip on the night. It was too cold to stay for long, so soon after he'd finished the slice of Beef Wellington, Lanigan headed off. He knew his territory well and chose a little pub just off the Kings Road, a regular with vagabonds, rogues and navvies. He pushed open the stained-glass panel door and was welcomed by its warm embrace. At the bar were a couple of the old boys, men of the road, like himself. Both looked older than their years. Lanigan knew them but gave them a wide berth. Neither were renowned for generosity but possessed eyes of hawks if there was money to be had. With a tenner clutched in his gnarly fist Lanigan waited to be served. He found himself a spot in the corner and contemplated his plans.

....

From the dining room came a raucous laugh. It was Berti's, he sounded like he was gargling a toad. All three looked up, Paddy happy at the distraction.

He appeared, "Darling they are trying to get me to stand on my head." It was a party trick from his younger days, standing on his head and drinking a glass of water.

He was followed by Melissa, Charles and lastly Philip.

"Come on get him to do it," Philip pleaded, hoping that Berti would either injure or make a fool of himself. "Come on, make him do it."

Berti looked to Paddy, eyes a whisky shine, "What do you think darling?"

Paddy grinned and let out a breath. "It's your back..."

Before she had finished, Berti was on the floor doing one arm push-ups. Although in his autumn years, he was still as strong as an ox. To loud cheers he managed ten on each arm and with a few practice movements was on his head. "Glass?" he called out, as his face turned purple.

"Bloody hell, we haven't got one," said Melissa, spluttering with laughter, "Quick someone get him some water."

"Whisky will do," said Philip.

Roberto dashed off to the kitchen, as Berti returned to his feet, saying, "For god's sake, have it ready." It took him four skips, but a few seconds later he again was planted head first on the floor.

Roberto was kneeling beside him.

Berti reached for the water, then changed his mind, "Wait, wait," once more he tried. On his third attempt he took the glass and a few sips but spluttered the water all over himself. He tried once more, with the same result.

As they looked on, Paddy knew this was why she loved him, forever the tryer.

After two unsuccessful swallows he collapsed down, with Charles and Melissa breaking his fall. He sat up, hair and face wet with water and saliva and shook himself. "Bugger me, that's the very last time."

....

With four whiskies' down, Lanigan returned to his seat with another. He took a sip and looked to the bar. It was a whisper at first, the two men were talking about him, and now not so discreetly. One was laughing saying how Lanigan was doing bob-a-job and door-to-door begging. Lanigan held his temper, turned an ear and took another sip. A young woman approached the jukebox at the far side. With deathly pale features and dark hair, she cut a look. She put her coins in the slot, then turned and slyly grinned at Lanigan. The jukebox cleared its throat, then came the sound of The Clancy Brothers, 'Little Beggarman.'

The bitch, she must be with them, Lanigan pondered. He began counting, *one, two, three,* before he'd gotten to ten, he had risen to confront the two at the bar. They looked terrified as he descended. Without warning he slugged the nearest, who cowered as Lanigan's justice rained down. Shocked the other guy swiftly made away to the far side.

In a flash the barman was out and manhandling Lanigan to the exit. "Out, out, out! he snarled.

Lanigan struggled, but he was on the backfoot. The barman was on his front foot and kept it that way. In seconds Lanigan was at the door, desperately gripping to the frame. Another push saw him sprawling on the pavement. Like two stags they faced each other. Lanigan said he wanted his drink. The barman wasn't having any of it, he knew how to handle a vagabond, a rogue or a navvy for that matter. Each time Lanigan pushed, he landed on his arse, after the third time of trying he gave up.

Apart from the whispers, the streets were silent, as he made his way back to the river. There she was again, pale and beautiful. This time he could see that she was pregnant, her belly gleaming like a second moon on the water. He waded in to his waist, pushing her further away from him. *Fuck off, fuck off! Why don't you fuck off!*

....

Roberto was with Paddy, "You know Paddy, I am intrigued." They were back in the garden; he was a few steps ahead. "How many years have you been with Berti, hmm?" Glancing back, "Somehow, so, I don't see him with you. Why? You are beautiful, successful. I know it is love, yes! But I ask myself, why Berti?"

Paddy smiled, but didn't answer, her eyes attracted by the moonlight which tinkled the leaves of the trees. Roberto was right of course, many people had said the same thing, family, friends, they were all shocked when she linked up with Berti. 'Berti, the clown or Berti the buffoon,' often she had heard when not quite out of earshot. But what was love? Sex was easy, but love, well love was a slippery fish, sometimes spontaneous and always difficult to hold onto.

"How many years?" repeated Roberto.

Paddy smiled, and linked into his arm as they walked on.

....

Lanigan looked up at the long elegant window. The curtains were pulled but some light was escaping. As he waited on the crow for an answer, the lamppost pointed a guiding finger. He had no choice; he knocked the door.

"Charles glanced at the clock, rose from his seat. "We're not expecting anyone, are we Julia?"

Julia looked bemused, "No."

There was something about the knock, or maybe it was the night itself, something that made Charles uneasy. He hesitated before going to the window, then pulled back a slip of the curtain. Lanigan was on the doorstep. "It's that bloody tramp." He went to the fireplace and picked up a poker, slapping it firmly across his palm. With a confident smile he strode to the door.

All they heard was Charles' raised voice and then nothing. Philip frowned and cocked an ear, he glanced to Julia. Melanie looked amused and it was her who went to investigate. In the hall Charles was remonstrating with Lanigan who was on his knees in the praying position. As soon as he saw Melanie he turned from Charles.

"Forgive me, please forgive me," desperately searching Melissa's eyes.

"What's the matter?" she asked.

"Please, please, leave me alone," Lanigan was crying.

Charles looked exasperated. "I don't know what's the matter with him. We're going to have to call the police."

Melissa knelt beside Lanigan and held his clasped hands, he looked terrified. "It's going to be alright." She glanced up at Charles, "Get him a drink for god's sake."

As Charles turned, Philip, Berti and Julia arrived.

"What's up with him?" asked Philip.

Melissa looked up frowning.

With a surge of testosterone Philip attempted to take charge. "We'd better call the police. Let them deal with this," he headed down the hall to where the telephone was.

"Wait, wait," said Melissa. "Let's give him a drink and see how he is."

Lanigan held tightly on to Melissa's hand. "I can't help you; it wasn't my fault."

Charles returned with a glass of water and a whisky bottle, Lanigan eyed the bottle with lustful intent. "I might of bloody known," flinging the water out the doorway Charles poured Lanigan a good-sized tumbler of whisky.

Lanigan snatched the drink and gulped it back.

Charles looked down at the pathetic figure, a wry smile appeared. He handed Lanigan the bottle, "There, take it. You'll be fine."

Lanigan let go of Melissa, clutching at the whisky bottle, holding it between his neck and shoulder. Melissa rose to her feet and looked down. Lanigan glanced up, and wiped away the snot and tears from his face.

With the manner of a brigadier consoling a shellshocked squaddie, Charles returned to Lanigan, "You are ok now, aren't you?"

Lanigan slowly nodded.

Charles called to Philip, "No need for the police. Our friend is fine."

Charles and Berti, each with an arm under Lanigan's elbow got him to his feet. "There we go. Everything is fine, just fine."

Melissa and Julia watched from the doorway as the men led Lanigan out onto the road. After a few steps Charles turned back. Berti walked on a few steps more and with a guiding hand sent Lanigan on his way.

Drama over, everyone returned to the drawing room. Paddy and Roberto arrived from the garden and were sorry to have missed the commotion. Charles played the hero and strategist as he lit a fire. Roberto set out the scrabble table, sitting himself alongside Paddy. It was to be girls against the boys.

....

Lanigan took a slug, the warming liquid hit the back of his throat and entered his stomach, it felt comforting. It was quiet now, he felt calm, he could hear the river and the towpath share a familiar song of sorrow. On the far side the lights were warm, warm and protective. She called out his name. He took a swig, then another one. The water was now up to his knees, not cold, not cold at all, it felt good. Another slug and he'd drained the bottle.

One for the Road

Ladies in their Sunday best were in full blather, letting slip a secret or two with a well-aimed wink. Melodious tones of an accordion swooped and bustled to be heard over the clink of glass and the babble of chattering voices. Seated grannies and grandpas scanned the room with the eyes of horse dealers, sharp and searching. Occasionally sending out a grandson or granddaughter to capture their quarry for a chat. Priests wandered in and out, demigods laughing at the jokes and banter whilst exchanging theologian intentions.

"Will you look at him? Jaysus he's grown?" said a red-faced navvy, of a tall gangly youth.

"Oh yes, he's top of the class" said the proud mother, her arm squeezing the boy's shoulder. "He wants to be a butcher. Don't you Eugene?" Eugene smiled disinterestedly.

Danny O'Connor was forty-eight, grey hair, grey beard, dark eyebrows like lintels, with a haunted look in his eye. Years of the road had hacked and battered the once pleasant face, only scaffold of bone and wrinkles was left. He was hunched and wearing a brown suit held together by dust and beer. Around his neck a bright yellow tie, sharp and bright against a frayed white shirt. A generous complement of shamrock hung from his lapel.

Twenty-eight years ago, Danny O'Connor cursed the day he'd stepped foot into The Fleece, vowing never to return. But time changes a man, softens his resolve; the past had gone. Today was a good day, a day for drinking, a chance to catch up with old friends. Although they hadn't recognized him it was nice seeing Sarah and Joe behind the bar pulling pints, though shrivelled with age they both looked well.

Across from Danny sat Michael, expressionless with black piercing eyes. The pair of them had linked up on a job in Scotland and now were the best of pals. Each had a small beer and a shot of Johnnie Walker in front of them, an overflowing ashtray held the middle ground. Michael slugged his whisky followed by the remains of his beer. He rose without a word, with nicotine-stained fingers he raised his cigarette to his lips, pulling out the last few puffs, then stubbed it into the ashtray. A trail of smoke clung to him as he wandered to the bar.

In the far corner of the room was a small stage, probably six feet by ten. On it was a fine dark-haired girl of fifteen or sixteen, her fragile voice struggling to be heard above the din. She was singing Carrickfergus, a melancholic Irish ballad. Danny strained his head to one side, listening to the wisps of sound of a tale of the doomed and the damned. He cupped an ear and began to sing along. As he stumbled through the lyrics, his mind drifted back to thoughts of Mary.

"You'll be as big as Sinatra himself, singing to hundreds," she had said in her innocence.

Shouts and screams and the sound of breaking glass bought him back to the present. In the middle of the room, two young lumps wrestled, like hippo's waltzing. Back and forth they tumbled across the bar. Tables, chairs, drinks and the odd person flew into the air as they grappled and tugged at each other.

"Boys, boys, boys," shouted Big Frank as he caught hold of the two. Although well into his sixties he had the strength of a bull and reputation to match. He had no problem separating the big galoots. He had one in a headlock, the other by the scuff of the collar. He released the two scrappers, fixing each one with an icy glare. The bums rush would have been the usual procedure, but Frank had a romantic heart. "You'll both shake hands; I won't have you's fighting, there are women and children here. You'll both shake hands," he repeated with malevolent intent. The two shook hands and with a slap on the back from Frank, returned to their corners, with brothers and cousins whispering seeds of vengeance for round two.

Michael returned from the bar, his hands full of drinks and a couple of bags of crisps tucked into his jacket pockets. He shoved over a beer and whisky, the crisps he'd leave for a late-night supper.

"Did you hear the girl sing?" Danny shouted.

Michael didn't respond but looked off in the direction of the now-empty stage.

"Did you hear the girl singing?" Danny repeated.

"Which girl?" Michael replied scanning the room.

"Did you not see the girl singing when you was at the bar?" said Danny, "Carrickfergus, she sang Carrickfergus."

"No," said Michael gulping beer, "No I did not."

Danny mumbled a curse under his breath and picked up the whisky, swirling the oily amber liquid. He looked around looking for her, there was something familiar about the girl. He raised the whisky to his lips, downed it in one, staring into the distance, transfixed by his thoughts.

....

Well, the story went something like this. The McGuffey's were a much-respected family back home in County Clare, they ran the only shop in the village. They were successful in business, generous in spirit and always pious in church. Mary was the eldest of seven, dark-hair, with a strong widow's peak, eyes that glinted like coal and skin as pale as milk. Not only beautiful, she was tough and strong-willed, forever in trouble at school. They said she took after her grandfather, a wild-hearted gypsy. Her school teacher Father O'Rourke, a mild and meek mannered man had tried his best but could never control her.

His soft pious voice, "Sit down Mary, please! Mary would you please sit down." When all else failed, his temper frayed to breaking. "Off you go to Sister Veronica! I've had enough of you Mary McGuffey."

Sister Veronica's rule was ruthless, but she didn't make headway either. After receiving the cane, Mary would laugh in the sister's face. Everyone knew she was destined for hell, but Mary didn't care a jot.

Danny worked as the McGuffey's delivery boy and Mary loved to tease him. In front of her mother one day, she asked if he wanted to practice kissing. Both Mary and her mother laughed as Danny turned scarlet and even more so when Mary pecked his cheek and ran out the door. When not working they'd wander up to the lough with Mary's dog Winky. Winky would splash about and if he was lucky, he'd catch an eel or two.

"The trouble with you Danny O'Connor," she'd remind him, "Is that you're too agreeable, you're too nice." Which was in part true, Danny was easy going, happy to follow. But unlike Mary's hotheadedness,

Danny's temper was cold and brooding, an anger he buried deep.

Even at the age of twelve, Danny dreamt of the day he'd marry Mary, and on his fourteenth birthday he asked her. She took the promise and his heart, saying they surely would, but let it be known that Cornelius O'Keefe had asked her too. The romance continued until one day in April Mary broke the news her family were moving to England. Two weeks later they left. Both their tender hearts were broken.

Mary wrote weekly with all the news and stories of England. Writing was not for Danny, so she didn't get or expect a reply.

Danny lived with his parents in a little cottage on the top of a very steep hill. On Friday's the mail was delivered by Barney the postman on his bicycle, always red-faced, puffing and blowing and out of breath, "Won't that girl leave you alone." He'd curse as he handed over Mary's letter, "You'll be the death of me."

Danny would take it outside to the toilet which doubled as a chicken coop. Once settled, he'd read as the hens looked on. A few showed mild curiosity but no real interest, they were too busy clucking about the new cockerel with fancy feathers who'd shown up a week ago. Mary wrote that her parents had bought The Fleece, a boozer with cheap bed and breakfast for navvies. Her dad's black Zephyr was a car so big the whole family could get in. There was a park near where they lived with a big pond where swans and ducks swam to their hearts content, but tramps lived there too and they'd cut your throat for the price of a pint. St Thomas's Church was at the end of the road, she was supposed to go every week but would head into the shops with her new friend Elsie instead. To get to school she caught the number 7 bus, the lessons were easy and the nuns were far kinder than the ones at home.

The following summer the McGuffey's returned to Ireland for a holiday. Once again Danny and Mary would head up to the lough and practice their kissing, until both became experts. Danny had been saving up his money, and whilst Mary was home, he was planning to buy her ring. Excited they caught the bus to Galway but it didn't work out so well. Whilst in the jeweller's, Danny spotted Mary outside chatting to the handsome fella selling ice-creams.

"You're an eejit, he only asked me where I'm from, and that's all!" she shouted, eyes blazing. With no ring bought; they fought all the way home.

Danny didn't speak to her for the rest of the holiday. On the day they were heading back to England, Mary called for him, but he wouldn't come to the door. She didn't see him wave goodbye; his burning heart dampened by secret tears. He moped about for days; all could see he was distracted. When his mother teased him, Danny would say he didn't give a flying shite about Mary McGuffey or any other girl for that matter.

A week later his father called out "Barney's halfway up!"

Danny rushed out as the red-faced postman peddled for all his might up the hill. "She won't leave you alone at all," he said, handing over the letter. "Good day to you," and back down the hill he went.

Years passed and with no work in Ireland, Danny too made his way to England. The crossing from Dublin was rough, he was sick the whole journey. An hour after landing Mary's dad Joe picked him up in the Zephyr, "A house on wheels," Joe joked. Danny had arrived with the promise of a job, and the hand of Mary McGuffey.

The Fleece was a big airy pub with high ceilings, it's beautiful stained-glass window faced out onto the road. Inside, the walls were decorated with faded photographs of farmers, spectre's locked in time. Irish music could be heard from streets away, Joe and Sarah knew the power of advertising.

Mary showed Danny to his room upstairs which he shared with four other men. She brought him a plateful of potatoes and bacon later, and in the evening Joe took him downstairs for a pint.

"No need son," said Joe, as Danny rummaged through his pockets. "I'll put you on the tab." Joe knew his people, and was smart enough to offer a thirsty navvy a pint and a plate of grub whenever they wanted. "We'll settle up on Friday," he'd say to any newcomer.

The following day Danny joined a gang of navvies and was put to work on the shovel, back breaking work but he soon got used it. Any spare time he spent his time with Mary.

Three months on and Danny formally asked Joe for Mary's hand. Joe agreed, saying that both himself and Sally would be delighted to have Danny in the family. The wedding was planned for the following spring. To celebrate Mary and Danny had a day out in London. They had hoped to see the Queen but were happy enough with the changing of the guard. Saint Paul's Cathedral was breathtaking. And in the evening they went to Leicester Square to see Old Man of the Sea, with Spencer Tracy, Mary cried, Danny hugged and kissed her weepy grin. They nearly missed the last train but were back in Coventry for midnight. It was a romantic walk back home, with a kiss and a grope before bedtime. The following weekend they caught a bus to Birmingham on the Saturday to see the Bull Ring. On Sunday, it was Stratford upon Avon and a boat on the river. Most of their courting however was a pint and a Babycham at The Fleece.

Danny continued working on the shovel, always an early start and often a late finish. Mary helped out at the pub, cooking, cleaning and serving pints.

As the weeks and months passed, the day trips became less frequent and any free time Danny and Mary had together was spent in the bar at The Fleece. One night after a blazing row, Mary told Danny she wanted more from life. Her dreams were bigger than a pint and a Babycham. With tears in her eyes, she called off the wedding.

Danny didn't get a wink of sleep that night, he was up early and went looking for Mary. Her dad said she was already up and out. Danny searched the streets for her but she was nowhere to be seen. The fact of the matter was that Mary was in her room, she had explained to her dad the situation and he agreed to tell a lie on her behalf. The work van pulled up; Danny knew he had to go. Mary wept as she watched the van disappear down the road. Danny wasn't good company throughout the day, he needed to speak to Mary. When they finally got back, Joe pulled him to one side, saying he was sorry but Mary had made her up mind.

Danny didn't go to work the next day or the day after that. It was on the Wednesday morning that he packed his bags vowing never to see Mary, The Fleece or Coventry ever again. He'd work in London, Birmingham, Liverpool, Glasgow, anywhere the wagon would take him and take whatever the shift would pay. On it went, work and drink, then drink and work until he remembered her no more. Years passed and so too the occasional girlfriend, but at times of stillness, she would come to him in his dreams.

Danny heard about the wedding. She'd married Paddy O'Rourke, a foreman in one of the factories; a teetotaler and a regular man at the church too. He didn't seem her sort but was a good catch. By all accounts it was a great bash, Joe and Sarah spared no expense, the food and drink were on the house, and as if he needed reminding, Mary looked beautiful.

....

"What time's the band on?" shouted Michael munching on a bag of crisps; hunger had got the better of him.

"What hurry are you in?" said Danny scowling across at his friend. "We're here for the night," then called across, "Not till seven."

Michael stuck a gnarly fist forward, holding the crisps towards Danny. Danny took a handful and began munching. He smiled and nodded to his friend "Them's good crisps, pickled onions!" and slugged down a gulp of beer. He was about to take another sup when a man slumped down beside him, splashing beer over Danny's suit. "Take it easy, fella," said Danny brushing the excess beer onto the floor.

Michael leant forward, eyeing the drunk, alert, assessing the threat.

"Do you not know me?" said the drunk, "Do you not know me, Danny?" His eyelids hung heavy and dribble glistened from his chin.

"No, I do not. We're here just to have a quiet drink," responded Danny. He turned away feigning casual indifference but kept one eye on the drunk.

The man eased closer, his weight now on Danny's shoulder. Once again, he slurred, "Do you not know me, Danny?" With a mouthful of decaying teeth, he grinned, then straightening himself, "Well, it's been a while alright." He raised a near-empty glass of whiskey and knocked it back, his top lip searching the rim of the glass, straining for the last of the liquid. Then as if starring in a comedy fil'm he saluted and cackled out "It's me, Paddy O'Rourke. Do you not know me now Danny?" he slammed down the empty glass on the table. "Will you stand me a drink?"

The veil lifted; it was indeed Paddy O'Rourke, Mary's husband. Danny chuckled to himself, thinking, *Well Jaysus, didn't she pick the wrong horse.* Danny glanced around the room, just a glimpse would be enough. His eyes returned to Paddy. In his time, Danny had seen many a man hit the bottle, and then there were others, others where it was the other way around. Paddy was in this camp. The bottle had hit poor old Paddy alright. It had hit him firmly in the kisser. It wasn't Danny's usual practice but he reached into his pocket and pulled out a handful of notes. Paddy's eyes followed in a hypnotic gaze as Danny peeled one-off. "There you go Paddy, take care of yourself now."

Paddy reached forward, clutching at the money, he drew the note to his chest and raised a hand in salute. "Thank You, God bless you General, God bless you," and kissed the note. He rose unsteadily, and looked towards the bar, his body swaying back and forth, his legs waiting for the instruction from his brain that had lost its way.

Something jumped in Danny's chest, he couldn't let him go, "Is Mary here Paddy?"

Paddy attempted to turn but staggered falling onto Michael, who held out a hand to keep him upright. He settled his hands on their table for support. "Mary, Mary!" Paddy repeated, his mind a maze of love, of loss and pain. "Mary!... Jaysus Danny! Mary's been dead for twenty years."

The Funeral

Rose made her way down to the kitchen; she hadn't slept well. Her feet were cold, particularly her ankles, she should have put socks on. As she filled the kettle, her mind was racing through impenetrable fog, her thoughts couldn't stop. Raising her hand to her chest she tried to reassure herself of something. From the cupboard, she chose her favourite mug, blue and pink flowers. She waited, then leant forward resting her hands on the work-top. The fog just would not stop. She hadn't expected it to be so bad. Moans crept up from her belly heaving through her chest, *he was gone, he was gone.* She wiped away the tears with the back of her hand, straightened and blew out a couple of blasts of air. The kettle's whistle brought her back to the present. Another long breath as she poured the water over the teabag.

At noon the doorbell rang.

"Hello mummy, how are you? Rupert's face looked angelic, yet solemn and consoling. A flamboyant dresser, he wore a cobalt blue three-piece velvet suit, a baby pink shirt with a collar so large his black neck-tie had given up. To complete the look, a cream and black silk polka dot handkerchief spilt out of his breast pocket, every inch the dashing dandy.

"You look beautiful darling," said his mother, as she embraced him tightly. "Stand back, let me see you."

Rupert performed a little twirl. He adored his mother and it pained him to see her so upset. As they hugged, he caught sight of himself in the large antique mirror that hung in the hall and teased down a few strands of his hair.

Rupert stood back from his mother and flicked off a few specks of fluff from his velvet jacket. "Everything bloody sticks to it," he said, raising his eyes in despair.

His mother laughed and wiped away a tear of joy, "Darling you look wonderful, absolutely wonderful." She knew he'd cheer her up.

"I know I do mummy," and with a wink, "If only I had a twin."

Rupert shared his mother's extraordinary good looks and emotional character, from ecstasy to despair. She'd doted on him and had even given him her name, Rupert Rose Irvin. They were devoted to one another.

"What time are we burying the old goat? I've got to be back in London later this evening," said Rupert, as he followed his mother through to the kitchen.

"But I've prepared a buffet," she replied.

Rupert knew that catering was not one of his mother's strengths and raised an eyebrow.

"Oh Rupert," she looked annoyed. "I really have made a special effort." Rose was dressed in a black dress belted at the waist, her waif-like figure had developed from her younger days, but at fifty-eight, she was still a very attractive woman. Unlike her friends, she had accepted her grey hair with genial aplomb, and now it had become very fashionable. Having cheered from this morning's episode, she made a promise to herself to stay strong.

"Where's he going?" asked Rupert.

"Well, he loved the orchard, so I've asked Ramsay to prepare a resting place there." At this a gulp of heartache sprang unexpectedly up hitting the back of her throat, she somehow managed to swallow it.

Rupert seeing his mother's distress, placed a comforting arm around her shoulder and warmly kissed the top of her head. "It will be alright mummy." He kissed her once more. "It will be alright."

A few tears and sniffs later Rose had recovered her composure. "Melly's asked the vicar to be here for three."

But Rupert had his mind on other things, "I know what would help," he jumped up from the table and disappeared into the pantry, reappearing seconds later with a beaming smile and a bottle of sherry.

"Why not?" said Rose with the glee of a schoolgirl.

"Yes, why not?" said Rupert, feigning enthusiasm. He had expected to find a bottle of Glenfiddich, mother's favourite tipple and only fished out the sherry as a poor substitute. The bereavement had affected her more than he'd anticipated. He took a couple of tumblers from an old dusty oak dresser, polished them with a tea towel, and poured two generous glasses. Rupert walked to the window, Ramsay's head was bobbing up and down as he dug the grave in the orchard. "Bloody hell, he's cutting it fine," Rupert glanced back at his mother.

Rose sipped her sherry "I know, I asked him to get it done last week but he was busy fixing his van, apparently the google pins... ends have gone, or something."

Rupert looked confused, laughed and shrugged his shoulders.

The doorbell rang.

"Ah, that will be Melly," Rose said as she went to answer.

Rupert wandered around the kitchen, on the fridge were stuck a few photos, he went over for a closer look. There he was in life, quite a physical specimen, a rugged face, bearded with dark wild eyes. Most were of him and mummy, but some included Rupert and Melly too. All were taken in the garden, which he'd loved. Rupert knew that mummy had been the centre of his world and although very different characters, he had depended on her for everything. It was hard to think he wasn't around anymore. *Funerals? The one time people have nice things to say about you, and you only miss it by just a few hours,* Rupert chuckled to himself.

Melly came bustling in, "Oh Ruppie, you look devastating. Like a tart on acid." Her lips were already pursed as she descended, "Where did you get that suit?" her eyes wide with approval. She rushed over and bear-hugged her brother with such force he almost spilt his sherry. Not waiting for an answer, Melly asked her mother, "Is there anyone else coming?"

Rose waited, she gazed blankly at Rupert and Melly, her thoughts in a distant, forgotten memory, "Sorry, what did you say?"

Melly repeated her question. She had a somewhat fuller figure than her mother, and although naturally a brunette her hair was blonde. She was a no-nonsense type, robust and direct, traits she took from her father, an ex-military man. At thirty-nine she was ten years older than Rupert. She'd married when she was only nineteen and three children and a house in the country later, she was blissfully happy with her lot.

"Oh, only the close family, and the vicar of course. Bugger the rest of them, they never liked him anyway."

"Well, he was headstrong and very hard-headed mummy," said Melly.

"Come on now let's all sit down and we'll have another glass of sherry. And yes; yes, I've erm...made some sandwiches, a buffet, I've spent an awfully long time on it," said Rose.

They sat at the table together. Melly munched heartily whilst Rupert, like a spoilt cat, picked his way through.

"Did you have any problems with the council mummy? You know, planning permission and all that," said Rupert, as he pulled out a slice of cucumber from a cucumber sandwich. "I mean it's a bit strange. He glanced at his sister, who was slicing off a piece of Dundee cake.

"As long as you've let them know, and he's 10 metres from standing water and fifty metres from drinking water, you're fine," Melly responded, passing the cake to Rupert.

Rupert recoiled, shaking his head "No thank you."

Victoria sponge maybe, but anything with fruit or currents ugh! Rupert's taste in food, unlike his taste in partners, was very catholic. "So could we be buried in the garden?"

"Oh, you are such a fusspot," said Melly as she took a bite herself. "I don't see why not".

Rose laughed and raised a hand to her mouth before answering, "Yes, but I'm leaving my remains to science. That's of course if they want me," she chuckled softly. Rose looked to her daughter who was sitting opposite her at the table, so strong and dependable. It was Melly who had taken care of all the arrangements, nothing was too much trouble. Then to Rupert, she shook her head smiling. She wouldn't deny she was a little disappointed when he'd announced he was gay, he was only fifteen. Well, they had never had a homo in the family before, not that she knew of anyway. But to be honest he was such a flamboyant child she should have guessed. It was Melly who had pointed it out saying, "It's not rocket science mummy, he's as camp as a Christmas tree fairy." *Now come to think of it, maybe uncle Percy?* But she was both happy and proud of her children and although she'd never say it, it was Rupert she loved most.

Melly glanced up at the grandfather clock which stood in the corner of the kitchen. It was almost two-thirty. "Shall we tidy up before the vicar arrives?"

At ten to three the doorbell rang; Melly strode

from the kitchen to greet him. The vicar was bald, soft-featured, stockily built with quite a noticeable stoop. His face naturally had a glum expression which was perfect for such an occasion as this.

Neither Rose nor her family were much for church. She chose her words carefully, one hand raised to her lips, hesitantly she asked nervously, "Would you like… something to drink?"

"No thank you, I've just had a cup of tea at the W.I." said the vicar. "Thank you kindly, but could I use your facilities?" The sides of his mouth together with his eyebrows raised as he finished his sentence.

Rose looked puzzled for a second, then responded, words bolting out, "Oh yes, sorry. It's straight down the hall. First on the left."

Rupert watched the vicar as he made his way to the loo. Once he was out of sight, he rose from his seat and mockingly performed an impression which resembled Quasimodo. Melly burst out a raucous laugh, but his mother's face was severe and rebuking. The sound of a flushed toilet was heard, and seconds later the vicar reappeared. All four stood silently for a few moments. The vicar looked down at his feet, with the solemnity of a bloodhound he said, "Shall we proceed with the service?"

Rose looked at her watch, it was five past three. She looked to her children for reassurance. Rupert touched her elbow whilst Melly supported her on the other side. They followed the vicar outside. Between two fruit trees was a large dark hole, and to the edge lay the body simply covered by a piece of tarpaulin, another sheet was hanging over the edge of the grave. The vicar began a short and simple service. Rose wiped away a tear, she was determined to stay strong. Once finished the vicar looked towards the family and nodded. Each of them stepped forward and picked up a piece of the tarpaulin. The idea was to gently lift the sheet so the corpse would roll forwards into its final resting place. But he was a lot heavier than anyone expected and although the three of them pulled with all their might they failed to shift the dead weight. The vicar, seeing their dilemma, lent a hand and slowly the corpse began to move forward. My god, thought Rose, this was ridiculous. Her whole back was straining, Rupert looked most uncomfortable, his face twisted into a face of a gargoyle, even though it was Melly and the vicar doing most of the heavy work. Suddenly the body tumbled forwards and then stopped, wedged against the earth.

A screech of tyres skidded onto the gravel drive and a middle-aged man jumped out of his mark 2 Jaguar. The resemblance between him and Melly was uncanny. He swaggered over in a grey flannel suit, "Am I too late?" he called.

"No Daddy" responded Melly, looking down at the grey woolly corpse, "But could you bring an axe from the house, his horns are far too big. That bugger Ramsay's made the hole far too small for a goat."

The Brute

The sun had just risen from its slumber, the sky was clear blue, it looked like it was going to be a beautiful day.

Staring into the mid-distance, Gustave stretched and yawned, He was huge, a real brute, with a large head and muscular shoulders, his barrel-chest reflected his power. He slowly blinked, twisted his neck to one side and then the other.

Nabbib his trainer wandered in, "Come on!"

Gustave looked up, he didn't answer, with a rolling gate he followed. He worked out daily, once in the morning and another at night. They gave him calm and helped subdue the demon, but never got rid of it. He was a fighter and had come from a long line of fighters. You could say he was primed for violence, blood lust on a hair trigger. At first, he liked it, the feeling of power was intoxicating. But now it was just there. It could start with just a look or a word of provocation, something would click, and in a haze of savagery his victim was left a bloodied helpless pulp.

The workout began with a long run, followed by basic strength training. They would then move to new techniques and finally wrestling moves to bring him down. It would take anywhere from one to two hours. Now and again Nabbib would turn up with a sparring partner, they were all keen and ready to have a go, but it never lasted long or well for the sparring partner. Once workout was complete, he ate some breakfast, which was exclusively high protein, mostly meat, he enjoyed making a glutton of himself. After that he went back to sleep for an hour or so. His dreams reflected his life, a world where lusts were sated.

With a yawn, he awoke and wandered down into the garden, finding himself a spot on the lawn. It was mid-summer; the sun was high and the heat on his body felt good. A rustling sound was coming from a tree overhead. He looked up, his huge head turned to one side to listen and then the other. Two birds were flitting back and forth between the branches, maybe discussing their plans for the day. After watching for a moment, Gustave lost interest, settled down and closed his eyes. *Yes, that heat felt good.* Apart from the chatter of birds the world was silent. His mind wandered to his youth.

He hadn't really known his parents. His sole recollection was watching them going at each other hammer and tongs. Once they'd frightened him so much, he'd soiled himself. Looking back, he recognised it wasn't their fault, they were living in chaos. The house was a constant mess, wrecked furniture, the smell of piss and shit everywhere. It couldn't go on and it didn't. The powers that be moved him and his sister Jesse on to a new family, which was great for the first few weeks, everyone on their best behaviour. But the honeymoon period didn't last. Fear returned into their daily diet, violence once again a constant companion. They didn't stand a chance. His only memory of kindness was of an old lady who lived next door who when they were hungry would feed them and occasionally take them out for walks. The abuse was plain for all to see and eighteen months on, the powers that be intervened again. He still remembered the day they came, a small nimble man and a burly woman, both in dark blue uniforms, they seemed so warm and friendly. The following day they separated him from his sister, with each going off to a different family. He was never to see Jesse again. From then on, he realised that kindness is easily fabricated.

His new family were not a lot different, frightened people who thought pleasure and security was gained in frightening others. As he got older, his strength grew and he became the one to dish out fear. He'd acquired quite a knack for it. Whether a smile or a snarl, every threat was faced down, and crushed into submission. Sure, he'd be your friend. *Yeah, we can have fun but fuck with me, I'll fuck with you*, was his philosophy.

Men and women would flock to see him fight. With demented faces they would whoop and holler as blood and guts were spilt for their deviant pleasures. And as with the perversity of nature, these people would bask in Gustave's aura of violence, he'd become a magnet to those pathetic figures who feared him.

Only once had he let his guard down. Heidi was beautiful with dark eyes that melted his icy heart. She was fun, and as if by instinct knew how to handle him. A time of joy; a joy to breathe, a joy to love. They hung together for a few months, it could have been a year, but maybe that was wishful thinking. But things change, she got pregnant, they fought, she disappeared, and once again his heart hardened. From that day he made a decision, he was on his own and would always be.

A noise broke into his meanderings, he looked up. It was the birds, squabbling in the branches. He studied them, watching their interactions, wondering how it would end. A few more squawks and one to flew off. Such beautiful creatures, he thought, able to fly, to soar, to raise themselves from this miserable existence.

He was about to settle back down when a flash of red caught his eye, it was a robin that had hopped down onto the lawn. Not wanting to frighten it Gustave stayed perfectly still. Shy at first, it kept its distance. Unblinking he gazed at the little creature as it hopped back and forth in front of him. It was now within a couple of feet and as he watched the bird, he realised it was watching him. Something drifted between them, a thought maybe, a belief, something, it was neither his nor the birds. Perhaps it was a pact, a trust, a hope.

In a flash he pounced, crunching the bird between his deadly jaws. Pleased, Gustave wagged his tail.

After all, he was a brute.

Galina the Mayfly

At the edge of Moorhen village is a lake, woods surround three sides and open hills and mountains are in the distance. It is beautiful, still and quiet, a great place to picnic or just to lie back and relax. All types of animals visit, deer, foxes, even a bear or two have been spotted. But our story involves something much smaller than a bear, much, much smaller.

Did you know that mayflies are sometimes called dayflies and that they live only for one day? Well, if you did, only part of that statement is true. Actually, they live for days, weeks, months and in some cases, years. Not as fully-grown mayflies but as nymphs, juvenile mayflies. Galina was a mayfly nymph. Her home was near the edge of the bank inside the spokes of an old discarded cart wheel. She wasn't the only nymph in the lake, there were thousands, maybe millions, trillions even.

1963 was the year of the big freeze, for months, the temperature had struggled to get above minus. Animals, even humans froze to death and the nymphs would have too but for a thick sheet of ice and snow insulating Galina and her friends from the worst of the weather. Trouble was, without rays of sunshine, the food they ate, weeds, algae and any vegetation really, didn't grow. Every day and every hour was a constant search for sustenance, many a creature turned to the filthy detritus which covered the bottom of the lake, hardly nourishing but at least it was something. But as winter stepped on into spring, shafts of light began to penetrate through the thick surface of the ice and a large hole opened up near the centre of the lake. At last, it was a time to celebrate, life was able to flourish once more.

By the way, as a point of interest, not all mayfly nymphs or larva are the same, some are crawlers, these as you can imagine crawl around over rocks and vegetation. Clingers, cling to weeds, anything really and are found in streams and fast running water. Then there's the burrowers, which as their name suggests make their home in the soft muddy bottom. The most elegant amongst them all are swimmers. Galina was a swimmer and as nimble in the water as most fish. Like most bugs, her head was round with a set of dark beady eyes, six legs, a beautiful long thorax, and the finest tail you are ever likely to see. She started life as an egg but who remembers being an egg? All she knew was her life as a nymph, bright and full of adventure. Like her friends, Galina didn't count days, or hours or seconds for that matter, but nevertheless, summers passed, winters passed and life went on. In Moorhen Lake there were nymphs of all sizes, some had only recently hatched, so small you would struggle to see them with the naked eye. Whilst others, well, they were as large as a segment of your thumb.

As the spring developed so did the supply of weeds and algae. Food was abundant and without boring parents to watch over them there was fun to be had. Of course, as a nymph you had to be aware of predators; trout, crayfish, dragonflies, leeches, to name but a few, all were partial to a fresh tasty nymph. Oh yes, you had to keep your wits about you, but as long as you were careful to keep out of their way you were okay. The favourite game of most nymphs was hide and seek, to tell you the truth it was more than a game, it was a way of life and Galina was good at it. She particularly enjoyed teasing the sleepy old trout who lived under the shade of an apple tree. She'd always wait until he was napping and just about to fall asleep, then creep up and nip his tail. The chase was on. Like lightening she would wriggle and slip through the tangled mass of reeds and pond life. The trout would follow raising mud by the barrowful, but he was slow and his eyesight wasn't too good either. With Galina out of sight, he'd give up and return to his slumber in the hope for peace and quiet, only to get nipped again. That was Galina alright, always into mischief, and that would have been fine if she had stuck to the old trout. The trouble was as she got older Galina wanted more of a challenge, and her mistake was chancing a pike. Now pike can move a lot faster than trout or mayfly nymphs for that matter. It took a nip or two to get the pike going but once started it went at breakneck speed. Swiftly twisting and turning Galina dashed this way and that, slipping between rocks and plants which would have left the trout for mud, but the pike matched her every manoeuvre. At one stage the snap of its jaws tidied up a loose piece of weed stuck to her tail. The chase went on for minutes, her little legs couldn't propel her any faster. Exhausted and with heart about to burst, she thought this was it, when suddenly a great sound of thrashing came from behind. She glanced back to witness the pike being swallowed by an even larger pike. From that day on she made a promise to avoid pikes at all cost.

If you are not a nymph yourself or into nature, you might not be aware there's something called, The Emergence, a Nymph's Ball. It begins on the stroke of midnight on the third Sunday of May and goes on for one week, sometimes longer. It is the celebration of birth, as the hatchlings rise from the bottom to join their elders. It is also the time when the oldest nymphs pass on to the next life. The build-up is something to see, all the larger nymphs gather to build an underwater castle, which is made up from the most nourishing weeds and plants they can find. This year Galina had helped to build one of the turrets, of which this time there were seven. Once finished the castle was huge, at least ten metres across and two or three metres high. It had a drawbridge that worked, a keep, battlements and an inner bailey that could hold millions. The idea of creating such a huge structure of the finest pond weed was that after the ball the baby nymphs could feast on it to their hearts content, ensuring a good start in life.

But like I said, the hatchlings were only one aspect of the ball, the other being The Great Emergence, and although tales aplenty, no one really knew what happened in the next life. Some said there was a lake beyond Moorhen Lake, where the weeds were as sweet as the apples and berries that dropped in autumn. Others thought it a place free of trout, eels, pike and leeches, where only friendly creatures lived, somewhere where they could dance, sing and play all day.

Galina, she had lost count of the many times she had shed her skin. For a nymph it was a way of life, like some mute calling and with each shedding they would emerge stronger. But yet, The Great Emergence was still a mystery.

On the day before the Nymph's Ball, nymphs collected forming processions and each procession was heading in the direction of the castle. Some were carrying banners and flags, for others it was their own colours which distinguished them.

From the outer edge where Galina lived, it would take a day to arrive. She was up early and took her place in line and was paired alongside a rather well-fed crawler named Henry. Henry didn't talk a lot and to the consternation of those behind was one hell of a slow walker. Unfortunately, nymph law dictates that during the march to the castle you cannot overtake and whomever you joined the procession with, you must also arrive with. Galena tried everything, pulling, pushing, cajoling but it made no difference, Henry simply plodded on at his own slow pace. He even cheekily suggested that she should carry him, which Galina wouldn't have minded, but in those days, for a female nymph to carry a male would have been considered outrageous behaviour. Fortunately, despite Henry's slow pace, they arrived before any of the real festivities had begun. Inside the castle was a crawling mass of nymphs dashing this way and that, feeding, chatting, playing. The young had already eaten a good proportion of the drawbridge and had to be spoken to severely by the water beetle guards. Galina spotted a few friends. Kitty, the most beautiful of all the nymphs, was surrounded by a group of admirers, all dressed in the latest fashions of the day. On the edge of the group was Engelbart, a shy, quirky, nervous nymph who was constantly made fun of, only because he tried to make friends with a fisherman's fly. But Galina liked him, so she wandered over. Engelbart smiled cautiously, eager for recognition but fearful of it too. She was just about to speak, when a trumpet sounded, everyone went silent and looked towards the castle keep. A moment later out strode two huge water beetles with glistening black shells. Between them appeared a nymph of tremendous height, twice as tall as your average. It was the King Carlos, king of all Moorhen Lake nymphs. Galina felt a flutter go through her abdomen.

Despite his noble status the King looked nervous, "My subjects. I am here today to greet you all and to join in celebrating new beginnings." A round of applause and a cheer went up. He went on, his manner was restrained, solemn. "Along with you, I will share this day and for whatever it holds."

Another cheer and a round of applause. He'd kept it short and sweet, which I think the audience approved of. Now the real festivities could begin. In the centre of the inner bailey sat a large rock which served as a stage. First to perform was an orchestra made up of frogs and newts, with a crab as the conductor. The first dance was a waltz, similar to a traditional human version but instead of steps 123, 123, 123, it went 246, 246, 246. Galina took Engelbart by the claw and led him onto the dancefloor. The ever-beautiful Kitty, taking the lead, was somehow managing to dance with six nymphs. It worked like this; each male held on to the other's tails as they courteously formed a queue. After a minute or two, Kitty would let go of the first, he'd peel off and go to the rear and Kitty would continue with a new partner.

As the evening went on the entertainment became a little wilder and less formal. The Crawfish Catapults, a renowned fiddle and banjo quartet played recent hits from The Pondlife Hit Parade, and a few golden oldies too. Dance after dance it went on, song after song. Later a delicious salad of Duckweed, Sago and water Hyacinth was served on shells of mother of pearl, with crystal clear water in tiny shells to drink.

The fun was interrupted by a shrill of a trumpet as the King appeared once more. Maybe it was the intensity of the occasion but a change had come over him, he looked different. Without saying a word he held out his arms, he bowed his head, then slowly began to ascend up through the water. With a tiny splash he broke the surface, a moment later their King was gone. Among the crowd there was mass of movement, as hundreds, then thousands of nymphs writhed in ecstasy and agony. Fearful, some thrashed to return to the lake bed, but however hard they tried, their ascent was predestined and they too ascended towards the surface

With every passing hour the number of those rising got bigger. One by one they heard the calling, first to leave was Kitty, then Samuel and Penelope. Engelbart looked terrified as he too rose in spasm. Frightened, Galina clung to her heavyweight friend Henry, who was firmly fixed to the bottom. She wasn't ready, not just now, maybe next time? But that all changed with a tingling, an urge, no it was stronger than an urge, it was an impulse, an impulse to leave her sanctuary, her refuge, the only home she had ever known. She felt pain, her body twisted, her back arching skywards as she too travelled towards the light. The sun was dropping in the sky, illuminating and shimmering upon the surface of the lake. It took all of Galena's strength to break through the meniscus and once she did it was frightening. The early risers had been decimated, it was carnage, the water awash with movement and death. She had never experienced anything like it as birds, fish, frogs, dragonflies and even spiders, were all present splashing and feasting like gluttons on the tiny prey. Galina tried to breathe but nothing was happening, she tried again, but again nothing, she was suffocating. A fluttering movement caught her eye, she looked to where once were her gills, and could see wings trying to move within. This shock caused her to open her mouth and finally she took a breath. With the rush of oxygen, her head felt light, then panic seized her, fear penetrating every cell. Another breath, then another, and as she did, her new lungs filled and began to calm her, slowly, slowly reassuring. As she twisted and turned her new body began to emerge, first her back and abdomen, and after a struggle her thorax broke free, then her legs, and finally, her head and wings. Galina had known moults before, but this was different, more painful and yet exhilarating. On the surface were thousands, probably millions of struggling Mayflies, all trying to free themselves from the waters deathly grip. Some had managed to fly and were in mid-air, others had drowned and were being picked off by the predators. Galina tried her wings but they were still soft, so after a few flutters she returned to the surface of the water. She looked up, a bird, that looked like a swallow was looming towards her, eyes fixed on its quarry. With all her might Galina flapped and flapped just managing a few skips as the bird soared on by. On her fourth attempt, her wings held and she broke free, lifting her higher and higher. Following the swarm, she found refuge in a tree and rested, but only for a moment as between the branches skipped nimble birds picking off the unwary. Galina could see it was movement that attracted the predators so tucked herself tight against a large bough and sat perfectly still. It was whilst looking up she spotted him high amongst the branches. It was King Carlos, he was surrounded by a multitude of followers, most were injured in some way and others barely clung to life. When the coast was clear Galina flew towards her king, rested, then higher again, until she arrived on his branch. He looked magnificent, his gossamer wings standing like sails of a yacht, his body shimmered pure gold. Galina spotted Engelbart amongst the throng and called to him, he looked up and flew to her. He said he had heard that tomorrow was the day when they would enter the new world. Galina was confused saying she thought this was the new world.

The King spoke, his voice soft and comforting, "Sleep my friends, for tomorrow is our day of calling."

With the sound of his voice a calmness descended like a fog. Galina felt a weariness that she had never known before. She wanted to talk, to ask Engelbart what else he had heard, but neither could keep their eyes open and despite the carnage that surrounded them they both dropped off to sleep.

On waking Galina felt ecstatic, every breath she took was intoxicating, every movement a pulse of energy. Then it happened, pain, agony, it was like she was being ripped in two. Her head twisted this way, then that, her body arched and she let out a scream as the skin on her back gave way. Slowly once again she emerged, it felt even more exhilarating than the day before. Engelbart stared, mouth agape, she looked breath-taking. Her body was a bright green, gold with dashes of brown, delicate lacy wings moving gently with the breeze, her tail was like a bridal gown, long and elegant. This was The Great Emergence and Galina was truly a magnificent mayfly.

"You look beautiful," said Engelbart, "Like a princess."

Galina blushed; she had never received a compliment before.

Mayflies were arriving in their thousands, covering the trees close by. Suddenly the King, along with his followers began to descend, it was like a carpet of silver flowing from the branches to branch. In the pushing and shoving, Galina lost Engelbart and was pulled along with the throng. Once she recovered her senses, she looked up to see an enormous cloud made up of millions of mayflies, hovering and drifting back and forth over the water with King Carlos at its head. It was only a flash but Galina was sure it was Kitty disappearing into the massive swarm. The water surface and above was alive with fluttering wings, every branch, every leaf, every twig. It was madness, the weight was crushing Galina, she tried to move, to free herself, but with energy fading, she was losing consciousness. There was no space to move, no space to hop, no space to fly. In her twilight, he came to her in a dream, a dream that could have been a million years old. It was the pike's snapping jaws, closer and closer and when he was about to clamp down on her, she jumped. She was now falling, tumbling through the throng towards the ground. This was it, the end, instinctively she flapped her wings, once, then twice, a third time and slowly, fretfully she began to flutter upwards. Blood and adrenaline pumped through her tiny body as she soared.

The King was aloft of the mayfly cloud, his golden body shimmering with graceful movement. Suddenly something caught Galina's eye, it was a bird, a hawk, circling, gliding, dipping closer, and with each pass the cloud of mayflies scattered and dispersed in fear, until only King Carlos was left, a single mayfly above his flock. The hawk swooped; eyes fixed and, in a nano, second, it snatched him from the sky.

That was the last Galina saw of her king.

The fluttering swarm began to reform as though a spell of madness had captured them. Unbeknownst to Galina the spell was moving outwards, and soon it would create a slave of her too. Closer, closer, she flew, she was now on the edge, movement and sound was beautiful, magnetic, and slowly the cloud engulfed her. Mayflies were everywhere, up, down, to the left, to the right. A large male caught hold of her, she resisted and pulled free, then another and yet another latched on, but again she broke free. A voice called out to her and through the mass of wings and bodies she could see him, it was Engelbart. He pushed and fought his way, getting bounced and bumped about like a pinball. Finally, he touched her, and they held onto each other.

Engelbart spoke, "This is it, Galina."

At first it was a warmth, a tingling, then a feeling of serenity, it was their silent universe, an embrace of a lifetime. Then it was gone.

Galena was in the water, a breeze dragging her over the surface. She felt exhausted, her eyes closed and opened again. Mayflies were falling like droplets onto the water. Engelbart was a few feet away and was making a hopeless effort to free himself, but the lake held him firm.

This was her stage, her final performance. She felt a contraction, then another and another as thousands of tiny eggs expelled themselves from her tired body. She would never see her children; this was the mayfly's destiny. Galina strained to flap her wings but they were wet and heavy. Her thoughts drifted to her days as a nymph, the old spoked cartwheel of her birth, the lazy trout, the shade of the apple tree, of Henry, Kitty and Engelbart. She wanted to say goodbye and tried to turn but the breeze felt like a hurricane. A mayfly landed alongside, it too struggled, all to no avail. Suddenly Galina felt a lightness as her body released her, Moorhen Lake was taking back what was hers.

She was travelling through a fog; aware but everything was distant. A voice called her name, she turned, it was King Carlos, "Galina," he called again, and leaving behind all she had ever known she followed.

An Evening in Paradise

Mrs Booth was on her way home on the number 7 bus. It was 4.30pm on a blisteringly hot day in June. She was eager to get out of her uniform and have a cool shower. Hers was the next stop, she organised herself, rang the bell and moved down the platform. She'd been on the bus for over twenty hot sticky minutes, just to be standing felt good, and with the front doors open there was a lovely cooling breeze. Her long dark hair danced over her face, she felt young and carefree. A falling strand freed itself, she touched it and watched as it floated backwards. The bus pulled up, she thanked the pockmarked faced driver and got off.

"Anytime love," he responded, with a wink of carnal desire.

A coquettish smile rose to her lips and a flush to her face, as secret thoughts glinted from within. *Fancy that, he could have been half my age.* She waited a moment as the bus pulled away and slipped off her jacket.

Tuesday was shepherd's pie night, she needed to do some shopping. Her heels clicked and hips swung with an accentuated swagger on the way to the Co-Op. In her day Carol Booth had had her pick of men and probably could now, with gym twice a week, she'd looked after herself. All had said Kevin had punched above his weight when she'd agreed to marry him. He was two years senior but looked at least ten, Father Time had not been so kind to Kevin, having gripped him firmly dragged him along at a hell of a rate ever since his teens. They'd been together for thirty years now, married for twenty-nine. There had been a sticky patch as she turned thirty, but apart from that it was a happy marriage.

She placed the pie in the oven and had turned to prepare some veg when she heard his key in the door. "Hello," she shouted from the small galley kitchen.

"Hellooo," Mr Booth called back. "What's for grub a' dub dub?"

"You know what's for dinner," she was short, but not aggressive.

Mr Booth poked his large freckled face around the kitchen door, pulled a gormless expression and disappeared to change. Carol glanced up and shook her head as he thudded and bounced his way across the landing.

Half an hour later they sat across from one another at the kitchen table. He'd changed into white jogging bottoms and a grey T-shirt; she was wearing a pretty pink summer dress. Two dinner plates sat on the table, his piled high, gravy leaking over the edge, with slices of buttered bread on a side plate alongside, hers a child's portion in comparison.

Without looking up Mrs Booth asked, "How was your day?"

"Oh, you'd have laughed," Kevin spoke with a broad Lancashire accent. "Steve from admin bought in one of them Billy Bass fish plaque thingies. You know the ones. You put them on the wall, a fish, they turn and sing. It sang Moon River, bloody hilarious." He looked up, his eyes filled with glee, before going on, "I took it into Jackie and Lynn's office, Jackie screamed," his face was beaming. Between mouthfuls he went on, "You can get them from that shop in town. I'll get you one at the weekend, they're only twenty quid." He turned back to his dinner.

No way was a silly novelty coming into her house, Carol knew exactly how she wanted her décor, her home reflected her elegance, *Billy Bass be damned. What was he thinking?* Before responding she caught herself and smiled saying, "I've seen them, they're advertising them on The Shopping Channel. I don't think we need one."

He recognised her disguised displeasure, nodded, then stuffed half a slice of bread into his ample chops, humming as he ate.

She looked across the table, a faint smile passed her lips, she wanted to tease him, tell him about the leery bus driver. Perhaps she'd feign indignation. With her head to the side, her eyes distant, she started, "Something happened to me…."

Kevin interrupted with an enormous belch. She shook her head and turned away in disgust.

No sooner had he closed his mouth, he went on, "You'll never guess what else happened? Sheila from cheques asked me if I knew anywhere, she could get a big end for her Fiesta." Grinning he beckoned a response, "Guess what I said?"

"What are big ends?" asked his wife.

Shrugging his shoulders, "You don't need to know. Go on guess what I said? Go on?" he implored.

"Halfords," said his wife with a shrug.

"Halfords!" Kevin repeated. He looked confused as he made his way to the fridge, pulling his joggers out from between the crack of his arse as he did so. Grabbing a can of beer, he opened it and took a gulp, letting go another belch from the side of his mouth, as if that made a difference. Glancing to his wife, "Halfords, what's funny about Halfords?"

"Why does it need to be funny? They sell car bits, don't they?"

"For her Fiesta, I made out she wanted it for her fiesta."

Carol looked totally confused; her eyes narrowed, "What the bloody hell are you on about?"

Kevin appeared shocked at his wife's attitude but went on speaking, slowly exaggerating his words, "I made out… she wanted… a big end… for her Fiesta." He moved around the kitchen dancing a pathetic flamenco, with arms in the air, clicking his thumbs, his huge backside swaying like a hippo's around the table.

"Fiesta Fiesta," he lisped out in a poor Spanish accent. "Don't you get it? She wanted a new big end, a new big…." he pointed towards his enormous rump, "For her Fiesta." Again, his finger pointed at his backside.

Carol wearily shook her head. At first, she'd liked his stupid jokes. He was always good for a giggle but by now she'd had her fill. She forced a smile and gazed trance-like at her food.

An hour later the dishes were washed, and the kitchen tidied, they were sitting in front of the TV.

"Can you pass me the remote please?" said Carol.

Kevin was sprawled on a pink velveteen couch; the remote control was sitting on his expansive belly. He picked it up and clicked over the channel,

Coronation Street was on. He looked across at his wife.

"I don't want to watch that; you know I watch the Corri' omnibus at the weekend."

"What do you want then?" he asked abruptly.

They faced each other in mild hostility.

"I don't know, I was gonna have a click," she replied. "Can I have it please?"

Ignoring his wife Kevin clicked through the channels one by one, his eyes glinting back and forth in her direction.

"Oh stop, stop, I like Morse, stop," she pleaded, as he continued through the channels.

"What do you want?"

"Morse, I want Morse," she shouted.

"You want Jaws; I'll see if it's on." He clicked up the TV guide, "Jaws?" he drawled, and read down the list of programmes. "Nah, it's not on."

She looked across, her temper egging her, nipping her, daring her.

"There's something on the Discovery Channel," he offered.

Carol was out of her seat and ready to scream, when Morse came up on the screen. She took a step back and snapped down into her chair.

"Just a little fun. A bit of fun my dear. I tease to please. Tease to please." He pointedly placed the remote control on his belly, grinning whilst tapping it with his forefinger.

Carol tried to calm herself, she took a deep breath and focused on the TV. Out of the corner of her eye she could see his pathetic grin of appeasement. She held her face of stone until he looked away.

Two minutes into Morse and he was up, "Cuppa tea love?" Raising his legs off the couch, he rocked back and forth until he rocked to his feet.

A single nod her response.

Five minutes later he returned with tea and a plate of biscuits on a floral tin tray. Chocolate fingers were Carol's favourites and placed nearest to the edge of the plate. She helped herself to a mug of tea and selected three fingers leaving two on the plate next to the fig rolls.

"Go on love, tuck in," said Kevin pushing the tray closer.

She hesitantly picked up the other two, scolding him mildly, "Are you trying to get me fat?"

He raised an eyebrow and with a wink, he smiled.

She munched the end of her biscuit and swung her legs over her armchair. Kevin placed the tray on the floor beside him and flopped down on the couch with a thud.

That night like every other they went to bed at ten-thirty, just after the news. She used the bathroom first and got into her nightclothes whilst Kevin, who had a fear of fires, would turn off all the electric sockets at night. Once he had done his rounds, he followed her up. She listened to the thumping steps, then to the sound of taps and the toilet flush. The bedroom light was off, Carol was tucked in and making plans for tomorrow. He moved quietly around the room and undressed. The bed creaked. In a moment, he was under the light cotton sheet. She shuffled back towards him.

"How's your day been?" Kevin asked, folding a huge arm over her delicate body.

"Not too bad, what about you?"

"Pretty good," he said.

"Night night. Night night. Don't let the bugs bite."

He brushed her hair softly with the tips of his fingers and gently kissed the back of her head. He pulled her closer, "Night night... love you."

"Love you too, she replied.

The Gift

Ma raison de vivre
La mia ragione di vita
My reason for life

Sarah had just finished adding nail polish to her little toe, when a rude thought came to mind, it made her grin. She went to her diary and wrote something down. The phone rang, it was her mother asking for details regarding her coursework and upcoming exams. Sarah was in her first year at university. She was studying chemistry and although never enthused about the subject, she found it easy. Her mother was now updating her on one of her cousins who was travelling around South America. Sarah was only half-listening; her mind had drifted and she wanted to hang-up. In an hour she was meeting up with Franklin, their first official date.

Her stomach was fluttering with that feeling that borders on fear. From her wardrobe, she pulled out a pair of denim cut-off shorts and a black tight-fitting t-shirt. They'd met at a soul night organised by uni. Franklin was black, tall, and muscular, with a hint of menace which she liked. He wasn't a student and was vague about what he did. Her friend Helen said he sold drugs, something he denied. It didn't matter to Sara what he did. They'd slept together on their first night, which wasn't great but hey-ho, what can you expect when you're shit-faced.

Sarah was bright, straight A's in her O levels and at A level, she'd got A's in Chemistry and English and a B in Art. To describe her, she was tall for a girl, almost six-foot, wide shouldered and flat chested. Her face had that satin surface of youth, flawless and perfect. The dark eyeshadow she wore accentuated blue eyes and contrasted with her blonde cropped hair. Standing in front of the mirror she pouted, then turned looking over her shoulder to check her look. As a very young girl she'd felt shy and awkward, but now at nineteen she knew how to turn heads.

They had arranged to meet at midday, but Sarah had decided to be late. Her aunt Rose, the black sheep of her mother's stuffy family, had a saying, *Loveliness is always enhanced by anticipation.* The longest she had left it was an hour, the guy had gone, but she hadn't cared. With Franklin it was different but she didn't want to risk more than fifteen minutes.

The bus pulled up, she stepped onto the platform and flashed her bus pass and was halfway down the aisle when the driver called her back. He examined her pass, eying her up and down as he did so. She smiled sarcastically as he handed it back, then took a seat.

They were meeting outside The Hat Shop in town. During the twenty-minute bus ride she daydreamed of how the day would go. *What would they do? Would they have sex? Would he turn up?* She feared he might not. *He'd better be there.* As the bus drew close, she moved over to an empty seat on the pavement side to see if she could spot Franklin, but there was no sign of him. Her heart fluttered to earth as she stepped off the platform and casually made her way over to The Hat Shop.

She was pretending to view the hats but was in fact watching the reflections of the passers-by. A loud whistle made her look around. It was Franklin, he was talking to a small squat black man on the other side of the road. She raised a hand to acknowledge his call and aware both sets of eyes were on her, stepped catwalk like into the road.

Franklin grinned, took her hand and kissed her cheek. Still holding on to her, stood back, "Man, you look good." His face was beaming.

Sarah smiled, "Thank you."

He introduced his friend as Dexter, who looked Sarah up and down but didn't speak to her. They quickly finished off their conversation, then did that hand routine that only black guys can do properly, before a bumping shoulder embrace.

"Laters," they said in unison.

Dexter turned and left.

As they walked towards the High Street, Franklin asked Sarah if there was anything she would like to do? Sarah thought for a moment, saying she was happy just to wander around the town. In a trendy vintage store, she tried on a couple of outfits, a clingy tube dress in black, some culottes and a vest top but didn't buy anything. From there they went into a designer boutique with a red rocket ship above the doorway. It looked great with a space orientated interior, but with t-shirts at over a hundred quid, it far too expensive for Sarah. Arm in arm they wandered on. She could see that window shopping wasn't really Franklin's thing and was relieved when he suggested they go for a drink.

The Queens was just off the High Street, one of those really old buildings, a long bar, lots of brass and low ceilings. He seemed to know most of the regulars but other than a lazy wave, didn't spend any time with anyone other than Sarah. They each ordered burger and chips with Sarah insisting on paying her way.

Like a gentle ballet, they talked about their favourite music, films, colour, the usual shite. Franklin described himself as a chauffeur, but only worked for his mate. When Sarah asked if his mate was a drug dealer, Franklin laughed. A skinny waiter arrived with the food. Franklin abruptly asked for ketchup, then proceeded to cover his meal with the sauce. He'd finished in no time and was eying up

Sarah's plate. Slightly embarrassed, she offered him her chips; he didn't refuse.

A few drinks made them bolder, the ballet had moved on to fleeting touches. Franklin said he loved her hair, gently pinching little tufts, Sarah giggled and playfully slapped him. Tenderly he traced the line of her jaw with his finger and looked deep into her eyes. Sarah blushed and took a sip of her drink. Franklin laughed; a throaty laugh, easy and hearty.

At three o'clock they'd had a few but neither were drunk. Franklin had to place a bet on a horse, so they made their way to the bookies. Sarah had never been inside a bookie's before and was interested. A race was underway, a couple of grey-looking men were peering up at the screen, the commentator's voice even and flat. Sarah watched as Franklin made his way to the front. He scribbled something on a piece of paper and handed it to the bored-looking lady behind the counter. He'd bet twenty quid on The Gift to win. The lady put it through a machine and handed him a slip.

The race on screen was getting into the closing stages, the commentator's voice animated. One guy clenching his fist was shouting encouragement. A tall nervous looking man was standing stock still, gazing intently at the TV. In a few seconds, it was all over. The tall man cursed and ripped up his slip, the other guy looked shocked that his horse had won. Sarah smiled at Franklin, who was checking the form on his bet in the racing post.

He looked up from the newspaper, "You up for coming back to mine?"

Sarah was surprised at his directness, and that he didn't want to watch his race, but without a moment's thought, accepted.

Franklin's flat was a ten-minute walk from the bookies. A high rise, nestled in a group of six other high rises. In the lift she stood alongside him, linking her arm in his. His flat was spartan and painted completely white and a lot tidier than she'd expected. A dark leather couch and glass coffee table stood on a shagpile rug in the middle of the room. In one corner were a set of weights and a workout bench.

Franklin disappeared into the kitchen, calling out to ask if she wanted a drink. Rum or vodka? Sarah wouldn't normally bother with spirits preferring a beer but did not want to be a party pooper, so opted for vodka.

Moments later he returned, vodka for Sarah, a rum for himself. He pulled from his pockets a small carton of orange and another of blackcurrant. "You want juice?"

She chose orange and after piercing the hole with the straw squirted it into her glass.

He put on some music, a classic Marvin Gaye album from the seventies and then stretched himself out on the couch. Sarah sipped her drink swaying to and fro to the music as she thought things through. She wanted him and it was now or never. Placing her glass on a coffee table she made her move. They never made it to the bedroom, half an hour later both were half-naked relaxing on the couch.

His phone rang, Franklin picked it up and disappeared into his bedroom. "Shit man," he said as he returned. He looked to Sarah, "Hey babe, you're gonna have to go, I got people coming around."

Sarah did not want to show her disappointment, saying simply, "No problem," and got her things together.

Franklin walked her to the lift, and made her promise to ring him, writing his number on her arm. He kissed her passionately and was gone.

A week went by, she'd called him three times but he hadn't got back to her. Six weeks later she was in a panic when she discovered that she was pregnant. Again and again she phoned, but no reply. Another week went by. She even went to where he lived but cursed herself as all the flats looked the same. That night she cried herself to sleep, the following day was no better. She went again to the flats, just in the hope that she might spot him, she even asked a few people, but it was no good.

She sat her exams but not being able to focus she failed them all. She began drinking and smoking far more weed than she was used to, some days she didn't even get out of bed. In three months, she had lost a stone and a half and looked dreadful. After countless unanswered phone calls, her mother turned up at her flat. After one look at her daughter, she insisted Sarah come home with her. Sarah didn't put up a fight. It was then that Sarah explained her predicament.

Her mother was furious, bitterness etched in the furrows of her brow, *Why was she so stupid and why on earth in this day and age had she not used contraception?* "Have you thought of…?

An angry scowl from Sarah stopped her mother mid-sentence.

Five months on Sarah gave birth to a baby girl, whom she named Irwin, which had a ring similar to Franklin, so why not?

Years went by and despite her mother's protestations she never went back to re-sit her exams. She got a part-time job as a parks attendant, and met and fell in love with Philip. He was a groundsman, tall, skinny, a fearless risk-taker. It was a passionate romance, but as the saying goes, *'Love is like a fire, but be careful it doesn't burn your house down.'* They married, six months later she found out he'd been cheating with a neighbour. He pleaded but by now she knew him too well. Sarah moved out and into a one-bedroom flat in a bad area of town. A decade tripped by like a walking holiday, pleasant enough but nothing to write home about.

Chris as he called himself, or Christopher as Sarah preferred to call him, was a neighbour, had helped to get her unreliable Morris minor car started one morning. They never said another word to each other for over a month. It was whilst shopping in Sainsburys they bumped each other, and after a bit of small talk, Sarah invited him around for a meal, as a way of thank you. Things blossomed, occasionally they'd go out if Sarah managed to get a baby sitter for Irwin, if not they were happy to stay in.

Christopher was not in Sarah's league looks-wise, and at forty-three he was ten years older. He was bald with a bit of a belly, but was kind and always ready to help, whether dropping off Irwin at school on his way to work or a bit of DIY. He wasn't the brightest, but his unworldliness made Sarah feel good. Life was going fine. Money was tight, but thankfully her mother would help her out if ever she was short.

Irwin like her mother was bright and enjoyed her studies. She had blossomed from a rather gangly youth and at eighteen she was beautiful. With her honey coloured skin, reddish-blond hair, long legs and lean figure, Irwin turned heads. She passed her A levels with ease and went to Bristol Uni, her first choice. In unfamiliar surroundings her first week was hard, she'd wanted to go home, but apart from that wobble, she breezed it. Three years one she had gained a first-class degree in chemistry.

Sarah, Christopher and her mother attended the graduation. Sarah looked elegant in an emerald green trouser suit; a floral scarf tucked under her jacket finished the look. Christopher had made an effort too, he'd bought a new suit, although with his belly it was a struggle to button up the jacket.

After taking their seats, they spotted Irwin waiting in line as she chatted to her fellow students, all in black gowns and mortar boards. She caught her mother's eye and totally at ease waved across.

After a lot of waiting, the event began with a speech from the Dean of the College, more speeches from the heads of department and them more from esteemed alumni. It seemed to go on forever. Finally, the students one by one took to the stage. After forty-five minutes it was Irwin's turn. Sarah sat up straight, he chest tightened as she watched as Irwin purposely stepped to the middle of the stage. She shook hands with the dean, smiled broadly and received her degree. Before exiting she turned to the audience, and waved confidently towards her mother, shouting. "For you mum!"

A loud cheer went up from the students. People were looking across to see who 'mum' was. Irwin was on a roll, she took a bow; another cheer went up. Christopher chuckled with embarrassment and glanced over at Sarah.

Sarah's mum was on her feet clapping enthusiastically, she nudged her daughter, turned and in a quiet whisper said, "That could have been you darling."

Sarah smiled and swallowed back her tears.

A Dish Served Warm

Mr Crème stormed off the bus, furious that it had stopped so far from its official stop. He opened his leather briefcase, took out a Staedtler pencil, a notepad and pointedly noted down the bus registration number. As he did so, a small pudgy freckled-faced boy, perhaps eight or nine was watching him from the wall he was sitting on. Mr Crème was determined to prove the driver's complacency. He chose a cracked slab as a marker and counting his steps strode back towards the bus stop.

"Forty-four," he muttered as he wrote it down. Just to confirm he repeated the exercise: only forty-three, this time. Frustrated by the inconsistency, he was about to start again, when the boy called out.

"Hello, are you doing a survey? The boy was on his feet, he looked keen and inquisitive, "My dad's an engineer. Can I help?"

Mr Crème knew it was best not to answer unsolicited questions, but also not to ignore the situation. He waved and smiled politely. The boy waited hesitantly before crossing the road.

A woman appeared, "George, you need to come in now," her voice was cool, perhaps fearful.

"I was just going to help the man, he is doing a survey for the police," said George, exaggerating his claim.

"He's not from the police. Come on in now!" she said, folding her arms across her chest.

The boy followed his mother, lingering a few moments before closing the door. Mr Crème knew what she thought, and was outraged. He quickly underlined the forty-four figure, slipped the jotter and pencil into his pocket, and walked on briskly not looking back.

Eight and a half minutes later he had arrived at a tired-looking Victorian semi. This was where Mr Crème lived. The house had deteriorated a lot in the twelve years since his mother had died. She had been such a tidy woman, and had kept it immaculately, but now she was gone. He'd pretended not to notice the tatty front door, the broken stained-glass panes or the peeling paint on the windows. He reached inside his pocket, pulled out his key and let himself in.

Inside he removed his thick grey coat, hanging it on a brass hook. A shaggy-haired black and grey dog ambled out from the kitchen.

"Hello Sam, have you had a good day?" said Mr Crème half-heartedly.

Only five years old, Sam had the lethargy of a much older dog, he responded with a weary wag of his tail, and sat down in front of his master. Mr Crème had got him as a companion, but they'd never really struck up a great friendship. From the start Sam was difficult. He had a habit of jumping up to lick Mr Crème's face, which repulsed him. They tried puppy-training classes, but still, he could not control Sam. He even asked if he could return Sam, but this was refused. It was instead suggested that perhaps neutering might make a difference. Neutering did make a difference, Sam calmed down considerably

"Good boy, sit-t", said Mr Crème, gently patting the dog's head. Sam ignored sit-t, and followed Mr Crème into the kitchen. Once the back door was opened, Sam lazily ambled out.

Mr Crème took a small Pyrex dish from the fridge, leftovers from yesterday's supper. He placed it in the centre of the microwave, setting the timer at three minutes, forty seconds, and began to set the table. Out of the corner of his eye, he could see the blurred outline of Sam waiting patiently behind the frosted glass door. He ignored him and continued with his task. On a small drop-leaf table, he placed a table mat, cutlery, and salt and pepper. He tore off a sheet of kitchen roll, made a precise diagonal fold and placed it on the edge of his setting. A fresh tumbler of water and the table was complete. He wondered whether bread was required, but decided against it, *Waste not, want not, use only what you need,* he reminded himself.

The sound of scratching on glass alerted him. He opened the door and watched as Sam went meekly to his bed in the corner of the kitchen. A ding' chimed! Food was ready, well almost. Before removing the dish, Mr Crème stood poised like a crane about to strike as he studied his watch. He counted, eighteen, nineteen… twenty seconds passed before he stabbed a bony finger at the release button. Giving the bowl a sniff, he smiled in anticipation. Supper consisted of a piece of chicken, one small potato, a portion of peas and a decoration of sweetcorn. He placed the napkin on his lap and sprinkled his meal with a small amount of salt, which he knew was bad for him, and a lot of pepper, which he knew was good for him. Between mouthfuls, he would place his cutlery on the side of his plate, and with his elbows on the edge of the table, clasp his hands. To an observer he might resemble a particularly pious clergyman in prayer.

Sam stared intently, eyes devouring every morsel, his nose making promises to his stomach, never to be kept. Beneath his thick shaggy coat, Sam was as scrawny as his master, but unlike his Mr Crème, he had a much bigger appetite. Dry, tasteless biscuits would be Sam's supper, he'd never tasted real meat in his life and was always hungry.

Mr Crème finished his food and washed up immediately. Once the kitchen was clean, he turned his attention to Sam's dinner. He filled a plastic measuring jug halfway, and poured the biscuits into Sam's bowl.

Sam waited; he knew the routine.

Mr Crème looked to Sam and called, "dinner". In a shot the dog skipped over, devouring every tasteless morsel in seconds. Mr Crème looked on, wishing Sam would show more manners.

In the hallway he changed into a cosy pair of tartan slippers, and neatly set his shoes down in their place. His plan for the evening was to start his jigsaw, have a bath at eight forty and be back down for nine o'clock to read a chapter of a new science fiction novel he'd picked up, then retire at ten-thirty. He checked his watch, it was seven-fifteen, this left an hour to start the jigsaw.

His lounge was dominated by a dark cupboard and bookcase. On the walls hung a tired selection of pictures of boat and ships, sailing this way and that. TV wasn't for him, *Constructive hobbies, feed the brain*. As he reached into the cupboard to retrieve the jigsaw, Bloody Hell!" he squealed out in pain." Then froze, terror-struck, fearful his neighbour might have heard the profanity. His forefinger had caught on an exposed rusty nail, the flesh was badly torn and blood oozed freely from the open wound.

From his bed Sam heard the squeal, sat up in his basket raised his muzzle and sniffed the air. In a second Mr Crème appeared, drops of blood splashing to the tiled kitchen floor. Hastily he tore off a piece of paper towel to make a temporary bandage, and fixed it in place with a bit of tape. Mr Crème looked down; the splashes of blood made him feel light-headed. He poured himself a glass of water.

Sam rose tentatively, head low, his body clinging the ground as he went to investigate the strange red spots that smelt so delicious.

Mr Crème pointed firmly in the direction of the bed. Sam obediently returned to his basket, watching as his master wiped and disinfected the floor. Going back into the lounge, Mr Crème checked for blood stains, dabbing a damp cloth here and there, but the Paisley pattern on the carpet was so busy it didn't really show. Once satisfied he returned to the jigsaw, spreading it out over the table. No sooner had he begun, a movement from across the room caught his eye. It was Sam standing in the doorway. Mr Crème's patience were wearing thin as he scowled across at his dog. "What are you doing in here? Bed.... bed!" he shouted, pointing in the direction of the kitchen. Sam did not move. Mr Crème shouted once more even louder. Sam's head dropped between his shoulders, he took one more sniff, turned and left the room. An hour passed; the puzzle was almost complete. Mr Crème checked his watch, eight-thirty, time to run his bath. He fitted two more pieces and went upstairs. In the bathroom, he turned on the taps, steaming water gushed forth into an old cast iron bath.

From his bedroom he collected a pair of striped pyjamas and laid them over the warm radiator alongside a clean dry towel. He poured rock salt into the water, an indulgence, but he felt it helped his bones, so the cost was justifiable. Two minutes later he eased himself into the piping hot water. The water felt good as it lapped up on to his chest. Sliding down he immersed himself, below the surface he could hear his heartbeat. He sat up; the bathwater was now towards the edge of the bath. Using his toe, he turned off the taps and laid back allowing the intoxicating heat to engulf him. It was almost too hot but he loved it. Closing his eyes, he was totally relaxed, listening only to the sound of his breath. His thoughts drifted like the steam which surrounded him.

A creak at the door stirred him from his slumber. Looking over he could make out a nose peeking around the door. "Sam" he shouted, then sharply, "Downstairs". The nose pulled back. Mr Crème listened hard but heard nothing.

It was then that he noticed the crimson colour of the water.

"Oh God!" he exclaimed. His heart raced and jumped as his lungs tightened. The bandage had gone and blood was pumping in gentle waves from his finger. In his panic he rose quickly, but the heat had scrambled his equilibrium, sending him crashing down. His head hit the solid edge of the bath. A searing pain, both dull and bright, shot through his brain.

Minutes passed as he lay on the floor, the tiles felt cool, he wanted to move but couldn't.

Something stirred through the fog, a furry shape was coming towards him. "Oh, thank goodness, Sam, get help, get help", but no words came out. He felt warm breath, the disgusting smell of dog biscuits and then the rasp of a tongue on his flesh.

ABOUT THE AUTHOR

Born in Donegal, Ireland, in 1958, Charlie McFadden with his family emigrated to Coventry in the early 1960s. He has worked in a variety of professions, including engineering, the rag trade, property development, and as an acupuncture practitioner. He now lives in Moreton-in-Marsh, where he is the owner and curator of the Moreton Gallery.